# THE GRIFT...

## DUANE LINDSAY
Copyright 2017

Duane Lindsay

*To Traci, the inspiration for everything*

TO GET YOUR STARTER LIBRARY OF BOOKS BY DUANE LINDSAY OR RAYMOND DEAN WHITE, PLEASE GO TO OUR WEB SITES AT:

DuaneLindsay.com
RaymondDeanWhite.com

If you enjoyed them, would you please write a review and put it on Amazon? We authors live by reviews and wither away like flowers without rain when we don't get them. And nobody keeps withered flowers anymore. Not like a long time ago when they got pressed and put in books that nobody looked at. Nowadays we just wait until they die and we chuck 'em.

So please write a review—We don't want to be chucked.

# INTRO
# THE TREASURE

*Oz Gorman is as crazy as a bag of squirrels.*

*Six-Five and bald as an egg, thick gray eyebrows and a grin like Jack Nicholson on a bad hair day, Oz paws through wooden crates in an antique warehouse, squealing with delight at each new discovery.*

*Outside Hurricane Katrina shrieks and moans like a TV wrestler as Oz scurries from room to room picking up packages and talking to himself.*

*The power has failed and the rooms are dark. He has to squint at each package as he fills a grimy mail sack with plastic wrapped treasure.*

*"Oh my, oh my, oh my!" Oz cackles like a witch, does a clumsy little dance step and waves his arms. He kisses the clear bag and says, "You call this crazy?"*

*Back outside, through the broken door into the biggest storm of the century, sloshing through waist deep water, he cries out at every slash of lightning that splits the swollen purple sky. The bolts sear his vision and he blinks in pain at the afterglow.*

*The fourteen-foot boat is tethered and he dumps the baggies to the floor where they float in the oily water alongside crushed Pepsi cans and soggy paper.*

*He turns back for more.*

*"So very clever," He tells himself. His tattered Army jacket, heavy with rain water, catches on a nail in the doorway and he tugs at it, cursing until it rips, freeing him. He studies the tear, frowns and trudges back up the stairs.*

*"Two more trips. Then I get the hell out of here."*

*Outside again he carries the long rifle to the boat, the damn thing grabbing at every branch, every overturned bench, every floating car. He throttles a fierce desire to throw it away but it is, by far, the most valuable thing he's stolen.*

*Two days ago he'd been a hired grunt from the Day-Labor place out on Biscayne, hired to pack up stuff from the auction house, save it from Katrina. The other guys, Harper and Spiccoli, Diaz and that fat bastard Cooper, wrapped things in bags and bubble wrap,* packed them away in wooded crates, nailed them shut. Oz and this greaser kid Mick, all stringy hair and buck teeth, had carted the crates up to the third floor.

A bunch of other guys screwed plywood to the windows, hurrying as the winds grew stronger.

"I'm not crazy!" He shouts and the dark empty stairwell echoes, "crazy crazy azy azy azy," until he puts his wrists against his ears to shut it all out. From the doc in the VA psych ward who dispensed the pills, to his neighbors in the run down place he lives in, they all think he's a wack-job.

Even the Health department has tried a couple times to take away his hoard of stuff— canned food, thirty-odd years of newspapers, the lion head, his clocks –but they don't come around much anymore, scared that he'll freak out again.

Oz pries open another crate. It hasn't been easy with them watching him, watching him, always...deep deep breath, exhale slooowly...watching him, but he marks each box with a tiny X like they did to the Jews homes in Germany that time.

He read about that. Oz reads everything, which is why he knows what to steal. Books, small enough to carry, each one worth a small fortune.

Two trips become four became seven, he just can't stop himself, but finally the boat is full. Oz bends over the gunwale, shoves off and immediately falls in, thrashing around like an upturned walrus trying to right himself. A bag slides off into the surging water, bobbing away like a tiny iceberg.

"NO!" He screams. "NO! NO! NO! NO! NO!" But it's gone. Furious, he pulls the cord of the Mercury outboard and flees into the night.

The journey home is a nightmare. Overhead, the clouds roil like a nest of angry, hissing vipers and at each block the storm rages harder until it seems to be throwing things at him personally, trying to kill him. Unloading into his house is a ceaseless battle against wind and water and airborne debris.

On his last trip a wooden shutter tears loose and dives at him like Satan on a hang-glider. He doesn't duck fast enough and rusty nails gouge deep red lines across his bald head when it slams into him.

*Laughing and crying and bleeding and triumphant, Oz falls over the threshold, kicks the door shut and rolls into a ball as the banshee wind wails like all the lost souls from Metairie.*

*"Crazy," he whispers in the dark.*

"Jeez, Dani; that's some story."

"Thank you."

We were lounging around a kitchen table in the dull glow of the overhead swag lamp or sprawled on the sofa; Cincinnati Bob Wilkerson, Sammy Hensel, Esteban "Ray" Sanchez and Merle Crookshanks. My crew.

"Sammy; you'll have to provide provenance."

Elegantly dressed, he sat up straight and nodded. "Sure."

"Ray, you'll create the store."

He dog-eared the lurid paperback he was reading. "A haunted house filled with worthless crap? No problemo, boss."

Cincinnati Bob raised a tentative hand. "Dani? Just what are these treasures?"

"Books, Bob. Rare precious books. I'm thinking autographed editions of *To Kill a Mockingbird* or a missing manuscript of Twain's *Huck Finn*. But use your imagination."

Bob smiled and began muttering about ink and paper.

"Merle?"

"Dani?"

"Are you in?"

He scratched his dog Buckles behind his floppy black lab ears. "I get to be a bald, scarred old pack-rat? Damn-betcha, I'm in."

I look around at them. "Okay. That's just the way we'll play the mark when we run The Treasure Hunt scam on him."

# CHAPTER 1

## MUSTANG DANI . . . AND DAD

"Don't this thing have air?"

I glanced at the bony little man complaining; my father, Leroy, "Pops" Amadeus Logan. He was slouched in the black bucket seat of my brand new old Ford, arms hugging his chest.

A 1965 fully restored Mustang convertible, fire engine red with leather interior, chrome dash, three speed manual with overdrive, you could get a speeding ticket parked at the courthouse. They just didn't make a better getaway car.

"Quit your bitchin', Pops. This here's the open road." I chinned to the highway through the windshield. "And that there's freedom."

"Damned hot, this freedom." He broke out the smile that had charmed so many wardens, twisted around to touch one of the large cases in the back, caressing the smooth mocha leather. "One point one million dollars. I never had a score like that my whole life."

"Neither have I, Pops," I said, trying to keep the giddy elation from my voice. Honestly, if we weren't driving I'd be dancing in the street.

The scenery outside whizzed past, barely noticed. Fields of seed rows waiting for spring to become green again, blue sky above, gray ribbon of the Ohio Turnpike in front and back.

The temperature had reached eighty and we weren't even past nine in the morning, hence my father's complaints.

On the lam, five hours out of New York City, heading nowhere, the sun rising behind us cast a giant shadow to the west. We drove after the shadow as if it was a destination we could never reach, like Moses near the Promised Land only, you know, crooked.

I felt a sudden rare fondness for my father. "I couldn't have done it without you," I told him.

"This is very true." Pops said and my feelings shifted immediately back to annoyance. Pops could make me angry faster than anybody; I guess that's what fathers are for. I tried again.

"Keeping Alexander from killing Nick and selling those phony blackmail photos to Richard...breaking in and taking the money. Oh, and being dead. Pops, you make a great corpse."

"A lot of people would agree." Leroy looked falsely modest. In my experience, he had never felt truly humble. He was simply the best con man still living –and he knew it.

"Even more would help it along."

I hadn't seen much of my father for a long time. Scamming this money represented our first real bonding in twenty years. Together we had just pulled off a major league long con –like a father/daughter science project – and the money was our reward.

With the dawn painting the sky with gentle pastels there came a surge of hope and confidence. I was beginning a new life.

"What about Nick?" asked Pops, after we passed a semi loaded with cattle. The odor wafted over us, making our eyes water.

"What about him?" Sore subject, this. I'd literally left Nick at the altar, agreeing to marry him, then sneaking off in the middle of the night with a briefcase full of his money. I felt bad about it but what can I say? I am my father's daughter. I was pretty sure Nick would have strong feelings about it, though.

"He's a smart one, Dani. You sure you did the right thing leaving him?"

"No," I said, but the sound was lost in the wind from all the freedom blowing over us.

A lot of miles later at a truck stop that served thick black coffee, Pops asked, "You think he's gonna look for you?"

"I'm counting on it Pops." I spooned sugar into a white coffee mug. "I am surely counting on it."

# CHAPTER 2

# A WHOLE NEW LIFE

We traveled west to Chicago, drifted south on Interstate Fifty-Five, leisurely passing St. Louis. I had no destination in mind and Pops seemed content with my company, or he just wanted to stay by the money. He lectured less than usual and was in a jovial enough mood to play cold reading, a game we'd been doing since I was six years old, freckle-faced and adorable, shilling in one of his countless scams.

We stopped at a diner on the Missouri side of Kansas where a waitress served me a very good blueberry muffin on a white china plate, gossiping with her customers while keeping an eye on my cup. Pops had pie with thick vanilla ice cream. He watched the woman work for a while and said, "She's from somewhere else... California? She's been married at least twice, divorced for over a year and lives with a man."

I knew his methods and studied her myself. Cold reads are a Sherlock Holmes trick we use to get inside the head of a mark. Small clues tell us what the person likes or hates, where she lives, what she does. In this case the shoes gave her away. They were way too fancy for a dive like this in the middle of nowhere. Something more expensive than Reboks, they did have a California feel to them. Worn at the heels so she'd had them a while. There were cigarettes in her pocket and no ring on her finger. But when I looked closer I saw the faint line of one. So, divorced. The color said it wasn't recent.

"No kids," I said. "And she likes to drink."

"But not beer," said Pops. He was a master at this. With a five-minute read he could convince you he was your long missing cousin. I'd seen him do an Anastasia on a mark without even knowing the guy's name.

"Something stronger, like scotch. Her name's Lilly," he concluded.

"It's on her name tag."

He grinned, amused at himself. "Just testing you. What else?"

"Current boyfriend's at the counter." Pops craned his neck and I added, "Third stool. She's been sucking off his cigarette as she passes and there's no check, even though he's done. She's comping him."

"Is that what she's doing to him?" He mopped up the last of his pie. "Want to take her?"

"I'm trying," I said, with dignity, "To go straight."

"Sure," Pops agreed. "But why?"

"You know why."

"Fine, I'll do it." He caught her eye from across the crowded room. I never knew how he did it but he could be as visible as a storm front one minute, as hidden as a politician's true motives the next. She came over.

"Ma'am," he said softly and she leaned in to hear him. Another trick –the mark needs to come to you. "Is there a place nearby to buy some liquor?"

"Oh, sure." She smiled, happy to help. "Bud's Liquor Barn, down near the tracks."

"I'm looking for a good scotch," he said. "Present for my daughter here," he added. Always put in small details; it makes the con more real.

"Your daughter," beamed Lilly. "Scotch is my drink, too."

"Is it, really?" Pops said with enthusiasm to her and a wink for me. "I picked up the taste in LA, just after my divorce."

"I know about that," Lilly nodded. "I did it twice."

"I'm a three-time loser, myself." He didn't have to confirm the California angle; we both heard it in her voice. He kept her talking until she had to pull away to her customers. Pops sat back, pleased with himself.

"You noticed the watch?" I asked.

"Of course."

"Real diamonds. A gift from lover boy over there."

"Means she's good in bed," he said.

"You always say that," I said.

"I'm always right, too."

When we finished, I drove slowly around the sleeping town for an hour before deciding to stay. Pops was, of course, horrified.

"Why here?"

I shrugged. "Good a place as any."

He studied the broad streets, the older houses, the utter lack of urban life. "No, it isn't."

"No one will find me here," I said.

"You got that right."

"I mean nobody. It's a good place to put down some roots. I can make friends here, buy a house..."

"Stop it! Dani, you can't be serious."

"Besides," I said. "Lilly serves a mean muffin."

Life decisions have been made on less than a mean muffin.

The next day I dropped Pops off at Kansas City's International airport, letting him figure out how to get his money through security. He was in a hurry to get back to Saratoga, Florida and continue what was possibly the world's longest losing streak –he hadn't had a winning year on the horses since nineteen-fifty-three.

He kissed my cheek when he left, an unaccustomed bit of approval, and vanished into the bustling airport, a small man with big bucks. I smiled at his retreating back and picked up the Mustang from short term parking and drove away, as free as a bird, as alone as a good deed.

# CHAPTER 3

# DANI MEETS THE NEIGHBORS

I bought the old house on the corner of Mason and Elm, two streets as American as apple pie in a town as forgotten as virtue. The real estate lady called it a restored two story farmhouse. I thought it looked forlorn. It jutted forward on its lot with a wide wraparound porch, tall maple trees with leaves pointy and proud as the Canadian flag, shaggy un-mowed grass, a lilac hedge in full bloom that smelled like heaven must and a big garage in back where I could stash my car.

I parked the Mustang in front with my two suitcases –everything I still owned in this world. The briefcase with my half of the money was hidden carefully in the attic along with an amazing assortment of cardboard boxes, clothes and ratty furniture left by the previous owners.

I'd be depositing it in the local bank in small amounts over the next few months. For now, anyone trying to steal it would choke on the dust.

"They passed away, poor souls," confided Adrianna, my realtor. "Carbon dioxide from a leaky space heater, ice fishing on Lake Palmyra." She made the sign of the cross, lowered her eyes to honor the dead and cheerfully showed me the kitchen, a gleaming space of copper tile, turquoise appliances and orange flooring. The renovation had been done in nineteen-seventy-six.

We closed in a tiny office in an ancient brick building right on the main street of Jamestown, Missouri, my new home. Adrianna handed across enough forms to paper Times Square, explaining as she slid them over, talking non-stop for nearly an hour while I wrestled with a hand cramp from signing.

I'd never owned a house before, or come as close to being a real citizen. Only the thought of hiding behind a phony name gave me any sense of security.

It's not as hard as you might think to create a false identity; it's kind of at the heart of being a grifter. I called Sammy Hensel, the best crooked computer technician I knew, and he made me a real person, as alive on the information highway as you are. Cincinnati Bob Wilkerson forged the documents that went along with it.

With a driver's license that would pass any cop in the world, a birth certificate and a social security card, I became Mona Pasternelli from Queens, New York. No longer, at least in this neck of America, Dani Silver, the grifter's daughter.

And now I had a house as well. Roots, a place to call my own. Her own. Whatever.

The excitement was a balloon filling within me. A house, a lot of money, freedom and, maybe, new friends, and it was all new. I felt like a girl again as I walked across the hot blacktop parking lot.

This was every first time. The first trip to the store with Moms' money to buy milk, the first kiss, the first time conning Billy Yaskoutis out of his lunch money after he beat up my little brother Petey.

Good luck finding me here, Nick, I thought. I didn't know where I was myself.

Jamestown, Missouri is a farm town situated in a river valley, a railhead more than a century ago with grain silos and neat geographic fences marking the acreages, fading red barns and white houses and a single street downtown with one café, three taverns, a two-story brick courthouse with diagonal front-end parking.

And no Wal-Mart or Starbucks within a hundred miles.

I bought a new bed at Hobart's Lumber and Mercantile down a block off Main Street near the abandoned water filling tank that fed steam locomotives back when Pops was still a boy. The tank squatted like a rusted alien, three-legged, graffiti adorned and sagging.

Hobart's took up two whole blocks, selling everything a small town could possibly need, many things it didn't and quite a few I had no ideas about. Farm supplies, I guessed, though what an "O'Dell Model Forty-Six self-propelling disc grader," might be I had no clue.

Missouri, in the midst of a late Spring heat-wave, sweltered under a cloudless sky with temperatures nearing a hundred. The natives buzzed with the news that this was the earliest in memory. Doom was forecast, gleefully.

I sweated along with them while settling in and buying a few groceries and that night I slept in my own bed for the first time since leaving New Orleans.

Later that night I woke to a scream.

Cicadas buzzed in the still night and the air hung as hot and heavy as a tar roof. I tossed and turned in sweat-soaked sheets, barely asleep, dreaming of air-conditioning.

"Brock; Goddammit! Let go!"

"Shut up, bitch!"

A fist smacked against flesh. A door slammed and silence returned.

I sat up in bed and blinked away confusion. A clock on the cardboard box next to the mattress changed to 1:47 and the temperature felt like living in a swamp.

The only light came from a three-quarter moon making a small pale square across the wooden floor. A cricket began to scrape its lonely legs and the sound reminded me of a horror movie, one where the creepy guy with the knife jumps out from behind the closet door.

I stared suspiciously at the closet door, ran a hand through tangled damp hair and looked at the open window. Softly, muted by distance and closed doors, the fight began again. Muffled curses, an occasional bang. I tried to remember who lived there but could manage only a vague image of a young woman and a bulky compact man in jeans and tee shirt.

Call the cops? No. Grifters never called the cops. I got up, wrapped the sheet around me and stumbled to the window. Next door, a mere thirty feet away, a small ranch house squatted like a dark menacing shadow. A lamp had fallen near the rear patio door, casting an eerie glow upward from the floor. A hand reached out, pulled the lamp up and switched it off. A few seconds later a man walked out onto the slab of concrete that served as a porch. Dressed only in a pair of cut-off shorts he was as jittery as a penniless junkie. He lit a cigarette from a lighter, clicking it shut with a snap that made me flinch.

The man radiated agitation. His hair was thick and black, his arms bulged with muscle and his bare legs swelled from ten thousand squats. The abs were as flat as the hopes for the economy.

He pounded once on the side of the house and suddenly looked up. For a long moment our eyes locked. I leaned back further into the shadow and tightened the sheet against my body, feeling like ants were crawling on my skin. He took a deep suck from his smoke and threw the butt away with a savage thrust, raised an arm and flashed his middle finger in my direction.

He went back inside, the patio door slid shut and the night quieted down again. Soon an owl hooted and crickets and cicadas took up their night-song. Frogs joined in for the chorus and bed beckoned me back to its stifling embrace.

Oh, goody, I thought; my new home.

Late the next morning I walked to the mailbox. The worn gravel driveway was dark with oil and age and my bare feet kept getting bruised by tiny rocks. I was leafing through the sale ads when a movement caught my eye. Next door, the fair-haired young woman neighbor walked to her own mailbox, glancing warily as she approached.

"Hi," I said, friendly, nothing more. "I didn't see you there."

She nodded, ducked her head, closed the mailbox—it was painted to look like a fish—and turned away. Slender and pale, her hair had that semi-styled, chopped look, the result of a cheap cut and little self-esteem. She wore tan slacks and a sleeveless white blouse, no jewelry and hardly any makeup.

"I'm Mona," I lied, and paused. "Is that a bruise?"

She shook her head, her shoulders hunched. I took her arm and turned to get a better look. The right side of her face was indeed a mass of discolored skin, purple and raw. I reached up a hand and she flinched.

"I won't hurt you. Who did this?"

"Nobody." She tried to pull away.

"Bull." I said. "He hit you."

"No."

"Yuh-huh." I tried a gentler approach. "What's your name?"

She threw a surprised glance up at my face and quickly turned away.

"Marcy," she said to the ground. "Garfield."

"Well, hello, Marcy Garfield." I pushed the anger back and made my voice small and comforting. "Would you like some lemonade? Or tea? I've got some cold."

The pause was long, with timidity battling with a real desire for human contact, before she bobbed her head three times in quick shakes.

Marcy Garfield huddled in on herself on my patio, feet tucked beneath her as if she could make herself smaller. She studied me over the rim of her lemonade as I sat patiently smoking too many cigarettes, waiting.

"It's not what you think," she said.

"Sure it is, honey."

"Well...it's not any big deal."

I stared, surprised. I'd seen this sort of behavior before but was still amazed by it. "Of course, it is. Man beats you up, seems pretty big to me."

"Brock doesn't mean to hurt me." Small voice, evasive eyes, frequent sips.

"Brock? The muscleman? Your husband?"

"Uh-huh. He says he loves me so much I make him crazy."

"Of course he does."

Marcy misread the look. She said, "You don't know him," like a mother hen defending her young.

"I don't huh? Let's see. High school jock, wrestling or football. Tough guy, had a car and a job before anybody else so he had money. You were thrilled when he picked you. He got a job at some construction company, makes good money, dumps it into some boy toy like a truck." I caught Marcy's gasp. "Uh-huh. He goes out drinking too often and comes home late and expects you to have the house clean and he hits you sometimes and then makes up, says he didn't mean it but somehow it's your fault. Did I miss anything?"

"He'd never...I don't...You..." Marcy got up so suddenly her chair fell over. "Screw you!" She glared at me and stormed away, around the side of the house. I hunched my shoulders as I heard a door slam.

"Right again," I said. Men.

# CHAPTER 4\

# LONG CONS, INCORPORATED

I didn't just take Nick's money with no thought of what I was going to do with it. I had a plan. A plan to go straight, more or less, while using the skills God gave me and Pops trained to perfection.

I was going to start my own business. In my head I thought of it as Long Cons, Incorporated, a name I was certainly not going to tell anyone.

It would work like this...

The long con being a nearly extinct art, practiced almost exclusively these days by my aging father, was ripe for a comeback. In the old days, the twenties and thirties, there had been the legendary Yellow Kid, Joseph Weil, and others of his kind. I grew up with stories about men who sold the Eiffel Tower, phony gold mines and even, in one memorable swindle, Pops himself selling the USS Mississippi, a WWII battleship. Twice. That one alone came close to making him con artist royalty.

Look it up, it's all true. Pops and his partner "Fast" Kate had committed some notorious scams. Besides the battleship, they created a computer game in the seventies that rivaled Frank Abagnale for sophistication and daring and pulled a memorable long con where he separated a group of crooked oilmen from a few hundred thousand dollars. He sold fake dinosaur bones, ran crooked horses, all sorts of jewelry and most recently, with me, conned a very bad man out of a whole lot of money. Half of which was resting comfortably in my attic.

But he was getting old. I knew in my heart that his days of running a game were rapidly coming to an end and though it grieved me in the way it does all children to see their parents lose their power, I was determined to carry on the family tradition.

I was going to resurrect the long con.

Sitting in my office, a front room the original builders would have called a parlor back when people still knew what those were, I'd set up a desk and computer and a man had come and wired up the internet so I could surf the web in happy solitude.

I was dressed for the heat in a thin cotton blouse, tight red shorts and a pair of sandals bought in New York. My nails were painted a shade of pink called coral mist and my hair was pinned up away from my neck. I looked, I knew, as wholesome as any housewife in a sitcom.

I typed, "Hey, Harpman, long time no see." Harpman Dan was a grifter working out of San Francisco. He owned a music store and played in blues bands but ran a pretty good back room poker game, siphoning tourist cash on the weeknights.

"I'm writing," I wrote, "about a new idea. I'm looking for marks to run the long con. If you hear of anyone who you want to take down, I'm willing to put up the front money and plan the sting."

A major problem with the long con is the up-front cost. Running a Big Store could cost between a few grand and hundred thousand, depending on the size. A rag required printers, the string needed expenses and more often than not refused to work for a piece of the action.

To do a first class raggle you needed a proper hotel, quality clothes, a decent ride. You couldn't expect the small players to bring in all the props for a sting; that was one of the reasons it was a dying art.

I intended to change that. I had a suitcase full of money that I planned to invest in myself. I'd spread the word, like I did with Harpman Dan, to all the cons. Cincinnati Bob, Alison Pinkney, Two Fingers Jake, Angel Face; I knew practically everybody who shaved a card or picked a pocket.

Bring me a quality mark and I'd set up the game.

The only consideration was he had to be bent. Oh, I know; you can't cheat an honest man and all marks are crooked. Sure, but some are more crooked than others. I wanted the ones who really deserved to be fleeced.

This was a new idea. Taking Nick's money had been the last act of my old life. I was going to go straight, sort of. I knew that Nick would look for me and I wanted to be ready for him when he arrived, someday. Innocent and sweet-smelling as a rose, and as rich as he was. Dani Silver, All American success story.

So I sent out my E-mails to as ragged a group as has ever haunted the dark corners of the web, letting them know I was available, was looking and could be had for a price.

A couple of weeks went by as I waited for the work to flow in. I wandered around my new area, checking out the rivers and dams, farms and fields, the occasional auction that seemed a high point on the social calendar. I felt like an anthropologist in the Amazon, not even close to being a member of the tribe. It bothered me a little, and I was feeling a bit sorry for myself, even reconsidering this whole hiding-out-in-the-country thing. What if Nick wasn't even looking? Not much of a game if one player doesn't even know there's a game on. I was beginning to think about conning someone local just to keep my hand in when Marcy Garfield came to the door with her arm in a sling.

"What happened?" I asked, though I knew.

"He...I didn't..." She broke down in tears and I wrapped her in a circling arm and led her inside. After two stiff drinks of Jack Daniels she got the sobbing under control and I heard the usual story.

"He came home late— it was payday—and he smelled of perfume. I asked him and he was like, it wasn't any of my business and he'd do...he'd do..." She choked and I patted her shoulder. I hadn't heard them fighting since the local Sears outlet had been in to install air-conditioning; my windows were now solidly closed.

"...Whatever he damn pleased and I was like, no, you won't and he started yelling and I started yelling and he hit me and I fell against the dresser. Nothing's broken; it's a sprain, that's all." She wound down at that point and I made a snap decision to butt in. I don't like men hitting women and anyway, I had nothing else to do.

"Here's what you do," I said. "Marcy, are you listening to me? You go get some things packed up and get out. Go to your parents..."

"I can't!"

"...for a while until he calms down. You can decide what to do later. Now go."

I led her back to her house and helped her pack, got her into a car and watched her drive away, then wiped my hands together as I walked back home, satisfied that this was now all over.

That thought lasted until ten that evening. I turned off the computer, stretched mightily, feeling bones and tendons creak, and what sounded like an entire cavalry stomped up my front steps. A heavy hand pounded mercilessly on my door and I hurried to it thinking it must be the police. I believed in always answering to the police because that's what innocent people do and I certainly wanted to appear innocent.

I opened the door and a man shoved me roughly aside. "Where is she?" he demanded. My radio was playing Donna Summers "Hot Stuff" until he reached out and swept it from the shelf. It splattered on the floor and went silent.

"What the HELL?" I demanded and he spun around, raised a heavy fist and yelled again, "WHERE IS SHE?"

Brock Garfield, dressed in blue denim jeans, an untucked baseball jersey and a Kansas City Royals baseball cap worn backwards, wild-eyed and clearly drunk.

"Settle down, big guy; she's not here."

He caromed around my living room, eyes searching and bolted for the kitchen. I heard him yell, "Marcy, Marcy, Marcy," like the yowling of a cat. Sighing, I closed the door and followed. I had no doubts about handling him. I'd been around drunks most of my life and found they were seldom effective fighters.

I heard boots clumping up the stairs, more yelling, the sound of furniture crashing, and I ran up to stop him. Brock stood weaving in the bedroom with the ruins of my dresser lying at his feet. My mirror was now many seven years of bad luck all over the battered wood floor and his boots crunched the glass as he stomped about.

"That's enough," I yelled. This had to stop while I still had furniture.

He backhanded me across the face. Pain exploded like a firecracker and a bright light flashed inside my eyelids. I reeled back and fell, banging my rear and the back of my head on the oak floor when I landed.

Brock grabbed my arms and jerked me to my feet like I weighed nothing. Heart beating like a machine gun I had less than a second to sympathize with bruised little Marcy before his face was in mine. He smelled of oil and whiskey and male rage as he shook me like a rag doll.

"Where IS she?"

"She..." shake..."Isn't..." shake..."Here."

Brock dropped me. "She is here. I know it!"

"Why do you think so?" I spoke softly to calm the brute.

"She called me. She said you told her to leave. She laughed at me." He lunged and I rolled away, any sympathy for Marcy already gone. The idiot.

Brock swung punches like he was taking batting practice after happy hour, clumsy and unfocused. I dodged and slipped under several before one caught me flush between my breasts.

Brock grinned and pumped a fist, "Yes!" and I bounced off the wall, scratching at his face. When he raised an arm in defense I kicked him in the balls. My father, normally a peaceful man, had taught me what I considered a valuable lesson. "Dani," he had said, "Never let a man hit you. It will give him ideas. But if he does, kick him purposefully in the groin area, which will serve to dissuade him."

Good advice, but in this case, ineffective. Brock gasped, his eyes grew to the size of saucers and he sucked in air. His raised arm swung and caught me in the cheek and when I stumbled he was all over me, cursing and whining. I remembered other lessons, took a calming breath and grabbed his nipples through his shirt. I pinched and twisted and Brock learned how to levitate. I let go and got to my feet.

As wary and confused as a wounded boar, Brock circled me. I decided it was better to out-think him than continue fighting so I said, in a soft, non-threatening voice, "Yo, big guy. Let's calm down and talk about this."

He feinted right and I went left, still talking. I noticed his high-school class ring and made a cold read. A Jock, missed the buddies. I figured him for football and lowered my tone. "Brock," I said. "You still playin' ball?"

He shook his head and made a half-hearted grab at me.

"Buddy," I oozed friendship. "Hey! You still see the guys?" It didn't matter who, there were always guys. Members of the team, drinking buddies. Guys like Brock always had guys.

Football didn't work so I tried wrestling. "You're still in shape. You seen the coach lately?"

"Coach Wilson?" He asked. His arms dropped to his sides as the steam ran out. "You know the coach?"

"'Course I know him! Who doesn't know the coach? Remember that match? What was it, senior year? You know...when you...?" I let it linger and took a chance. I stepped closer and lowered my guard. No threat here.

Brock said, "Senior...? Oh, you mean when I took third place in my weight class?"

"That was it!"

"Sure," said Brock. He was down from his rage, reminiscing now, and I put an arm around his shoulder – had to stretch for that – and led him out of my bedroom. He talked all the way down the stairs, out the door and back to his own house.

When I led him in I caught sight of Marcy hiding behind a door. Her eyes were as wide as full moons as she watched me ease her husband into his bed.

Alone.

"How did you do that?"

It was nearly midnight and Marcy had been talking non-stop for an hour.

"I don't get it," she said. "You got Brock calmed down like he was a baby."

To beat off the nervous energy I was doing card tricks. I shuffled, cut, nullified the cut, made the Queen of Diamonds appear on top, then in the middle, then the bottom. Marcy, involved in herself, didn't notice and I was doing it by rote, lessons drilled into me by my father from the time I could hold a deck.

"A person who can handle cards won't ever starve," he told me. I was eight at the time and equated starving with being out of Pop-Tarts. Over the years he'd proven his point a dozen times when I hit lows or needed getaway money. Now I kept a deck handy and could do most of the tricks David Copperfield did.

"How do you do it?" asked Marcy again

"Marcy," I said. "Go home."

"I can't go there," she said. "He's there."

"He's always been there," I said. I was tired and sore where her husband had hit me. I'd taken off my bra and noticed the deep bruise between my breasts. Brock would have to pay for that, for sure.

"But this time..." Marcy let that trail away.

"Go home, Marcy."

Crestfallen, she left.

# CHAPTER 5

## I KNOW WHO YOU ARE

Ah, but she was back by nine, arm in a sling, with as determined a look as a mousy, beaten down woman could have.

The doorbell rang and I swept across the scarred wood floor like an avenging homemaker to see her standing on one foot twisting a handbag like a chicken neck.

"Speak of the devil's wife." I held onto the door.

Marcy wore a blue dress with white flowers. Her choppy hair was clean and the dress, though inexpensive, nicely fit a well-curved body. Her makeup almost covered the bruises on her cheek. "Can I come in?"

I hesitated. I was of two minds regarding my new neighbor. On one hand she had a tough life with Brock. On the other, she had sent him in my direction. Add in my strong opinion about women who let themselves get beat up and I was leaning toward shutting the door. Once, I believed, was a surprise; twice a habit. Three times and you had yourself a lifestyle.

Seeing my hesitation she spoke firmly. "I know who you are."

"What?" I asked, shocked. I had visions of paddy wagons, cops, sirens, handcuffs...all the things I thought were far behind me in New York or Louisiana. When you live on the outside of the law your whole life, the phrase, '*I know who you are*,' takes on a certain significance. Like taking that last step that isn't there, it's a teeth-rattler.

I'm not often at a loss for words, but that did it. Marcy waited, nervous and aggressive at the same time. She wore an expression that said, '*This is my big break, I'm not going to back down. Okay?*'

"Come in," I said, knowing it was an admission of something. What did she know? Who did she think I was? Was a lie going to work here, or would I have to resort to the truth?

I escorted her to the kitchen where she sat at the island on a tall stool beneath a wrought iron pot hanger. The pots were gone but I imagined that when they were there you wouldn't be able to see under them.

I made coffee to busy myself while Marcy waited quietly. I poured some into brightly colored Fiesta cups, one red, one yellow, and set the red one in front of her.

"Is it your father?" she asked. I raised an eyebrow. "The bony old guy who was here when you looked at the house? Your father?"

I nodded. Pops had come house-hunting with me, not with interest but for the chance to convince me I was out of my mind. Evidently Marcy had seen him. Evidently, I was.

"I've been watching you," she said. I got a funny feeling of being spied on and mentally ran through the list of things I'd been up to. Nothing illegal recently, I decided, and relaxed.

"You do such strange things over here," Marcy said. She sipped from her cup, made a face and added sugar. "You're up at all hours, you don't have a job, you got that funny little car."

"What's funny about a Mustang?" I asked. Where was this going?

"Nothing. It's odd here, 'cause we never see something that sporty. I kind of got the feeling you're hiding from something."

"I'm not."

"Sure. But I was, you know, curious. Not enough to do anything, but interested. Then last week on TV...do you watch TV?"

"Um," I said. "No." A lie; I was addicted to those stupid reality shows. God knows why.

"So you didn't see *America's Most Wanted* last week?"

I shook my head.

"He was on it. The old guy, your father. They did a story about con men, maybe because there's this show on another station with a gang of con-men."

I'd seen it. It had as much in common with what I do as Celebrity Poker.

"His name's Leroy Logan, isn't it? They say he's the last of the old fashioned con-men. They even said there was a reward."

Oh, Pops, I thought, what have you done to me? I refilled her cup and she smiled thanks. She added three sugars, some cream, stirred it carefully and took a tentative sip. All the while I watched her. Was I going to have to run again? I was happy here and didn't want to find someplace else, start over again, again.

"What do you want?" I asked.

"First, who are you?"

What to do? My first inclination was to lie. But what could I make up on the spot to convince this suddenly aggressive woman that I was who I said I was. Ah, hell. I decided to take a chance.

"My name's Dani," I said. "Dani Silver."

She looked confused. "But the show said your Daddy's' name was Logan."

"Leroy Amadeus Logan," I said with a sort of perverse pride. "I changed it so I wouldn't be associated with him."

"Oh," she said, as if understanding. "Why not? He's your Daddy."

I considered everything that Leroy was, everything he'd done, and 'Daddy' wasn't in the top ten. I loved and respected him and was just as often frustrated by him.

"What do you want?" I asked again.

"I want to get rid of my husband."

We ate pizza and drank beer on my hot back porch while the sun poured through the cheap bamboo shades, painting them with shadows like jungle camouflage. "So where is he?" I asked.

"I don't know. He always goes somewhere for a couple of days when it happens. I don't know where."

"This happens a lot?"

"Once, twice a month." She hung her head and waited for sympathy.

Not from me. "Are you *insane*?"

Marcy looked startled. "You don't understand."

"Sure I do. The guy slugs you; you cry and he knows he can slug you again. This goes on until it's part of who you are and you no longer see how sick and stupid it is."

Marcy shot up, her back and face stiff, her expression rebellious. "I don't have to listen to this crap."

"Oh, shut up and have another beer." I stretched out and opened the pizza box; one slice left. "Let's talk about Brock," I said.

# CHAPTER 6

## WE'LL TIVO THE BASTARD

I was being blackmailed by a Missouri housewife too timid to stand up to her husband. I said, "You're not going to tell anybody."

She said, "Well..."

I felt a little bit of pride concerning her, like she'd done something that I would have done. Can't face your problems? Get the neighbor to do it. In that spirit, I decided to open up to her. What the hell, I'd never had a confidante except Pops, who didn't count since he was far too judgmental. Real friends, the kind you tell secrets to and giggle late at night, had never seemed like a good idea. They wanted to talk about boys and I wanted to discuss scamming the local school board.

But Marcy knew about me, at least a little, and for reasons of her own didn't disapprove. And it was nice having someone to talk to.

"I need to know more about him. Where does he go, what are his hobbies, friends, anything."

"You're really a con-man?"

"Woman. A con-*woman*. What does he like? What doesn't he like?"

Marcy focused on me. "He likes beer and naked women and he doesn't like me. Okay?"

"Look, girl, running a con, even a little one like this, isn't a matter of just doing stuff. I have to know what I'm dealing with so I can plan it. The more you know about a mark, the easier it is to take him down. So talk, what's he like?"

"Oh." She considered, shrugged and told. Brock had, as I figured, been the high-school stand-out. The cocky All-American boy with the world just waiting to roll over for him. He went to college on a wrestling scholarship, found out that everybody in sports was the best in their school and he busted out.

He'd come back home with his tail between his legs and got a job at a warehouse, bringing in enough to pay the bills and get drunk. Slapping around his wife seemed to be just a release from the pressure of the lost glory days.

"What does he do, nights?"

"Sits around. Watches TV. Drinks a lot of beer."

"Does he still do sports?"

"God, no. That would take effort. Brock's looking for the easy way out."

As I grifter, how I loved hearing those words. Anybody looking for the easy way was a sure target for my kind. "What else?"

"He likes bowling."

"Nope. What else?"

"He goes to the *Bottom's Up* every payday." She saw my expression and explained. "It's a strip joint out on the interstate. Draws a lot of the truckers."

No, I thought, still not it.

"He plays the Lotto."

"What?"

"The Lotto," Marcy said. "He buys five tickets every week down at *Bud's Liquor Barn*. We have to watch the damn giveaway every Saturday night."

I sat up straight and thanked St. Dismus, the patron saint of thieves. "That's it," I said.

"Marcy looked blank. "What's it?"

"We are," I said happily, "going to make Brock Garfield the luckiest man on the planet.

Except for having to explain everything to Marcy, running a TIVO scam was about the simplest con possible. I'd even read where some college guys did one as a prank on a buddy.

It's a variation of the ancient Golden Wire, the scam used in the move *The Sting*. It's based on delaying the result of a sports event until the mark can get in a bet. That way he's got a sure thing.

TIVO was just the modern device that took the place of a telegraph.

I told Marcy, "What we do is tape one week's show, buy a lottery ticket with that week's winner, and slip it in with Brock's tickets. Then we play last week's tape instead of the new show and he believes he's won."

"Uh-huh," said Marcy, dubious. "And what happens?"

"I don't know, he's your husband. What will he do when he wins a couple of million dollars?"

She wanted to say he'd share it with her, I could see it in her eyes. But she didn't. He lips grew tight and she sat rocking on the porch for the longest time before saying slowly, "I guess there's only one way to find out."

That Saturday we recorded the Lottery broadcast. Marcy paced back and forth, telling me every few minutes that this couldn't *possibly* work. I was trying to quit smoking and had decided that half a pack a day was a good target. As she paced I carefully lit the day's seventeenth, sipped from a glass of Chablis and tried to calm her.

I said, "Trust me. It'll work."

When the show ended I wrote down the winning numbers on a scrap of paper. *32, 37, 14, 51, 7 and 23*. I had already made Marcy order a satellite video recorder. She and Brock had an old gigantic dish, about the size of a billboard.

"Now we wait until Friday."

"How can you stand this?" She asked. "I'm a nervous wreck."

"Wait until Friday."

At five o'clock we staked out the parking lot of *Bud's Liquor Barn* waiting for Brock to get off work. Marcy got wide-eyed and ducked in the seat. "There he is!" She pointed.

A big blue pick-up with all the toys roared onto the asphalt lot. Brock's truck had road warrior wheels, running boards, halogen beams and yellow fog lights, chrome roll bars, a chrome spare gas tank and for all I knew a helicopter. He gunned the engine the way all jerks do, opened the door and slid down to the ground. He swaggered into the huge blue corrugated metal building and came back with a brown paper bag that he carried by the neck.

He clambered back into the brute truck and drove away.

"Quick," I said. "Go and buy the next ticket. It's important that the time is the same as the one's he just bought." I handed her the paper. "Make sure it's these numbers."

Marcy looked pale but obeyed. I watched her scurry across the hot-top, enter the building and come back, shoulders hunched as if it were raining or she could be seen.

"I got it!" She was bubbling with excitement. "Now what?"

"I already told you." Several times. I relented, remembering when I was new at this. The excitement and fear could be overwhelming. "Tonight, when he's asleep you swap out one of his for this one. But remember, make it the last one."

"Why?"

"Because people always expect it to be the last one. It makes it more believable." She gave me a look like she thought I was crazy but how many times have you found your keys and said, "There they are, in the last place I looked?"

Being a grifter requires a lot of knowledge about what makes people do things. As Pops says, "You've got to have a feel for what makes the frog jump."

I drove her home. "And Marcy? Get me invited for a late dinner."

Brock was clearly uncomfortable having me around and I made every effort to convince him that what he remembered hadn't happened.

"Didn't I...?" He asked, not really wanting to finish, "Get drunk and beat you up?"

"You came over after a few drinks," I said innocently. "But you went home with Marcy."

"Oh. Okay."

After that he settled in, annoyed that I was there but unsure what to do. We made small talk and finally ten o'clock came along. Brock went to the living room and Marcy dashed in before him.

"Let me get it," she said, a bit manically. Her face was flushed, as if she'd been running from the undead, and her smile had that forced look of a wax museum figure. She blocked his view as she turned on the set and pressed play on the recorder.

Brock, sitting back in his recliner with the ninth beer of the evening, never noticed.

The announcer was an aging game show host named Chuck Whimpole who, with the help of a pneumatic blonde in a tight red sequined gown, made the selection of numbered ping pong balls an event to rival the Super-Bowl in excitement.

He pressed a button and a ball rose in the clear plastic tube to fall down a chute. I sat down on the far side of the sofa where I could get a sidewise view of Brock.

"*Seven!*" Chuck bellowed. The blonde held both arms up as if in religious ecstasy. Her gloves were as white as her teeth.

"*Twenty-Three!*" Chuck wore a gold lame jacket and black pants with a stripe down the leg.

"*Thirty-Seven!*" A synthesized group of horns blatted, "Ta-Dah!" Marcy fidgeted in the doorway, went out, brought her husband another beer, went out, fidgeted in the doorway and came back in.

"*Fourteen!*" The woman's eyes shone with manic glee. Her eyelashes were long and black. Brock had already thrown away four of his tickets. The remaining one was clutched tightly in his fist.

"*Thirty-Two!*" Chuck's microphone was shaped like a wand, a phallic symbol of impossible dimension. Brock dropped his bottle and beer sloshed on the brown carpet.

"*Fifty-One!*" The lottery was twenty-six million dollars. Chuck leaned into the camera and said, "Now for the power ball multiplier!"

A drum roll began and the horns played a sustained E-flat demented chord.

A red ball rose into the tube, hovered and fell.

"*Nine!*"

The imitation crowd went berserk. Chuck and the blonde grinned like Incan death masks and the station went to a Toyota Sell-a-Bration commercial.

Brock screeched a cowboy yell. His face was ashen and his mouth opened, closed and opened again. Marcy sat on the couch watching him carefully. She wore a long red nightshirt with a white Snoopy carrying a lit candle. Her feet, in pink fuzzy socks, were pulled up under her.

She said, "What?"

"I won," said Brock. His voice could barely be heard over the screeching of the Toyota buyers. A Land-Rover for Twenty-Nine-Nine? Oh-My-Gawd!

I grabbed the remote and turned it off. The silence was deafening.

Marcy sat up straighter. "Won what?"

"The lottery." Brock leaped to his feet, shaking the ticket at her. "I won the freakin' lottery!"

Marcy jumped up. "No way," she said, over and over. "No way, no way, no way."

"I can't believe it!" Brock, in gray gym shorts, chest rising and falling like a trampoline as he gasped for air, held the ticket in disbelief. He had forgotten I was even there.

"We won the lottery," Marcy said, like a non-believer seeing an actual miracle.

"We? The fuck you mean we?"

"The ticket," Marcy pointed and Brock tightened his grip. "It's ours."

"Like Hell! This is mine. I won it. It's all mine." He sounded like Daffy Duck in the old cartoons and I had to stifle a laugh. The end of a good con always gave me the giggles.

Marcy gaped at him in surprise.

"But we're *married*!"

"Not anymore." Brock strode from the room and came back in a few minutes with a sports bag stuffed willy-nilly with clothes. The sleeve of a baseball jersey stuck out like a drooping arm; the casualty in a bitter war.

"Screw you, Marcy, if you think you're getting one red cent from me."

He stormed away and we heard the roar of his truck as he peeled off into the night.

For a long time we sat still in the silent empty room. Marcy's breathing came in soft pants as if she was exhausted. Her eyes were unfocused in shock.

The ticking of the clock, an inexpensive imitation wall clock from Target her mother had given her when she married Brock was the only sound in the room.

Until Marcy began to cry.

# CHAPTER 7

## A FINE TURN OF EVENTS

Brock's meltdown was spectacular. We watched it all on TV Monday morning.

In a scathing attack he burned any chance of ever working at the Klipmann Metal Works where he'd been a fork lift driver for five years. He ridiculed his co-workers, sneered at the foreman and, in a wonderfully misguided act of 'take this job and shove it,' mooned the entire front office, causing an uproar of laughter and appreciative hoots.

Security hastened him on his way, not gently.

Marcy and I watched the news with a mounting sense of elation (me) and dread (her). Brock called the two local television stations, announcing the winning ticket and inviting them to his victory speech at the lottery headquarters in Kansas City. He invited the KC stations as well before roaring the 80 odd miles south.

At 9:00 he climbed the steps of the lottery building, raising his arms in a sort of Rocky fist clenching salute.

At 9:01 the doors opened and a chunky man in a black suit came out to a lectern mounted for press conferences. He shook hands with Brock.

"Oh my God," whispered Marcy, watching intently. "That's his best suit. He only wears that at weddings and funerals."

"Which is what this is." I felt like laughing. This promised to be good.

The lottery man gestured and Brock handed over the winning ticket, looking down on the reporters with a big goofy grin. He didn't notice the man compare the numbers and frown. He went on beaming at the reporters while they saw the reaction and quieted in confusion.

Finally, Brock heard the silence, turned around to see the lottery man glowering and said, as he would be saying a lot for the next several days, "What?"

"Is this a joke?" said the lottery man.

Open mouthed, gaping like a flounder, Brock demanded an explanation. "That's my ticket," he shouted. "That's my TICKET!"

"These are last week's numbers." The lottery man held up the small paper and the news people crowded in to get pictures. Within an hour it would be in every news feed in the country.

By six that evening it would make it all around the world. By the following morning Brock would hear from *America's Stupidest Criminals*.

I felt that glow I get from pulling off a successful scam. Sure, it was possibly overkill to use my talents this way but hey, justice was achieved. Maybe Nick was right to insist that I only con those who deserve it. I solemnly shook Marcy Garfield's hand and smiled at her.

Brock Garfield was screwed.

# CHAPTER 8

## THE BAT-PHONE

I sat high in the seat of a hated new exercise bike, pedaling gently while watching the television on the temporary bookshelf. Marcy lay on a green mat, caught in the middle of a leg lift to observe the coverage of the Brock Garfield lottery fiasco. She wore red shorts, a yellow Tee-shirt and big white Reeboks. Her curly hair framed her face like a bobbing halo. With her leg stretched at a taut angle she looked a bit like Robin, the Boy Wonder.

"He's really screwed," she said conversationally, then began to giggle. I wondered at how much abuse a woman had to take to feel such glee at the fall of her husband. However much, Marcy had undoubtedly lived through it.

"Totally," I gasped. Even slow the bike was a struggle. Damn, I was out of shape. I looked at my reflection, generally liking what I saw. Long legs and hair, slightly exotic features, a drawback to anonymity, five-eight and a hundred-twenty-pounds. Not bad for thirty-five.

"You're free of him," I said. "What are you going to do?"

"I dunno." She resumed her leg lifts, apparently without effort. I frowned and resumed pedaling harder. That's the problem with youth, I thought, it's totally wasted on the young.

"Gonna have to think of something," I said. "School?"

"Ugh."

"A job?"

"Are you kidding? I'm trained for nothing. I can sit at home, clean house and cook a few things. I'm not even a mother."

"You could teach aerobics," I suggested. She was certainly in good enough shape. Unlike me. I vowed right then to not waste any more time. I'd eat right, lose those five pounds I always carry, quit smoking, get in shape and stay that way. I made the same promise every time I worked out. I glanced down at the speedometer and saw that I'd been pedaling less than a mile. I swear the bike was mocking me.

"I guess," Marcy said, but she sounded dubious.

Downstairs the phone rang. In the silence of the house, the loud ring sounded nasal, like a Bronx cheer.

It rang again. Marcy looked up and said, "What is it?"

I side-saddled my leg over the bike and trotted to the door. "Holy Mother of God," I said. "It's the bat-phone."

# CHAPTER 9

## WHY DID IT HAVE TO BE JIGGS?

I said, "Hello?" and a voice from the past begin babbling in my ear. A voice I had last heard in New Orleans cursing me when I told him to get out of my life. Jiggs Roche, my first serious boy-friend.

He spoke rapidly and Cajun accented words spilled over me in a flood. His voice, high-pitched and whiny, as if he was constantly trying to justify something, sounded like the buzzing of gnats. I shook my head to dislodge them and saw Marcy enter the room with a yellow towel wrapped around her shoulders.

"Who is it?" She mimed as I pressed the phone back to my ear.

"Dani," it said. "I can't believe I'm talking to you, it's like we never were apart, I'm so happy to hear your voice…" So far I had said, "Hello."

" - And I know we didn't part on the best of terms but I really need your help and I heard from the grapevine that you were willing to set up scams and I have the perfect person for you if you'll just give me a moment to explain."

He went on and I considered how I had last seen him. Pops was holding the shotgun, an Ithaca 12 gauge I believe, while I explained to Jiggs in no uncertain terms that if he ever spoke to me again I would find a way to get him arrested for everything from drug dealing (he did) to contributing to the delinquency of a minor(me) and anything else I could invent.

He seemed to get the point and hadn't been heard from since.

Until now. I said, "Jiggs," but it was stopping the tide.

"I don't know who else to turn to, Dani. My Moms is dead and she gave the house away before she died and the lawyer says there's nothing I can do about it which isn't fair at all…"

Nothing was ever fair at all as far as Jiggs was concerned. But I stopped for a moment before hanging up, remembering his Moms, a gentle good woman with a bad son, resigned and weary. Mary, I recalled, though I had been too young to call her anything but Ms.

Roche or Moms. She baked bread and cooked the best spicy hot crawdads I had ever tasted.

My mouth began to tingle with the memory and I interrupted again. "Jiggs."

"...Briscoe," he said. "He's a televangelist..."

"Jiggs."

"...Got his own station and everything but he's a crook, Dani, and he stole Moms' house, just *stole* it."

"Jiggs!" I bellowed. "Shut the Hell up!" Marcy, seated at the table drinking a designer water, began to smile.

"Why are you calling?" I knew why, of course; he wanted a favor. Jiggs Roche always wanted a favor. He lived like a cockroach, on the kindness of strangers. "Speak slowly and to the point or I'm hanging up."

"Just please don't hang up, Dani." I also remembered his habit of saying your name a lot, as if it made you more likely to do whatever he was after. I had learned to resent it then. I hated it now.

"Moms died."

"I heard. I'm sorry."

"But she gave away the house to this phony TV guy and I want it back."

"Uh-huh. But why call me?"

"Well..." This, I knew, was the pitch. "I heard from somebody that you was starting a business and that you'd help people get even and stuff..."

"I am," I said. "But not for you." Tell the truth I was tempted. Not by Jiggs – I'd learned that hard lesson long ago – but by the prospect of getting the business started. This was, after all, my first request. How could I turn it down?

"Aw, Dani," he whined.

Then again, how could I not?

"You can't!" cried Marcy, following me upstairs with the bleating persistence of a sheep. I pulled out one of my just un-packed suitcases and began transferring clothes into it.

"Not now," I said.

"But..."

I stopped, holding a light aqua blouse – the color of my eyes – to my chest, and looked at her. She seemed to be in a state approaching panic. "What?" I asked, perhaps more testily that I should.

"You can't go to New Orleans."

"Why ever not?

 "You can't leave me."

"Of course I can. I have to. That's where the con is."

"No. I mean you can't go anywhere!"

That got my attention. "What are you talking about?"

"Brock's just been tricked and humiliated. Today, Dani. What if he comes after me?"

"Bosh," I scoffed, recalling a favorite scoff of Leroys'. "He's long gone. He won't come back."

"You're right, maybe he won't. But what if he does? Dani, he'll kill me this time."

"He won't," I said

Marcy stared at me.

"He wouldn't," I said

Marcy waited silently.

"Damn," I said.

# CHAPTER 10

# THELMA AND LOUISE

We left for New Orleans the next morning with Marcy's three suitcases, a make-up kit, three bags of groceries, a traveler mug, light jacket, heavy coat and seven pairs of shoes.

"You want to just hook up to the house and drag it along?" I asked. My own luggage was crammed in that small space Ford called a trunk. The bulk of my money was buried in the back yard.

Marcy bounced with a frantic excitement. She sat on the doorframe, swiveled tan legs in a wide arc and dropped into the passenger seat. I opened the door with stately dignity as befit my years.

"I never went anywhere before," said Marcy. Her hair floated around her face like a cloud as we breezed past the Conoco station onto the Expressway. "This is just like Thelma and Louise!" She gave out a loud whoop as I raced through the gears and the Mustang hit the highway at seventy.

"Just remember that Jiggs isn't Brad Pitt," I suggested, but my words whistled away as soon as I said them.

We drove east to St. Louis and south through the soupy heat of Missouri with the top down, along the well-traveled interstate into the cradle of the Civil War. We ate at truck stops, always fending off truckers, and I bought a half-dozen celebrity magazines at a gas station outside of Greenville, Arkansas and read them when we stopped for the night. I don't know why I care about movie stars but I do. Marcy had a paperback Grisham that she read while I drove.

"Who's this Jiggs guy?" asked Marcy. Jackson was in the rearview mirror and soon we'd be in New Orleans, my home town. The memories were getting stronger. "How long were you with him?"

"Too long."

"Why'd you break up? Did he hit you?"

I laughed out loud, a snort that would have been inelegant on anyone else, at the idea of any man hitting me – he'd wake up dead,

buried in a swamp – but especially of Jiggs Roche doing it.
Violence wasn't Jiggs' style, nor was working. He lived off women,
sponged off society and smoked a lot of dope.

"He stole things," I said eventually. My heart for one, and later,
my stereo for drug money. I'd been younger and, and less mature,
but Jiggs walked funny for a few months.

"You steal things," Marcy pointed out.

"I do not," I said, thoroughly outraged the very idea. "I'm a
grifter, a con woman by training and profession."

"Sorry. What's the difference?"

I thought about it a while before answering. I suppose, from her
point of view, that a crime was a crime was a crime, but I knew
better. What I did was an art. Sure, people lost money when I was
around, but never by violence. The long con was an elegant
undertaking, refined and civilized.

Or, like anyone else, I was bullshitting myself, hard to tell. I
resolved to show Marcy what conning was all about.

"Wait and see," I said, as the car glided down the exit at Glen
Martin. I turned left on Jefferson Davis Boulevard and looked for a
Hotel. "Tomorrow we'll meet Jiggs and see what's what. After that
you just might have a ringside seat to the best con ever attempted."

We got a room at a Holiday Inn with a flooded out of order pool
and flowers in the lobby, ate a late breakfast in the attached diner
and met Jiggs in the moon walk park in the early afternoon. He was
late of course. Jiggs had never gotten up before eleven or been on
time in his life.

He came up like a vision from the past beneath the hanging
vines of an acacia tree, wearing sagging jeans, an armless tee-shirt
and a swagger that said he was above every loser he met. He had the
skinny build of an addict and his hair was gelled and spiked as if he
was nineteen and liked Rap music. His shoes were worn down and
he had stereo headphones in his ears. Jiggs was forty if he was a day.
I felt all the old feelings rush back.

Lord, how I disliked him.

We waited at a wooden picnic table on the banks of the
Mississippi near an old white bandstand. Bougainvilleas, Hyacinths,
Forsythias and willows weeping golden showers framed the

impossibly blue sky and the humidity made it feel like we were deep in an undersea kingdom. Even breathing was an effort.

"Dani!" He held out his arms for a welcoming hug which I ignored. His arms fell without resentment as he turned to Marcy and smiled hugely, revealing a gold capped tooth.

Marcy, to my horror, grinned back as if she liked what she saw and accepted his hand, which he bent to kiss, making her laugh.

"How long has it been?" He asked and I held my tongue from saying, "Not long enough." Instead I beckoned impatiently and he sat backwards on the bench, leaning his elbows on the table.

I studied him, wondering how in Hell I could have ever imagined I loved him. Sure, I was young and stupid. I had to be or else I would have never come near him. He was everything I loathed; dirty, ignorant, lecherous and a user. I began to question why I was here.

"So tell me the story," I said.

The guy's name, said Jiggs, was Hailey Briscoe and he ran a small local Christian radio station somewhere west of town. He'd only been on the air for a couple of years, and Jiggs saw his billboards sometimes or on buses and bus-stop benches, strictly small time, targeting the poor and desperate.

"He's real hard core, though, the whole Hell-and-Damnation thing. Says New Orleans got Katrina because she was ungodly and deserved to be smited." He looked confused. "Smitten? Smote? Anyway, he's broadcasting and you know me, like, live and let live and all that shit and I'm like paying no attention at all and my Moms dies."

"I'm sorry," I said and Marcy touched his arm in sympathy.

"Yeah, well; we weren't all that close, not after the last time I went up to Angola—that's the state prison." Marcy looked startled and impressed which was, I'm sure, the reaction he'd been after.

"Moms didn't have a lot of use for me but I'm her only kid so I knew the house would be mine when she died."

He held out his hands in a 'See what I mean?' gesture and I stifled the desire to bite him. Jiggs had always been this way, telling the part of the story that interested him, needing to be goaded into filling in any gaps. Like what the Hell he wanted from me.

"So...?" I prompted

"So? She dies and I went to this lawyer—"

"Which lawyer?"

"I don't know, I got his card. I went to this lawyer and he told me Moms had given the house to this guy—"

"Hailey Briscoe," I said and now Jiggs looked annoyed.

"Yeah, of course," he said, like anyone would know that. "I said, "what about me?" and he was like, "what about you?" and I was, "the house, man!" and he was like, "the house was *given* to this guy." and I was like, "that ain't right, man.' and he just sort of shrugged, you know, like they do? You know, lawyers." He shook his head like he had a right to be aggrieved.

"So what happened?"

"I hate them fuckin' lawyers, man, they just..."

I interrupted or he'd go on forever. "What *happened*?"

"Oh, yeah. Well, I was like, "fuck this." and he told me to leave."

"I would, too," I said. "Let me get this straight. You think that, because your mother gave away the house that you think should go to you that this guy—"

"Hailey Briscoe."

"Right, the televangelist. That he did something wrong."

"Uh-huh," said Jiggs. He kept playing to Marcy, like she was an audience who approved of him rather than to me, who didn't, and she was eating up being the center of attention from someone who didn't hit her.

"Why?" I asked.

"Why what?"

"Why do you think he did something wrong?"

Jiggs gaped at Marcy with a 'who *is* this person?' look, shook his head and said, "Because, why else would Moms give away my house to some stranger?" He rolled his eyes and Marcy turned to me for an answer like she was buying this guy's act.

"Maybe she gave it to him for being there for her. Maybe he comforted her in her old age. Maybe he was available instead of in jail or selling dope."

Jiggs considered it. "Nah, Moms loved me."

I said, "Not likely," which got me a look, and he and Marcy waited, watching me with eyes that would be sad on a Beagle. I wanted to walk away, just forget the whole thing. I wanted to forget

I ever heard of Jiggs Roche. It was clear he hadn't changed; he was still the same old tool he'd always been.

But I was here and the situation had possibilities. I resented phony preachers, which the South seemed full of. Always pushing for money, demanding cash. I figured if God was that bad off he'd hold his own fund-raiser without the help of a two-bit TV charlatan. Maybe a bake sale.

And besides, I did like his Moms.

So I said, "I'll check into it," regretting the words as they left my mouth. "I'll see if this guy's real and if there's anything there for us."

"Us?"

"A crew. If I need to bring in a gang to get your mother's house back, I'll have to pay them."

Jiggs looked confused and hurt, an expression I remembered well from the past. It meant he understood totally and wanted something else but knew better than to ask. I believed in that moment that if I was Jiggs' Mom I'd have given away the house long ago. With Jiggs in it.

"But I thought...?"

"What?" I said wearily. Honestly, the man had no limits.

"Well, I mean..." He looked to Marcy for support, got an encouraging smile and pushed on. "Word I had was that you were *paying* for this."

I burst out laughing. "Who told you that?"

Jiggs didn't like being laughed at; it happened too often. "Leroy told me." He rushed on before I could interrupt. "Not to me, okay? He told some other people and I heard about it from somebody and I called you."

"You got it wrong, Jiggs. I'm not in the charity business. What the deal is, I'll pay the expenses up front to run a long con, but I expect to get paid back and I intend to make a profit."

"Shit," said Jiggs. "Does that mean you won't help me?"

"That means I'll look into it," I got up to leave, brushed some dirt from the back of my shorts. "Where do I find this guy?"

"I don't know."

"What does he look like?"

Shrug.

"Oh for Heaven's sake, Jiggs. You must have seen the billboards, at least."

"Sure. He looks like a guy, okay? Old, a suit, a lot of hair. Big white teeth."

"I'll look into it." Easier to do my own research than continue this conversation.

"You'll call me?" Jiggs made a phone with his hand and held it to his ear.

"You bet, Jiggs. I'll be sure to call you." I was trying for sarcastic, forgetting that Jiggs didn't get it. It was nice to see an old boyfriend who deserved it fall this low, but I was tired of him now and wanted to be gone.

"Right. You'll call me." Jiggs walked away backwards, still with the hand phone, nodding as if his agreement would somehow be binding. "You call me."

# CHAPTER 11

## THE MINISTER WILL SEE YOU NOW

The Hailey Briscoe Ministries operated out of a run-down building well outside of town, a typical blond brick, low profile, one story flat roofed former grade school that a couple of generations of children had learned in, except for me whose formal education had been sketchy at best.

"It's just like Parker Elementary," said Marcy, proving my point. We parked near the front door on a faded blacktop drive where the Mustang looked like a hooker at a pot-luck dinner next to the staid old building.

Inside were the same halls, the same blond wood doors with little windows in them but the classrooms held no desks or students. Instead they were crammed with bunks and looked like a war zone evacuation area filled with hundreds of soggy woebegone survivors. From somewhere far off came the shrieking of opera.

We hurried past these grim reminders of Katrina's wrath, marching along the low ceiling narrow halls with our feet clacking against the industrial brown and cream square tiles. A sign on the former attendance office written in black magic marker said, "Studio is in the gymnasium."

Which would be that way. We entered the first room with an actual ceiling high enough to allow a sense of proportion and walked through a field of cheap folding chairs to the stage, a raised platform covering the entire far wall. The usual lectern and American flags had been replaced by a simple pulpit with a microphone and huge speakers. Cables snaked across the floor, covered with silver duct tape to lessen the tripping hazard. Hulking cameras on tripods stood like dinosaurs, covered in gray plastic.

A large man in a pastel green suit stood at the pulpit, studying a script. He had that look of barely contained energy common to some politicians and all fighters, like a caged lion, poised and calm but ready to erupt. Even from across the room I could feel his presence.

He looked up and held out a large hand. "We're closed right now. No interviews."

"We're not reporters." I reached the stage without slowing and walked up the four stairs, holding out my hand. People almost always stop what they're doing to return the handshake, except in Montana, which I didn't know first person, but Leroy swore it was true.

"How come?" I had asked.

"I dunno, but it's a fact." I'd probably been ten years old when he told me, but I remembered.

We were both dressed in well-tailored suits bought for the purpose at a shopping mall in Memphis. I'd told Marcy, "Good dress is the most important first impression. It trumps everything except an introduction from a VIP. Remember that."

"Why?"

Surprised, I had shrugged. I'd forgotten that Marcy wasn't a grifter and realized I was enjoying having someone to talk to. And maybe show off a little bit. "Just pick out something medium priced and low attention-getting."

Hailey Briscoe stared at us as if we were insignificant but he set down his papers to shake hands as I made introductions. I had decided, as a first approach, to be a policewoman. The authority usually got results.

"I'm Carly McNair and this is Bonnie Renaldi, from up north." I confided that last part. Another lesson recalled; "always end an introduction with a non-sequitur. It makes them think of that instead of who you aren't."

"Hailey Briscoe." In addition to the last pastel green leisure suit in America he wore polished black shoes that matched the thick hair combed back from a widow's peak to a full wave in the back. Elvis Presley himself would have envied that lush mop.

He wore rings on three stubby fingers, one ruby, one emerald and a purple monstrosity that I took to be an amethyst. My first appraisal said they were real; this guy wouldn't accept fake stones. His hands were large with dark hairs, his shirt was white, his expression wary.

"What can I do for you?" His voice was his gimmick, a southern drawl as rich as honey, with deep undercurrents of subdued electricity that I knew would make women breathe a little deeper and men feel a little less secure.

A preacher's voice, or a grifters, not that I saw a lot of difference. Both of us were selling snake oil by the case and getting paid for it.

I found myself disliking Hailey Briscoe on some deep level where words fail and instinct takes over. I sensed a barely concealed violence under the polished veneer. Beside me I felt Marcy go tense and realized she was having a similar reaction.

I said, "We're with the New Orleans Police Bunco Squad. We've had a complaint from a..." I took out a battered spiral notebook, flipped it open and read. "Jiggs Roche. He says that his mother, one Coretta Roche, donated a house to this organization on or about the fifth of this month. Mrs. Roche having since deceased, Mr. Roche, the son, feels that the said ministry took advantage of his mother's frail condition and failing faculties to take unfair advantage."

This barrage of legalese often caused people to bend over to co-operate but Hailey Briscoe, eyes sharply focused, merely regarded us without affection.

He said, "Miss...?"

"McNair," I said.

"Do you have any identification?"

"Of course." I took out a battered wallet, flipped it open to a card that said I was who I said I was. Hailey took it, studied it and returned it. Cincinnati Bob, I thought fondly, was a master at forged documents.

"What's this about?" Hailey sounded like a busy executive who couldn't be bothered with details, a harried televangelist with sermons to write, souls to save.

I explained, referring to my book. "A Mrs. Roche, of Seventy-Five-Forty-Seven Riverwalk Way..."

"Yes, yes," said Hailey. "I remember now. A sweet woman, Mrs. Roche."

"Sweet enough," I said. "She gave you her house."

Hailey shrugged. "I can't be responsible for people's actions." He made it sound like he considered them fools, these people who believed in him. His sense of superiority, even arrogance, surprised me. I would have thought a personality this negative would be disadvantaged in his profession.

Whatever spiritual cod liver oil he was selling seemed to me as phony as a three-dollar bill. Of course, I should talk.

"Unless they're coerced by fear of the afterlife," I suggested.

"Miss...uh..." He snapped his fingers impatiently.

"McNair."

"I resent your implication."

"Sure, I would, too. But speaking of the house, what did you do with it?"

"I wouldn't know." He waved an arm that took in the cameras, the stage, the seats. "I have so much to do here. Sermons, missionary work –I can't be expected to know every detail."

"Of course." I thought his evasions sounded rehearsed, like he'd been questioned before and was no longer bothered. Still, I wondered as we studied each other, there seemed to be something behind the bluster, some secret he kept well hidden.

"I listened to your broadcast," I said, fishing.

"Which one?"

"The one about sin." I said, wishing I'd actually prepared for this.

"They're all about sin," said Hailey. His frown was Biblical in its disdain and his blue eyes suggested hellfire and damnation were just a matter of time. God was patient they said, but I'm not.

Hailey Briscoe reminded me of another Baptist preacher I had known, a man as insincere as a horny teenage boy. Winston Grimes believed in a God of everlasting punishment and fervently wished it would happen soon. In the meantime, he offered—for a price—indulgences that just might give the sinner and even break.

I wondered at Hailey's effect on the poor and needy. His accent was Deep South with a trace of education slipped in and I realized this was not an ignorant man.

I tried again. "I'm impressed by the frugality of your operation, Mr. Briscoe. You certainly aren't spending much on luxuries, are you?"

"Is that part of your investigation?"

"Speaking of contributions," I said smoothly. "Mrs. Roche's house...I wonder if you have any financial records. Perhaps in your office?"

"I won't allow you to see them," he said immediately. He drew back his large head and regarded us down his considerable nose, trying for imperious, succeeding at arrogant.

"Separation of Church and State, right?" My voice dripped sarcasm, like I'd heard it all before and wasn't buying.

"Exactly," said Hailey.

"Precedent," I said.

"Precisely."

"Mr. Briscoe, would you care to come downtown with me? I can have a warrant for obstruction in half an hour."

Hailey regarded me for a long while, and said. "No, you can't."

"What?"

"I said you can't get a warrant. I've done nothing wrong and, without a lot more than a vague accusation, you won't be able to get any judge to issue anything. Especially in these times."

"Which times are these?" I asked, annoyed despite myself. I was beginning to really dislike this guy.

"Post Katrina. The entire government is overwhelmed by the challenges they face. Prison records missing, *prisoner*s missing, the courts are in chaos. Finding a compliant judge will prove a formidable task Miss..." He snapped his fingers again.

"McNair."

"I'm terrible at names," he admitted.

"You seem to know a lot about the law, though."

"Are we through here?" He said it so suddenly that I had no response.

He turned back to his papers and, after a few awkward moments, we left.


Once we were back in the car Marcy asked, "What was that all about?"

"We were checking him out."

"Did we learn anything?"

"We have no idea."

"Is he...what's the word? Legit?"

"Legit? Dear, you watch way too much TV."

"Well, is he?"

"I don't know."

"What *did* we learn?"

I considered as we drove past a dilapidated turn of the century shack. I imagined ancient share-croppers working the soil, a mule pulling an old plow. Women in red bandanas, children on their hips as they hung clothes on the line, God fearing people who went to a clapboard church and gave what they could, a pig or chicken, maybe a dime if they had it. I shuddered.

"He knows an awful lot about the law for a Baptist preacher," I said. "He knew Mrs. Roche but denied it. He wouldn't let us see his records. He drives a terrifically expensive car."

"How do you know that?" asked Marcy, sounding fascinated. Her life until now had been beatings, boredom and television. She must have thought she'd fallen into a detective show.

"I saw it in the parking lot. A new white Cadillac Escalade."

"How do you know it's his?"

"It's parked in a space marked 'reserved for Reverend Briscoe,' and the vanity plates read, "God's #1.""

"Good eye."

"I'm a professional." I said solemnly.

"So he's a crook?"

"I don't know."

"Did we learn *anything?*"

"He has nice hair."

Jiggs Roche, wriggling to music from the spheres, was predictably upset.

"You didn't find out anything?" he demanded. His jeans had gotten, if possible, even dirtier, his hair was still jangly and the I-Pod hanging from his belt with the tiny wires running up his shirt to the earphones just *had* to be stolen.

I reached out and plucked them from his ears. Jiggs winced and tinny tiny music squawked from them as they dangled, something Jamaican and upbeat. Bob Marley maybe, and the Wailers.

Aggrieved still further Jiggs demanded, "That's my tunes, dammit!" He swore at the world in general, since he didn't dare swear at me. Our last meeting, though twenty-odd years ago, was still fresh in his memory. "What about my Moms' house?"

"I don't know. He may be legitimate."

"Crap, he is. He's a thief. He stole my Moms' house. She wouldn't have given it to him when she was gonna give it to me."

I considered the likelihood that Coretta Roche was going to give anything to her pig of a son. She'd thrown him out about the time I did and I saw no improvement since. When I was sixteen I'd thought of Jiggs as daring, an outlaw and a reason to annoy my mother and usually absent father. I'd grown out of Jiggs within the first couple of months.

"Maybe," I offered tactfully, "Your Moms *wanted* to give the house to the church."

Jiggs goggle-eyed me as if I was insane. "Are you crazy? My Moms loved me."

Somebody had to, I thought, though I doubted it was Coretta. "I don't know, Jiggs. Hailey doesn't seem to be the devil you think he is."

"I agree with Jiggs," chimed in Marcy and we both turned to look at her in surprise.

"You do?"

"Sure. I can't believe a mother would give away her son's inheritance like that. It just doesn't seem right, you know?"

"Yeah," said Jiggs, nodding. "She wouldn't." He studied Marcy with new interest and she faced him squarely, her chest out in full display until I grabbed her by the arm and pulled.

"No," I said. "Nope, nope, nope. We are going now." I imagined what he would do to an innocent like Marcy and shuddered. "Jiggs; I'll investigate, I promise. I'll find out about the house. Good-bye."

Marcy went along with her arm but she was watching back to the park where Jiggs Roche stood like a statue honoring the disreputable.

# CHAPTER 12

# A STUDY IN PATIENCE

We drove back into New Orleans, making the transition from rural to urban by getting trapped in a nasty traffic jam. By the time we reached the Holiday Inn I was grouchy, tired and hot. My feet hurt from riding the clutch and I craved a drink, a bath and my magazines. Simultaneously.

Marcy, though, wanted to talk. She found our first day more exciting than I remembered it and was running down every moment, squeezing out the juice. She concentrated especially on Jiggs, which I found disturbing.

"He's kind of cute, isn't he?"

"God, no!" The elevator taking us to the fifth floor had bright lights and signs advertising actual Cajun cuisine in the downstairs restaurant. Since we'd eaten at a real crab shack an hour before we didn't bend to the temptation.

But I had to stop this budding infatuation. "He is not cute," I said firmly. "Not at all cute. He's a user and a drifter and a walkaway Joe."

"A what?" Marcy laughed.

"A guy who's born to leave you. Can't stay with any woman, has the attention span of a flea and the morals of a catfish. A bottom feeder."

"Dani, you're jealous!"

"Oh, Lord." I had to nip this in the bud. As I remembered my youthful discretions I considered that, of them all, Jiggs was the worst. Even more than the time in Tulsa with that ensign from the Naval Department. No way could Marcy be allowed this mistake.

"Listen." I was unused to being the voice of sweet reason— usually I demanded full speed ahead and never mind the seat belts. "Jiggs is not a good person. He's worse than Brock, he's..." The elevator opened and we went down the hall. I stuck the plastic card in the slot, the light turned green and we went in. Got to move somewhere better, I decided. Maybe rent a nice place in the Quarter. "Bad," I concluded.

"Never mind, Dani. It's not like I want to sleep with him or anything." Marcy was laughing at me but I remained stricken. Don't even think about, I telegraphed, trying to be telepathic. Read my thoughts, girl—the man will spit you out more surely than your husband ever did.

Marcy turned on the TV and I fled to the bath tub where two glasses of wine and a lot of suds made me a new woman. Angelina was adopting again, a Diva got busted for possession and telephotos showed more beachwear cellulite than a weight-watchers convention. Bliss.

Basically, I'm a creature of comfort. A hot bath and room service are pretty much the absolute minimum. I read about a Diva's current meltdown and the Hollywood baby boom and forgot, in the snooping into celebrity lives, that my own once again contained Jiggs Roche.

By the time I emerged in a white hotel terry robe, faced freshly scrubbed, hair up in a towel, Marcy was already in bed, remote in hand, hysterical laughter on the set.

"What are you watching?"

"Dunno."

"Is it any good?"

"No." She went back to the show and I read a book until midnight.

The next morning at breakfast Marcy said, "So, what's next?"

Swallowing—why do people always ask a question just when you've taken a bite?—I answered, "Research."

"Really?" Somehow that impressed Marcy. "Like at the library? I love libraries. I used to go there when I was younger, before, you know, Brock."

"Brock was against you going to the library?" How was that possible?

"Brock was against anything that wasn't all about himself," she said and I took the opportunity to reaffirm my point.

"Jiggs is worse, Marcy. He is so much worse."

"How bad can he be? He had you." She turned back to her eggs and I shuddered. Yes, he had me. He certainly had.

The New Orleans library had been, like almost everything else, damaged by Hurricane Katrina. The smell of wet paper filled the nostrils and made the eyes tear.

We went up broad old marble stairs, worn smooth by a million feet, to a vast chamber of copper and dark oak. The hushed echoes felt like a cave as we checked computer screens and pulled out financial records. I was fairly good at this sort of thing as I had to be to plan long cons. The lever—that particular piece of information needed to rake in a Mark—was usually found in these dusty or mildewed shelves and stacks.

After three hours and pages of notes and a hundred photocopies, we were both sneezing and rubbing our burning eyes. I wondered how the harried librarians could stand it.

It was overall a sad experience, like seeing a beloved Aunt who filled your childhood with laughter and Kool-Aid, now reduced to feebleness and dementia. I wondered if the ancient building and its contents would survive. I hoped so.

We broke for lunch at Wimpy's, ate salads and French fries to balance the calories and headed to the Parish courthouse.

"Why?" asked Marcy.

"It's where the records are."

"It's boring."

"Astoundingly so," I agreed.

A very well-dressed man in a cream suit held the door for us, as any southern gentleman would, and we entered the courthouse. I nodded politely as my eye caught the glint of a diamond tie clip. Nothing avaricious, merely interest.

We filed slowly through the metal detector and took a paneled elevator to the sixth floor (archives) and read records, pulled log books and spun microfilm for the balance of the afternoon. To her credit Marcy remained helpful and, as far as any human could be in this place, good spirited.

Back at the hotel she watched American Idol while I studied the results and compared notes and threw papers all over my bed and drank coffee, smoked cigarettes and mumbled.

"I'm trying to *listen,*" she complained.

"Why?"

Around nine (local news, Marcy bored) I gave up, took a shower and got into bed. The blankets on the other queen bed rose and adjusted and Marcy appeared on one elbow.

"What'd we find?"

I looked over. "Nothing."

"Is he a bad guy?"

"I do not know." I sighed. It was frustrating. A long day of research was supposed to provide a clue to the Mark's character, a glimmer into his finances or marital status or personal property. Cars owned, real estate purchased, boat registrations, lawsuits, even traffic tickets were accessible if you knew where to look, and I was very talented at looking.

But this guy? "Nada," I said with annoyance. A nerve in my neck twitched and I rolled my shoulders.

Marcy eyed the littered room. "Nothing at all?"

"Zilch. There's no indication Hailey Briscoe exists. There's not even a registration for the broadcasting station."

"But doesn't that tell you he's bad?"

"No. There could be a lot of reasons he's not on the grid. Most of the records around here got screwed up by Katrina. Maybe they didn't get put back together right."

"You believe that?"

"Nope. There's something wrong here. I can't quite put my finger on it."

"Soooo?"

"I have to bring in an expert. A forensic accountant."

"A crooked money guy?" asked Marcy.

"Girl, yeah."

"Cool."

Lights got turned off and in the darkness, I wondered, was it? Really?

# CHAPTER 13

## ANGEL FACE AND THE LONGORIA

I called Angel Face from my cell phone, sitting on the edge of an unmade bed, sipping bad hotel coffee in a paper cup. After this we were going to *have* to find something better.

Sally Rakowski—Angel Face to her friends in the business—answered on the third ring and I pictured her as I'd last seen her, an overweight woman of middle-fifties, skin the color of mahogany, always smiling. She worked as an accountant in the artfully designed Clark County Justice Center in Las Vegas, Nevada, was married to a framing carpenter named Raglan and had a son, Bryce.

Her voice dripped like warm taffy as she answered with a loud, "Hey, Dani! Scammed anybody lately?" I held the phone from my ear and wondered what her fellow workers were thinking.

"Angel Face," I said. "How do you get away with saying stuff like that at work? Doesn't the State of Nevada have *any* standards?"

"None whatever."

Sally worked for the Securities and Fraud Division, favored red tailored dresses in a plus size and could track the ebb and flow of money through a business like a bloodhound on a hot scent.

"They make allowances for me," Sally said. In fact, she made her boss Jeff Fleeny look so good he let her get away with murder. Sally Rakowski could get a job almost anywhere and Jeff knew it.

"How's Bryce?"

Her voice softened. "He starts a new course of chemo next week. Rags and I are keeping our fingers crossed." Her eight-year-old boy had been fighting for life since his birth as a preemie. His latest battle involved a mysterious blood disorder requiring endlessly exhausting tests and expensive treatments, not all of which were covered by insurance. Thus Sally Rakowski, alias Angel Face, took an occasional part-time gig.

"How's Rags holding up?"

"He's a rock. He gave up working to take care of Bryce. But you didn't call just for old times' sake. Dani, what's up?"

"I have a job."

"Yeah?" I could hear the interest in her voice. Sally wore her emotions on her sleeves, the main ones being her hopeless love for her son and the endless challenge of financial mysteries. "Where?"

"New Orleans."

"You're back home," she said, delighted. Sally had been after me for years to set down roots. I wondered how she'd react to Jamestown.

"I'll tell Jeff I need some personal time," she said. "But Bryce starts his chemo this week. If anything happens..."

She didn't have to finish that thought. I remembered her son, a skinny kid with big eyes facing a death sentence. Sometimes life wasn't at all fair.

"Not a problem. This should be a quick one."

"What's the setup?"

"A church."

"A church?"

"Not a *Church* church," I explained. "One of those televangelism places. On TV with free giveaways for a love donation. That sort of thing."

Sally, a deeply religious woman—I guess she had to be—heard the tone in my voice. "They're not all crooks, you know."

"Never met one who wasn't." My feelings about TV preachers were strong. Real churches I believed, didn't feature crying virgins or plastic vials of holy water. They didn't sell autographed photos of Jesus—and yes, I'd seen that scam run, back in Arkansas in the seventies. Real churches didn't take people's houses as a ticket to Heaven or act like carnivals.

Even the carnies were more honest. Sure the games were fixed but you could still win a stuffed Hippo for your girl and maybe get lucky that night.

Not many televised churches could make *that* claim.

I'm biased, I admit it. I said, "I can't get a feel for this one, Sally. Guy named Hailey Briscoe runs it, it's grown big in the last year, taking in a whole lot of money. He's accepting people's houses as donations."

"Uh-oh," said Sally. Being bent herself she recognized the signs. "What do you want me to do?"

"Run a sweep on the guy. Tell me if he's crooked or straight. I can't play a con unless the mark is hungry." I gave her what information I had.

"Okay. I'll give it my best. You want me to call you?"

"Sure, and send whatever you find to..." I gave her my internet address and we said goodbye. Sally Rakowski, my friend.

"Now what?" Asked Marcy.

"We wait."

"I'm bored. Can I take the car and go someplace?"

I looked around the darkened room. The shades were still drawn and bedclothes littered the floor. Cardboard food boxes, newspapers and our luggage competed for the small space. We needed something better.

"Let's go get a nicer place," I said and Marcy's face developed a grin. She looked about twelve.

"Race you to the shower," she yelled, and dove past me on the bed.

The Longoria had seen its best days in the early nineteen-fifties. A three-story brick palace built in the French Quarter with black wrought iron balconies over flowering Acacia trees, it had been converted to rented apartments in the sixties, renovated in the seventies and was now a faded Grande Dame, elegant and well past its glory days.

Expensive, but the apartments had kitchens and two bedrooms and, best of all, two vacancies, one on the second floor and another on the third. Perfect.

I negotiated a slightly lower rent on the second floor, using neither my Jamestown name nor Dani Silver. Marcy had the good sense to stay quiet when I answered, "Connie Romweber," to the manager's question. I'd forgotten to warn her of the change.

We took the room after I learned that the night manager would be in that evening. Compared with the Holiday Inn, the Longoria was a palace. Brocaded wallpaper in rich gold and fiery reds, wainscoting of honey varnished maple, a double bed in each bedroom and ceiling fans whirring softly, making me feel I was in a movie.

The balcony held a pair of loungers and a black table with four comfortable chairs and an umbrella against the sun or rain. I loved it.

Marcy dashed for the largest bedroom while I settled in the one with the view of the street. We moved suitcases and went for a long walk through the humid afternoon air, ending up at a sidewalk café that served fried catfish.

Marcy said, "Ugh," and ordered a hamburger with French fries. She watched the crowds going by with the interest of a virgin traveler, marveling at the diversity.

This part of the New Orleans had been spared the major damage from Katrina but even so we saw signs of high water lines, broken trees and boarded up buildings. I wondered if the city would ever recover.

Back at the Longoria we sat around the pool until evening when I went up to change. "I need to see the night manager," I told Marcy. She wore a yellow bikini that stopped all eyes and put down her paperback book, a biography of Oprah that I wanted when she was done. My own two-piece was turquoise and received lesser attention alongside hers. Getting older strikes us all, I considered, not that it felt any better.

"How come?"

"I need to rent the other apartment."

"How come?"

"For a bolt hole," I answered. "I'll explain later.

The manager, a young man named Peter, greeted me when I walked in from outside, still wrapping myself in a towel. I explained that I wanted the third-floor apartment, that my name was Cher Delecrois and that I was moving here from Minnesota. I showed him paperwork that agreed with these lies and we negotiated a lower rent than they wanted, a higher one than I would have liked.

Having money allowed me to live at the Longoria but it didn't take away the habits of a lifetime. I'd been stone broke more often than not in my life and couldn't see paying two-thousand a month for a furnished apartment I might never use.

Still, if I did need it, I'd be thankful.

Marcy said, "Explain, please" when I returned. She muted the TV—someone shrieking when they opened a case—and waited.

"Pops taught me," I said. "It's always possible for a scam to go down wrong, he said, so always have a way out. I got the apartment upstairs in case the mark catches on and I have to hide really fast."

"What a great idea." Marcy was still wearing the bikini, an abbreviated model I think she would have been embarrassed in back in Missouri. I'd been noticing changes in her as she came slowly out of her shell, like a hermit crab hesitantly testing the air currents.

"Hey," she said, "Can I borrow the car?"

"Sure. Where you heading?" Before she could say, my cell rang. I made a 'just a moment gesture' and answered. "Sally!"

I cupped the phone and listened. Marcy got up, went to her room and came back out a few minutes later dressed in a short dress and low heels, snapping on imitation pearl earrings. She caught my eye, held out her hand and mimed, "keys."

Distracted, I fumbled one-handed in my purse and gave her the keys to the Mustang. Marcy smiled like a teenager, waved and left.

Why did I suddenly feel like I'd just made a dreadful mistake?

But Sally was talking and I forgot the idea. She said, "I've been checking out the financial life of Hailey Briscoe and his Church of Divine Faith. Since the church is a nonprofit organization its records are public record—not that I needed them to be."

"What did you find?"

Her voice, small and distant, expressed doubt. "Nothing really...and everything."

"What the hell does *that* mean?" I shifted the phone and poured myself a glass of Merlot. The deep red wine glistened in the light from the kitchen. A photo in *People* showed a current starlet-du-jour in a low-cut dress.

"It means there's something there," Sally said. "But I don't know what."

I was shocked. What Sally didn't know about finances didn't exist. What was up with this Hailey Briscoe character that could shake her?

"The money," Sally began. She paused to collect her thoughts. "There's something odd about this church. His money is behaving strangely."

"*Behaving strangely?* What does that mean?"

I heard the rare uncertainty in her voice when she answered. "I don't know, Dani. He's bent, I can tell you that. I don't know how, or why, but there's a lot more money going into that church than there should be and far too much going out."

"Where's it going?"

"I don't know yet."

"But he's crooked?"

"He's...something. Dani, I've got a bad feeling about this. The last time I saw books like these was a mob operation."

"What! You're saying Hailey Briscoe is *connected?*"

"Yes. Maybe... I don't know."

"Well," I said. Connected? This kept getting weirder and weirder. What was Jiggs involved in? "Keep looking, will you?"

"I'll find it tomorrow." Sally assured me. "And Dani?"

"Yeah?"

"Be very careful."

# CHAPTER 14

## ACE, THE WATCHER

Everyone hated the Ace.

Darren Lane—"the Ace"—was the most unlikable person imaginable; racist, obnoxious, misogynist, fat. Not fat like overweight, but fat like rolls of blubber cascading over his belt.

He spoke in the third person, bathed infrequently, cursed often and chain smoked. Insufferably smug, his personality was unflaggingly negative and outspoken and for the Ace, no project was ever worth doing. All in all, it was a damn good thing for the Ace's friends that he didn't have any.

Still, he was the best watcher in the business. I considered while dialing, that Ace was the reason people thought of con men as criminals. Not all of us, I realized, are slick and professional. Some of us are the Ace.

"Yuh," said the phone. I imagined him, a flabby man of poor clothing and poorer hygiene, somewhere in America. No one knew where the Ace lived. He answered the phone and showed up, when he bothered, from wherever he happened to be. I always figured he lived in an abandoned school bus parked at the edge of a dump.

"Ace?"

"Yuh," said the phone.

I sighed and launched into her story ending with, "I need to know about this guy. It's a week, maybe two. A full watch, all expenses."

After a long silence the phone said, "A split or a fee?" Meaning, do I get paid up front or do I get a piece of the action?

I hesitated. Sally got a flat fee because of Bryce, but I didn't want that kind of overhead. I was new at being a businesswoman but an old hand as a con. Besides, everyone worked with Pops for a split. "A piece."

"How big's the pie?"

"I don't know yet. Maybe a..."

"Fee," he said.

"Half-million," I finished.

"Fee." He said, adding a number that made me laugh out loud.

"You're not that good, Ace."

"Fifty."

"Ten," I countered. "And expenses."

Another silence while I pictured him as I'd seen him last, a dirty unshaven man who could have been a street corner panhandler, in grubby jeans and a Megadeth tee shirt. His hair was worn straight and styled with enough grease to lube a tractor. Finally, he said, "When?"

"Now. Take the next flight in. I'm at the Longoria Hotel in the Quarter." I gave him the address and hung up, shuddered and went to take a shower. Ace had that effect on people.

"Fuckin' doorman, he complained. "Didn't want to let me in."

I could see why. He was dressed in garbage chic—torn jeans, grubby high-tops, obscene tee-shirt. He could give Jiggs a run for the most disgusting. What I couldn't see was how he ever got on an airplane.

He came in, declined coffee, accepted a scotch at ten in the morning and said, "Who's the mark?"

"His name is Hailey Briscoe. He runs a televangelist station that brings in big money."

"Why are you after him?"

"Does it matter?"

"No." He lit a cigarette. "The Ace doesn't care. Could be the Pope for all of me."

"Fine. Sally says..."

"Angel Face?" He nearly smiled, as close to a compliment as he could get. "She's in? The Ace likes her."

I sighed, something everyone did around the Ace. He liked anything in a skirt. "She says the money's 'behaving strangely,' but she can't figure why. So I want a full time watch on the guy to see what he's doing. I know he's bent. Find out how much."

"Sure. I'll need three cars, two from rent-a-wreck, one from Hertz. I've got my own kit." For a watcher, the kit consisted of the changes of clothing that would make him blend into the crowd. A watcher wasn't as much of a chameleon as a "face" (who could be anybody) and generally became a watcher because he liked being sneaky. This shoe fit The Ace perfectly, though I had often wondered how such a slob could tail someone without them noticing.

"Do you need backup?"

"The Ace doesn't need anything." He looked around and spotted Marcy watching him with curiosity. "Who's the quail?" He asked. "The Ace *likes*." He grabbed at his crotch and leered. "C'mere, honey; talk to the Ace."

"Marcy. Leave," I commanded.

"You don't need to tell me." Marcy hurried from the room while The Ace stared at her ass.

"Ace," I said. He continued to stare. "Ace," I said, more loudly. He was oblivious, as if in a trance. I slapped him—hard. "Ace!"

"What?" The Ace returned his attention, unfazed by the slap. "Gimme my money and I'll get on the guy."

"You're kidding; I'm not paying you in full. Half up front, half when you get back."

"I get the full week even if I find something on day one."

"The hell you do. Daily rate only."

"Full week," the Ace insisted. He crossed his arms across his thick chest and waited.

"Fine," I said, breaking first. "Full week."

"Whether I find dirt or not?"

"As long as you look."

Ace looked as offended as a disgraced detective could possibly look. He'd worked the force in Detroit for a dozen years before being brought down by a grand jury appalled beyond words. The fabled blue shield—cops hiding and protecting their own—didn't apply to violations as outrageous as his. The Ace had been drummed out of the police department and barely escaped prison.

"I do my job, Dani," he said softly. His voice was the low rumble of a disturbed bear and I had a moment where I actually might have respected him, just a little, which he ruined immediately by saying, "Just give me the fuckin' cash."

"Sure." I peeled off a sheaf of hundreds, handed them over and the Ace shoved them in a wad into his front jeans pocket.

# THE ACE

He parked the rented Ford outside the televangelist station and waited four hours for Hailey Briscoe to emerge. He watched the mark get in a new model Cadillac and drive away, started the car and followed.

They got on I-10 and went across Lake Pontchartrain on the Causeway, leaving the Ace wondering why anyone would build a twenty-four mile-long bridge. They exited in Mandeville and drove, a parade of two, down a series of side streets to a cul-de-sac in the Beau Chene subdivision. Hailey parked in the driveway of a two and a half story, orange brick, Georgian-style mansion, walked unaware up the sidewalk and vanished through a pair of ornate wooden doors. Home.

The Ace noted the address and appraised the house with the expertise of a man who once patrolled in Grosse Pointe. Four large, white, framed dormers stuck out of a gray slate roof. Eight large mullioned, double-hung, windows with heavy, thick, fully-operational, gray-green shutters adorned the front. The large southern oaks along the driveway showed fresh chainsaw scars where broken limbs had been removed. Pink Peace Rose blossoms had been wind-whipped and scattered over a large oval flower garden centered along the front of the house.

An oriental-looking man, probably Vietnamese, was down on his hands and knees trying to repair the damage. Hungry, fearless Robins feasted on the worms and bugs he exposed every time he lifted a bunch of dead flower stalks.

The Ace shifted back into drive, u-turned and drove away. He'd need a better car.

The next day, in a new model Chrysler, the Ace continued his surveillance, following Hailey Briscoe back to the station where he waited for three hours, then to Brennan's Restaurant, down in the Quarter on Royal Street, where The Ace ate cold Circle K hotdogs and drank warm beer while waiting. Hailey came out after a while and the Ace tailed him back to the station.

At four-thirty he followed him to the mansion. The Ace didn't wonder how a small-time televangelist could afford such a house; he merely assumed, as he did of everyone he met, that the guy was a crook. If he couldn't earn enough to enjoy the good life, he was scamming it somehow.

He put a discrete illegal phone tap on the house late one night under the cloaking eye of a quarter moon. Every day had its hour or two of rain, all adding up to a drenched swamp of a city, baking in the desolation caused by hurricane Katrina. The Ace sat in the nice car and waited, listening. Sometimes a woman made calls or a servant called a market or a salesman made an attempt to sell siding or time shares, and sometimes Hailey Briscoe called City Hall and spoke to a woman named Cora Lynne Jackson in the Mayor's office.

Those last calls were interesting to The Ace, not because they revealed a crooked plan, but because they didn't. But maybe they were talking in code, somehow.

The days went by, the Ace watched and ate and cat-napped and followed and learned absolutely nothing. On Sunday, the weathered old school filled to overflowing with the faithful, the hopeful and the desperate, all driving cars more disreputable than the junker the Ace squatted in. They swarmed into the double doors seeking salvation or ease or at least a few moments of hope. The heat was oppressive, the mosquitoes buzzed and fed and the Ace, as patient and unblinking as a frog, waited dead-eyed and silent.

On Monday, Hailey met with a building official named Victor Windham but The Ace couldn't pick up the conversation with his Big Ear device because large green and purple Komaratsu construction machines were making too much noise.

On Tuesday, nothing happened—again.

On Wednesday, he "bumped" into Hailey Briscoe as he exited a Cracker Barrel restaurant and lifted his wallet, hoping for secrets, but getting nothing but sixty bucks and some gas cards. He kept the cash, tossed the wallet.

On Thursday, The Ace washed up at a Texaco station, slathered on enough deodorant to cover himself or choke a horse, dressed in a passable suit and canvassed the neighborhood near the television station. He carried a clipboard and made comments about, "census survey," or "water department." People answered his questions without resentment; it was that type of neighborhood, beaten down enough to accept any official at face value.

He learned nothing of interest.

Friday, he somehow insulted the married night manager at the Circle K and she caused such a ruckus that you'd have thought he'd actually done what he suggested rather than just suggest it. That got him banned from that store so he took his meager business a mile down the road to the EZ Serve on Magnolia.

Saturday, he tried the survey again in Briscoe's own neighborhood, getting few replies and considering the entire day a waste of time.

Sunday night he called Dani from a pay phone at the local bar. "He goes to the church and he goes home. That's all he does. He's not playing the ponies, sneaking out to gamble or to pork some broad. He sometimes talks to people in local government but that's what Ministers do. As far as the Ace can tell, he don't have a life at all."

"Stay on it, Ace. I need a handle on this guy."

"Sure. I'll do another week, but if he don't move by then he's not going to."

"Right," I said. "Another week."

As it turned out, the Ace only needed another day.

The wiretap phone buzzed softly at 9:30 Monday night rousing the Ace from a bizarre and disgusting sexual fantasy. He sat up, rubbed his eyes, felt the stubble on his cheek scratch his hand and picked up the phone and pressed "on."

"See you at ten?" Hailey said.

A woman with a Creole accent answered, "Sure thing, hon; I'll be waiting."

Hon? Could this be something? The phone went dead and a few minutes later the garage door opened. Hailey's Cadillac backed out in a blaze of red tail lights, shifted and sailed away serenely into the dark night, pursued, unaware, by the world's most disreputable tail.

They drove across the Causeway Bridge into New Orleans, idling at red lights, goosing through the yellows and greens to an old apartment building in Metairie. Hailey parked at a curb, left the car and pressed the lock remote. The Ace watched him enter an unassuming door halfway down from the corner, got out, grunting with the effort, and went to the door. A small name tag said, "Carver, Phyllis."

The Ace knew; he absolutely *knew* what he'd find if he busted in. He'd been a vice cop, and filled with vice of his own for too long not to know, but he was being paid pretty well to be certain. He looked around for a way to find out. He crossed the street and looked at the building and saw a light on the third floor. A rusty fire escape beckoned on his side of the street. Maybe he could see in from there, but lowering the ladder would be noisy. He took one half-hearted jump to try and snag the lowest rung, lost his footing and landed on his butt with an, "Oomph!"

"Screw this," he said. He wasn't being paid *that* well.

## DANI

"He's shackin' up," the Ace reported the next morning at my flat in the Longoria. He looked around hopefully for a sign of Marcy, saw nothing and appeared disappointed.

"You're sure?" I was dressed in thick, non-revealing clothes, the way any sensible woman would when in the presence of the Ace. Most women would gladly wear a Burka if he was going to be around. I'm sure the Ace didn't care since he was probably picturing us naked anyway.

"Sure, I'm sure. I saw 'em, didn't I?"

"I don't know. Did you?"

"I said I did. Jeez, Dani." Affronted dignity was beyond him but he tried for—and failed—at hurt. Eight days on stakeout hadn't improved him and I tried to stay downwind.

"Just gimme my money," he said, holding out a fat paw as if I had it ready for him. "I'm in week two," he reminded. "That's the full two weeks."

"I know, Darren." Whenever anyone wanted to annoy him they called him Darren. For some reason it made him crazy. "I'll get it for you." I walked out of the room as the Ace stewed in his own thick juices.

I returned as the Ace was eyeing my purse, saw the look and moved the bag farther away on the counter. I hadn't offered him coffee or anything, being eager to get him out and have the place fumigated. I handed him a fat white envelope which he opened and slowly counted. When he was done he sniffed and said, "Okay. Good-bye."

"Wait," I said. The Ace stopped.

"You're sure?"

He placed one hand over his heart.

"God is my witness, the minister is porking some broad." He turned and left the apartment.

# CHAPTER 15

## FISH OR CUT BAIT

I had a decision to make. Hailey Briscoe was a crook or he wasn't a crook. He had taken Coretta Roche's house or it had been donated. He was as phony as a three-dollar bill or merely a victim of his own delusions.

I sat down with a glass of Merlot and a yellow legal pad and made notes to myself. Traffic below was short on tourists, long on the stench of recovery and filled with the noxious fumes of diesel machines plowing up the debris. I tried hard to ignore the constant reminders of Katrina's visit.

I wrote, "Against" on my pad and listed the reasons why Hailey Briscoe shouldn't be a target. They were few and weak. The list for "For" was stronger, possibly because that's the way I wanted it to be. He looked, I thought, like a swindler, he had a mansion and a new car, his business had swelled beyond all reasonable expectations in the last year. His wife was a trophy model unlikely to be impressed by a loud over-dressed Southern preacher and he was, according to the Ace, having an affair.

And I personally couldn't stand him.

In the end it was two considerations that made my decision. The woman stashed away and the fact that I wanted to run this con so bad I could taste it. I made all the mental convolutions and twists necessary to convince myself I was being objective, but in the end the choice was made when I accepted the call from Jiggs. I had something to prove—to myself and my father— and I was going ahead.

This, it turned out, was not my best decision.

Marcy joined me on the terrace with a bottle of some sweet drink and a copy of the new '*US*' magazine. It had the current celebrity couple on the cover, he looking serious, she in a bikini and I almost put aside my pad to read the story. If I had an addiction, it was to gossip magazines. And reality shows. And bubble baths and…stop it.

"Whatcha doing?" she asked. She was wearing a yellow bandeau and mint green tight shorts against the humid hot air. Her hair was damp from the shower. From somewhere I heard the sound of the Beatles doing some song I remembered from long ago.

"Deciding on the con," I said, watching her leaf through the pages. I thought I saw a lurid headline about a popular soap actress suing a producer for harassment and wanted to read over Marcy's shoulder but she closed the magazine and seemed interested.

"Yeah? What do you do?" She twisted in the chair and tucked her feet beneath her.

"Well, I have to decide what to run based on the mark's habits. I have to bring in a crew to actually do the work..."

"You won't do it yourself?"

"Some," I admitted, though I knew I had trouble letting go of any of it. Pops said I had a control problem and needed to trust more. I replied that being a con meant not trusting people. We settled on a standoff on this point.

"But remember that Hailey's seen me. I'll have to be careful how I play being around him."

"Can I be part?" Her eyes were large as if star-struck and I realized she was good and hooked on this lifestyle. I could sympathize with her escape from Brock. This new life included sleeping late, lounging around half-naked and swindling ministers. Not a trace of reality anywhere.

"No," I said firmly. "This is no place for amateurs." But even as I said it I wondered—what was I doing playing in this league? Was I ready for this?

Marcy accepted this and appeared to lose interest. She returned to flipping pages and I wrote down names and after a while she got up, stretched high and bent to touch her palms to the floor. Somewhere a voyeur whistled, which we both ignored. The faraway radio began playing 'Stairway to Heaven' and Marcy asked for my car keys.

"Sure," I said. "Where are you going?"

"Out," she said, vaguely. "Shopping, maybe just see the sights..."

"Fine," I said. "The keys are in my purse. I was back to considering names for my crew when she left. I didn't notice if she changed clothes and later didn't wonder when she failed to come back that night, or the next.

That was my second, and most serious mistake.

# CHAPTER 16

## HELL HELL THE GANG'S ALL HERE

"Bob, this is Sam. Sam, Bob." I made the introductions with amusement, watching them appraise each other. Cincinnati Bob Wilkinson was tall and angular, like a cross between a stork and an exercycle. His clothes were mostly Hawaiian shirts of red Hibiscus and green ferns over tan knee length shorts, too casual for wherever he was. As the paper-man, he'd be printing all the bogus documents, magazine articles, brochures, licenses, IDs and whatnot the plan would need.

Sammy Hensel, eyeing him with apparent unease, was the technician. His job would be to hack into computer systems, surf the internet and do all the high tech low social skill things we'd need.

A computer geek, Sammy had been kicked out of several colleges for hacking, database theft and, in one dramatic but unproven charge, had once created a Playboy photo shoot at the University of Minnesota ("The Girls of the 10,000 Lakes") that resulted in 230 semi-naked women flocking the campus dorm.

Astoundingly well educated, Sammy dressed exclusively in British high style; Carnaby suits, Eton collars and whatever the fashion magazine du jour dictated. He spent whatever time and all the money from his jobs to browse fashion malls all over the country. Tall, bald and exceptionally, good looking, Sammy could have been a Roper except for being black and the regrettable lack of personality.

"Pleased," said Cincinnati Bob, not meaning it.

"Charmed," agreed Sammy, not meaning it.

"Do you want to come in?" I asked.

"Yeah."

"Certainly."

They joined me and a vaguely Hispanic man lazing on the rattan sofa beneath the slowly revolving ceiling fan. He wore tan slacks and a thin white dress shirt. His hair was black and slicked and he had a thin mustache over a crooked smile. Both Cincinnati Bob and Sammy the technician were instantly charmed, for different reasons.

Sammy, because he was well dressed, unlike this Cincinnati person; Bob, because he hoped the new guy was gay.

"Ray Sanchez," I said and Bob said, "No; don't get up," before he could, and Sammy dashed over and shook hands heartily.

"You've just got to be the Face," said Bob, belatedly getting his own hand in there. Ray shook it.

"Nope. I'm a Fixer."

"No kidding," said Sammy, sitting down next to him and removing a paperback book he'd just sat on. He glanced at the title, saw it was some popular trash with a jet plane on the cover, and threw it behind him.

"Hey! I was reading that." Ray got up and retrieved his novel, brushing away the attached cobwebs. He pointedly sat down on the single chair opposite the two new guys. Esteban Ramirez Sanchez liked books almost as much as he liked women and was rarely seen without one or the other, often both. As a fixer he was the guy who'd get anything: hotels, cars, tickets. He could gain access to anywhere, anytime, and was always trying to scam something.

I offered drinks, was refused and sat down. I was feeling a little giddy to be beginning a long con all on my own and secretly delighted in watching the reactions of my team to each other.

"Let me tell you the details." They all turned various degrees of attention my way. "First, I've got Patty Krill on the mark doing a raggle. We're still looking for the handle."

"You don't have a plan yet?" Sammy, showing off those nonexistent social skills, stared at me like a very well dressed lizard, perched on the edge of the sofa to save the crease in his perfect pants. Bob and Ray looked intent.

"Not...yet," I admitted. I coughed into my fist. "But I'll have one soon. I just need to find..."

"That's not how Leroy did it," complained Sammy, and Bob nodded like a spastic bird. Ray Sanchez merely waited.

"Yeah. Leroy never called us in until he had a plan," agreed Bob.

"I've got a plan,"

"What is it?"

"Will you guys just shut up and let me explain?" I took a deep, *deep* breath and let it out slowly, counted to five, considered my audience and counted another ten for good measure. I was, truth be told, feeling a little stage fright. I'd run a major con before but the crew had come in with Pops. This was my first solo.

"I've got a mark. He's got money. He's bent. I'll find a way to fleece him." I spoke firmly to overcome any objections. Keep control, I thought, stay in control. "In the meantime, I have things for each of you to do."

Ray finally spoke. "What's in it for us?"

"A piece," I said. Please let them go for a piece.

"A piece of what?" Asked Ray. "What's the pie?"

"I'm not sure." I cursed myself for stumbling. Ray caught the gaff and spoke for everyone.

"I want a flat fee. Not profit, no piece." Ray and I had a thing once, a few years ago, and now I remembered why I'd broken up with him. He was cold at heart, uninterested in anything but his books and money.

"Me, too," said Sammy.

"Yeah, me. Too." Cincinnati Bob was slower but got there eventually.

Crap. I'd been hoping that at least some of them would take a cut of the action rather than having me pay up front. I mentally totaled the costs so far and shuddered. I still had expenses and, if things worked out right, a big store to pay for.

And I didn't have any idea what the take would be even if I figured out a way to take down Hailey Briscoe. Damn; this was getting out of hand.

"How much?" I asked.

We settled on a number that made my heart sweat and I paid them, up-front, half of it. In this business you had to trust your people, but I wasn't crazy; they'd get the rest when something actually happened.

But Sammy wasn't satisfied. "This isn't right, Dani. Pops would do it different."

"I'm not Pops, God Dammit!" I regretted yelling as soon as the words left my mouth. These guys, Ray Sanchez included for all his cool façade, were mostly children. They'd never had a real job or responsibilities, never been saddled with the cares every other human being took for granted. They were used to doing things in a particular—and peculiar—way.

"I'm trying to do this by myself. Can you guys respect that? That I might want to be independent of my father?" I watched their eyes, windows of the soul and all that, and saw I was reaching Bob and Ray, not Sammy, who looked bored and mulish.

"I don't want to take orders from a woman," he said.

"You're taking money from a woman." I got up and held out a hand, palm up. "Give it back. I don't want you here."

"Hey!" His hand went to the elegantly tailored breast-pocket of his jacket. "You can't take it back."

"What do think; this is grade school?" My voice dripped scorn. "No take backs? Gimme the money back, Sammy; you're no use to me." I waggled my fingers.

Sammy looked like a little boy who'd dropped his ice cream cone. He glanced at the others for support, got none and gave in.

"Fine," he said. "You're in charge." He ran a hand over his bald head to cover his embarrassment. "What do we do?"

"Okay." I relaxed a little. This was like directing a kindergarten; a very expensive kindergarten.

"Sammy, I want you to do the usual internet stuff. Find out everything there is to know about this guy. Where's he from, what did he do before, does anybody have hooks in him? Skip the financial, Sally's already covered that. But give me everything else."

"I'll need a set-up," he said sullenly, meaning a computer.

"What's wrong with yours?"

"I need a better one."

"Get what you want, I'll settle up at the end."

"Now." His eyes were on his perfectly polished shoes and I realized this was an attempt to save face: pick a small point and win that.

"Sure." I offered an amount to easily cover any computer on the planet. "That good?"

"Fine." He glanced at Ray with a sly smile, like he'd just won a major victory. Ray looked away.

"Bob."

"Yessam?"

"Find a printer, get a pad, get ready. I'll have moves for you in a couple of days."

"You got it."

"Thanks. Ray?"

"Yes, Dani?" Ray answered seriously. I saw he was stifling amusement. The little bastard liked seeing me squirm.

"Scout out a medium sized store location in southern California. Good neighborhood, not a strip mall."

"You're setting up a store?"

"Yeah; I've got something in mind. I'll need stock, books and cards mostly, and a lot of Bible stuff. Maybe you can find a going out of business auction or something."

"Or something," he agreed dryly.

"Posters, banners. High class, I'm going to lure a big money player. Get with Bob and he'll print up whatever you say."

"That's it for now. Let me know where you're gonna crib and keep in touch daily."

"We're not staying here?" Asked Ray. I interpreted the look; *with you*?

"Not hardly. I've barely got room for two."

That's when I noticed that Marcy wasn't there.

# CHAPTER 17

## PATTY AND SAMMY AND BOB; OH MY!

## PATTY

Patty Kreel liked to crochet. Given the opportunity she'd be at home in Proctor, Maine sitting in her favorite chair, watching *"The Price is Right"* while making Afghans and comforters for her family. She'd already done three this year; a brown and gold for the Jordans, an American flag for her mother and a nice red and blue throw for her own sofa.

But, like everyone else, she had to work, so here she sat, sweltering in a revealingly low cut tight midriff shirt, a skirt that could pass for a belt and three-inch high heels. Her hair was a pricey blonde wig from Fredericks of Hollywood, her makeup was expert and her handbag was a saucy little red number with sequins. She looked like a low-price hooker and proud of it. Tarty, but with class.

The heel of her right shoe was specially made to break when she stepped on it a certain way, which made for very careful walking, but a guaranteed meeting when she wanted.

She sat in her rented Toyota outside an old school waiting to play her variation of the flop, and age old scam usually committed as a medical fraud. The con would "get hit" by the mark's car then claim an old injury as a new one.

The early evening was humid and alive with all the humming buzzing creeping things that didn't exist in Maine and Patty kept the windows up to ward them away while she peacefully knitted one and pearled two and clicked her crochet needles. She studied her work critically. This one was going to be a lamp table cover, as large a project as she was willing to bring with her to work. She liked the way the brown yarn mixed with this particular red.

There he was, unmistakable in the greenest leisure suit she had ever seen. Hailey Briscoe, preacher of the Church of the Divine Faith. He stood on the stairs with one leg bent, turned back to talk to somebody inside, leaving a last instruction perhaps, or just shooting the breeze after a hard day of soul saving.

Patty got out of the car, steadied herself to avoid a real broken ankle and took a few wobbly steps forward toward the white Cadillac. She saw Hailey wave and turn to walk down the stairs and she calculated the distance they each had to go.

Walking slowly, just another working girl heading for the bus, Patty kept a close eye out for those humming buzzing creeping things but still managed to give a small indifferent nod to the preacher as he neared her and his car. She waited until he was busy getting his keys and let the shoe do its work.

"Oh!" She gasped as the heel broke away, sending her and her small bag crashing down on the worn concrete sidewalk. Her knee scraped and her nylon tore as she braced herself for the fall she'd taken a hundred times over the years. She felt a pain in her leg that wouldn't have been there even five years ago and thought, "I'm getting too old for this," as she landed in the thick grass of the median.

"Ow," she groaned realistically and Hailey Briscoe dropped his keys and raced to her aid. He bent to one knee—*that* was gonna leave a stain—and got an arm under her head as he tried to comfort her.

"Are you all right?"

Patty turned slightly to settle her left breast firmly in his hand which he pulled away hastily. "I'm fine," she said. Her voice was Deep South, with little education but an undercurrent of sexuality that promised pleasure and non-commitment. She looked up from the cradle of his arms and whispered throatily, "Thank you. My heel just broke."

She pointed. He looked and sure enough, the heel was flopped at an awkward angle. The gesture was calculated to make a man run his eyes all the way down the long length of her stocking clad leg and Hailey, like anyone would, did just that, letting his gaze admire the free view.

Gotcha, thought Patty. "I must have hurt my knee," she said as he helped her up. His hands didn't roam and his eyes locked on hers as if he was really truly interested in how she felt. Patty frowned.

"Shouldn't wear shoes like that," said Hailey. "They could cause some serious damage. You ought to be more careful."

"I was just going to work," she said. Keep them talking, that always worked. She steadied herself on one leg like a tall over-sexed stork. "What do you do?"

"I'm a preacher. I work at that station over there."

"A television station? Are you famous?"

"No." He let go of her, turned and studied the ground. "I dropped my keys somewhere...oh, here they are." He bent to retrieve them and gathered up her purse. He handed it to her. "Do you need any help? An ambulance or a ride to the hospital?"

"Uh, no. No, I'm fine." Astounded, she thought, but fine. He was ignoring her. Patty couldn't believe it.

"Well, if you're all right I'll be on my way. I have an appointment to keep, things to do." He smiled, a little come and go trick of the mouth, and stepped away. "Goodbye."

Patty watched him get in the huge white car, back up in a wash of red lights and drive away.

The car vanished and darkness settled over her. The humming buzzing creeping things resumed their evening noises and Patty shuddered. She bent to take off her broken heeled shoe and limped back to the Toyota.

## SAMMY

Sammy Hensel drove his personal midnight-green Jaguar X-6 into the parking lot of Qual-Cast.Com, a huge steel and glass building in the north suburbs of New Orleans. The lot was an ocean of black asphalt and yellow painted lines with islands of plantings. The suburb was far enough away from the low-lying areas that it escaped the major power of Katrina but evidence remained in the form of cracked trees and stripped vegetation on the mounds that surrounded the tower. Several windows were boarded with plywood, like acne on the face of the building.

He parked near an overhead light, locked the car with a clicker—*fweet!*—and strode to the main entrance. With his gleaming black attaché case, his expensive well-tailored suit and air of bored confidence, Sammy was obviously one of the rising young executives who worked here.

As a hobby or a quirk, Sammy liked to do his computer work on someone else's computers. He could have brought his own—could have, actually, worked from at home, but what fun was that? The money he'd taken from Dani to buy a computer he considered a bonus.

Besides, the big servers were better anyway and left no traces.

So whenever he had a large job to do Sammy Hensel would research prospects and select a good sized new company to set up shop in. He thought of himself as a Cuckoo bird who left its eggs in a Blue Jays nest; a changeling in the family.

He'd taken the effort to create a forged personnel badge before coming here this Monday morning at nine and was swept with the flood past the two uniformed black security guards who sat unaware that they'd been flanked. At random he chose the elevator marked 12-20 and got off at the seventeenth floor. He nodded absently at the receptionist in the lobby, at her post with the first cup of coffee already finished and the E-mail checked.

Half an hour of wandering around gave him a feel for the place. He discovered that the technical support group was on ten and he invaded their department as easily as he did seventeen. He found an unused office in a far corner with a full desk and a terminal, located the break room and the men's room and looked up a company directory. For the next two hours he created a fictitious position for himself and learned the names of who his bosses would be if he had any.

His story in place Sammy turned on the computer and began hacking into the life of Hailey Briscoe.

He did the easy stuff first. Birth date, place, parents, schools, awards, publicity and, repeating a little of the early work of Angel Face, his basic financial records and history.

Like Sally, he was a little surprised to find how thin a trail Hailey had left behind. He found hardly a trace of the usual things like credit cards, home loans, car loans.

Puzzled, he expanded his grid to wider searches, looking for anything anomalous but coming up empty in each case.

He spread some papers on the desk, went for coffee and returned. At eleven-fifteen a head stuck itself into the door and a middle-aged man in a white shirt and tie followed, saying, "Hey, there."

Sammy looked up with real interest at his first challenge.

"I'm Gibb Sutter," said the guy and Sammy got up to shake hands. "I'm the department manager." He was typically overweight with office flab, too busy or unmotivated to fight the battle of the bulge.

"Sam Winters," said Sam, using the name on his freshly forged company ID. "Pleased to meet you."

"Your first day?" asked Gibb.

"Yeah." He gestured at the computer. "I'm the new financial internist." This was a position that didn't actually exist but sounded corporate enough to impress without admitting to any real function. Managers hated talking accounting.

"What do you think, so far?"

"Pretty nice," admitted Sammy. "Seems like a good company. How long have you been with them?"

"Ten years next May."

They talked for a few minutes before agreeing to do lunch. "I'll introduce you around," said Gibb. "Pick you up at noon?"

"Noon," smiled Sammy and just like that he was in.

## BOB

"Gorgeous," said Cincinnati Bob Wilkinson, running a tender hand over a gently rounded curve.

"She is that," agreed old Hank. "Gantry-5000." He nodded with proprietary pride. "Mark six model. The only one like her in the state of Louisiana. She'll do whatever you want her to do."

"Computer interfaced?" asked Bob, though he knew the answer. He'd read all the technical sheets and product bulletins on this baby. At night he dreamed about her. Asking was merely conversation, pure social pleasantries among connoisseurs. Wine fanciers or cigar aficionados probably did the same thing while stroking their stogies.

But Cincinnati Bob didn't drink wine and hated the smell of cigars. He lived printing. He considered the smell of ink to be God's aphrodisiac and could tell you about every major innovation in printing since Gutenberg stopped pressing grapes in favor of paper.

"It'll print plastics, too," said old Hank, a medium sized man of over seventy and under a hundred who'd been in the printing business since World War II. He knew everything from mimeographs to Xerox and *United Specialty Press* kept him on salary for the prestige of saying they worked with old Hank.

He looked more like a farmer than a printer, with faded coveralls and a weathered face, but on his head was the old pressman's hat of folded newspaper. He still smoked cigarettes despite the smoking prohibited signs, he mouthed off to customers and cussed the bosses frequently. Old Hank was a coot.

"It can turn out a thousand pages an hour and you can't tell them from the original."

"That's nice," approved Bob.

"What do you have in mind, sonny?" asked old Hank.

"Oh, this and that," said Bob, studying the elaborate control panel on the top of the gigantic green machine that squatted like some prehistoric monster in the front of the huge press facility out in Kennora. The plant was nearly 100,000 square feet of pulleys and belts and rolls of paper and vats of ink. There were catwalks and cranes overhead and a constant din of motors. The Times-Picayune was printed here and the smell of newsprint was like a Chanel No. 5 perfume to people like Cincinnati Bob and old Hank.

"This and that, huh?"

Bob shrugged and looked around. "And so on. Brochures maybe, not a lot in quantity but long on quality. Some documents." He looked intently at the printer who ran a grizzled hand across his mouth.

"Machine like this ain't much good for what did you call them? Documents?"

"*Private* documents," stressed Bob.

"*Private* Documents. Uh-huh." Old hank paused to light a smoke, offered one to Bob, who declined. "Who'd you say sent you?"

"Pete Conesco," said Bob.

"Pete..." Old Hank considered this for a while through the clouds he was making. "From Austin?"

"Pete's never been in Texas his whole life. He lives in Hartford, Connecticut on Irving Street. His wife's named Doris, his daughter is Hannah."

"Oh, right; him," agreed old Hank.

"He uses the Simpson double-ought-fifty-seven." Bob said, naming an older model press favored by counterfeiters. In fact, a husband/wife team had been busted a year back in Arizona when their Simpson broke down and they sent it to the shop for repairs. The mechanic found it clogged with the remnants of the prettiest fake twenties he'd ever seen. He called the Feds, of course.

"A smaller press would be better for your needs," said old Hank. "And someplace...quiet."

"Quiet's very good," agreed Cincinnati Bob.

"I know just the place," said old Hank. "Why don't you buy me dinner tonight and we can discuss it?"

Old Hank was as bent as a cheap nail.

## RAY

Esteban Ramirez (Ray) Sanchez studied himself in the window of *Chez Paris* and liked what he saw. Thin, elegant, good hair, a killer smile, Ray would have had to beat off the ladies with a stick if he had anything but passing interest in them. Oh, he liked sex, but it wasn't the reason he lived.

Ray loved books, *lived* for books. Any kind of fiction, but mostly the military high-tech stuff like Stephen Coontz and Tom Clancy, would make him stay up all night. He read at least three novels a week and visited every used book store he came across. He'd once found a copy of *Flight of the Intruder* for a quarter at a run-down store nearly ten years ago. The memory was still sweet.

He went through the door held open by the smiling waitress, looked around and spotted Sammy across the room. They waved at each other and Ray slipped through the crowd.

"How's it hanging?" he asked. Sammy was already drinking something red and sweet-looking and Ray snapped his fingers to call somebody, sat down and ordered a Harvey Wallbanger.

"Hanging tough," said Sammy. They bumped closed fists and Ray studied the menu. He settled on a New York strip steak, Sammy order the Filet of Sole and they talked.

"What do you think of all this?" asked Sammy.

"You mean Dani? She's okay."

"A little flaky if you ask me."

Ray, who had once dated her, thought Dani to be the smartest women he'd ever met and sexy as hell in an overachiever sort of way. He would have defended her but he really didn't care enough to do so. Someone, annoyed at Ray's constant inability to care about anyone, had once remarked, "See this saucer? Esteban is about as deep."

Everyone called him Ray to his face and Esteban when they referred to him and almost always negatively.

"She doesn't seem to have a handle on this," complained Sammy.

"No?"

"She doesn't do it right."

"Like Leroy?" Asked Ray.

"Well, yeah."

"Listen, my friend. Leroy's day is done. It's time for some new blood. I think Dani'll do just fine."

"I guess," said Sammy, but sullenly.

The food arrived and was sampled. "I need some things," said Ray. The aroma of cooked meat rose over the table.

"Like?"

"An out of business book store, I think. Or a remainder outfit that'll give a good price on books and stuff if you buy the lot."

"How come?" Sammy wore a pale linen suit that conveyed leisure and power, as if it was being worn by an important man who was—for this moment only—relaxing.

"We're setting up a Christian Book store," Ray explained. "Dani says they're big out east and on the coast."

"What am I looking for?"

"Find me a couple of prospects in Southern California or Nevada, near Vegas or Henderson. Quality doesn't matter since the mark won't get that deep into the store. We'll flash roll him with some primo stuff at the door." A flash roll referred to the old grifter trick of rolling a hundred-dollar bill around a thick stack of singles to make it appear you had a lot of cash. For the big store con it meant salting the good merchandise in front of cheap junk to make it look like a huge inventory.

"How big a lot?" Sammy tasted his Filet and found it good. He touched his thin lips with a linen napkin. "In dollars."

Ray considered. "A couple thousand books, I don't know...maybe a few grand. Go up to ten. Dani doesn't seem to be too worried about money."

"That's a problem, isn't it? This whole idea of a self-financed long con? Ray, whoever heard of such a thing?"

"Nobody, I guess. But they used candles before electric lights."

Sammy stared at him. "What the hell is that supposed to mean?"

## DANI

I *was* concerned about the money; it was going out in buckets.

Sitting on the patio at the Longoria I studied the list of all the expenditures to date. Travel, by car and airplane, hotels, all four-star, food at the better joints, cars from Hertz, not Budget and the fees to all the contractors, which added up to over a hundred and twenty thousand dollars. God, why wouldn't *any* of them take a piece of the action?

I sipped a latte, dark with chocolate and cream, and fretted. Maybe I'd made a mistake I thought, feeling something like panic settling over me. I thought about what I was doing, running it through my head until I was damn near depressed. Nothing was going right. I still hadn't made contact with the mark, Patty hadn't lured him in, I was hemorrhaging money and worse, now I was doubting myself.

Was it always like this, being the boss? Did Pops have these moments? I couldn't imagine it. He was such a strong character, surely he'd never failed.

I wished that Pops was here to talk to. I'd never realized how lonely this could be. Last time I had Pops around and when he left, pretending to be dead, there was Nick.

I missed Nick. I could use the feel of his arm around my shoulders, the comforting way he told me everything would be all right even though, at the time he was saying it, people were trying to kill us.

I even missed Marcy, the irresponsible little goof, and wondered where the girl had gotten herself off to. Marcy and Jiggs, I thought, what a recipe for disaster.

I went back to the notepad. I'd paid for Sammy's computer even though I knew it was a scam. I knew his working habits and made allowances for his eccentricities the way all good bosses did with brilliant technicians. Put up with their ways or get someone else equally eccentric, but you're never going to change them.

We still hadn't set up the big store yet. That was going to cost and I wrote a few practice numbers on a spare piece of paper to see how I'd react. Not well. When the number got past $20,000 I felt myself getting nervous.

This small business stuff was a pain.

## PATTY

Patty was in pain. Her ankle *hurt.* It was that damned trick shoe, she thought, it gets harder every year to pull that off. She was back in her room soaking in a tub filled with thick suds, feeling the dull ache all the way up her leg. It would figure if she'd pulled something, and didn't even get a rise out the guy.

What was his problem anyway? She gave him a good look *and* a free feel and he walked away as if she didn't tempt him at all.

Well, when the going got tough the tough got going. Wasn't that a saying? If it wasn't it should be. She pictured it embroidered on a sampler, something simple, maybe red letters against a cream background with, I don't know, an American Bald Eagle flying overhead for that inspirational feel. She could see it spelled out in thread, *When the going gets tough—the tough get going.* Uncle Pete would like one, she decided, and went back to rubbing her ankle.

Two days later she was back in a different car looking nothing at all like a tart. Today she was a brunette wearing a professional outfit of powder blue with low black pumps carrying a thick day timer. Cincinnati Bob had supplied all the credentials she could possibly need, Dani had set up an appointment for an interview and she strode to the door of the church as Carolyn Baker of *Modern Religion Magazine.*

Hailey Briscoe met her at the tiny office that had once held a principal, a school nurse and unruly children. He pumped her hand and offered her the guest chair across from his desk. Patty launched into her story, showed him the sample magazine Bob had created, an authentic looking fraud that even had her convinced.

Dani helped prepare the interview questions and things went well. Patty suggested lunch—the interview had been scheduled for eleven o'clock for just this reason—and Hailey accepted with a delighted smile.

"I don't get out much," he admitted at the table of a small catfish joint on the river road. They chatted and she led the conversation back to him.

"Tell me more about you," she said. "Not the details, but the personal stuff; the *interesting* things."

"For publication?"

"Off the record. I'm just so impressed by what you've done." There, she thought, no man could resist talking about himself.

"Not much to tell, I'm afraid. I got into the ministry when I served in the Army, became the squad relief padre. When I got out I took classes at Divinity but didn't care for it." In fact, Patty knew, Hailey had been thrown out for excessive drinking. "So I went on to another University..." California Coastal Ministries, Patty filled in, an unaccredited diploma mill.

"I got my degree and served at several small churches."

He drank Pepsi-Cola in a tall glass without ice and ate like a man who hadn't seen food since last Tuesday. She had no idea how his suit stayed so clean, with fish and fries and Cole slaw—they made a great Cole slaw—being shoved into his mouth between words.

"You got married recently?" she asked.

"Un-huh, uh-huh," Hailey nodded, swallowing a thick wedge of Key Lime pie. "Wonderful woman! We were wed only two years ago."

"That was about when you started the ministry here, wasn't it?"

"Yes, Ma'am, it was. I see you've done your homework."

Hailey beamed like a man asked to show pictures of his grandchildren. "I was looking for something to do with my calling— something meaningful to the world, yet spiritually fulfilling. I met Sara Jane and while we were dating she suggested that a television ministry would be wonderful."

"So together you...?"

"Started the ministry, yes. And it has gone better than I ever dreamed, praise the Lord." Hailey actually glanced upward when he offered this and Patty sipped her Soda water—with ice, thank you; *she* wasn't crazy—and wondered, was this guy for real?

She had a sudden unhappy thought that maybe, just maybe, he was.

# SAMMY

Sammy Hensel, on his third day at Qual-Cast.Com, was enjoying himself hugely. He still had no idea what the company did, or what he would be doing if he actually worked here, but he liked his co-workers, delighted in going to lunch with them, loved chatting up the secretaries on his way to his office.

He was certainly glad that he'd given himself a window office. The view of the artificial pond was soothing when he took a break from the computer. The fountain in the middle, the ducks and geese paddling about...he sighed, filled with peace.

Back to work. He hacked in and picked up where he'd left off last night before he went out for beer with Gus and Ely and the guys at Skelly's Bar. What a great group! Once again he approved of himself for thinking up this scam. It was so much better than working alone in his own home. The company made him more productive.

He was halfway through patching together a history of *Golden Bower Books*. His work was so good it would have passed a basic inspection by the FBI so he had no fears that Hailey Briscoe and his little church would pierce the carefully crafted web of lies he was building.

He made up articles and placed them in the files of prestigious newspapers and magazines; Time, Newsweek, the New York Times, even Forbes and Inc. It was amazing how easy it was to hack into their archives. The articles were canned, piecework from real stories done on other businesses. Sammy just changed the names and particulars to fit his vision.

A web site, a corporate headquarters in San Vicente, California at an address that was actually owned by Prudential Insurance, not that anyone would check that far, and all the bric-a-brac that made this a real business.

He added a note: the company was moving to a new headquarters sometime in the third quarter. Yes, that was a nice touch.

He went to lunch with Janelle and Tony from Sales, enjoying their company immensely, came back and finished a very nice corporate income statement when Landry Calhoun, VP of Management and Personnel Placement came into the office.

"Sam," he said. "Just who in hell are you?"

"I beg your pardon?"

Landry, a beefy guy with black glasses and a frown, held up a red folder, shaking it once for emphasis. "This says you're not employed here."

"It's wrong," shrugged Sammy. He got up and stood casually, clearly not intimidated or guilty. "Paperwork just hasn't come in from Human Resources yet."

"I am Human Resources," yelled Landry. "I would have known if you were hired." He paused, clearly uncomfortable with confrontation. "You, sir, are a fraud."

That's when the stripper came in.

With the balloons.

# CHAPTER 18

## THAT'S JUST NOT FUNNY

## RAY

Ray Sanchez studied the empty store and looked at the manager in amazement. "Eighteen-fifty? Are you insane?" He gestured at the piles of debris left over from a former tenant, the scarred drywall after that tenant pulled down the mirrors, the half-dismembered mannequins lying about like victims of a shopping mall bombing.

He widened his arms to encompass the neighborhood, implying deep criticism where none was deserved; the area was up-scale yuppie, exactly what Dani expected. Still, you had to bargain.

The manager, a pretty young woman of middle twenties with big red hair and too tight skirt, clutched her appointment book to her full chest and looked determined. "Eighteen-fifty is actually very reasonable, Mr. Sanchez."

"Call me Ray," said Ray. He touched a pale torso on a silver stand which toppled to the floor. Dust poofed up from it.

"The area is exceptional for your type of business. The foot traffic is over one hundred per hour and the square foot price is only $4.25. That compares with..." And she went on, droning her facts and figures, handing him supporting paperwork, graphs and pie charts in color, getting into the fact that she was a grown-up until Ray interrupted.

"Ms. Penderby."

"Tiffani," said Tiffani. "With an i."

"Tiffani," accepted Ray, knowing she put a little heart above the i. "How long is the lease?"

"A year, minimum."

Ray didn't care, it was part of the game. "And the deposit?"

"One and a half months rent."

"Uh-huh. I see." He nudged the mannequin with the toe of his rattlesnake skin boot. "And this junk, when can you remove it?"

"Today's Wednesday...how about by Monday?"

"All right." Ray sighed as if making a monumental decision. "I'll write up an E-mail to corporate, tell them it's a go." He made a note to have Bob print up some good quality checks with a California account code. They'd bounce of course, but not before they were done here.

"Let's go back to your office and fill out some forms. What do you say to some lunch?"

"Why Mr. Sanchez; I would love that." Tiffani lit up like a Christmas tree.

"Please," he said. "Call me Ray."

# BOB

Cincinnati Bob liked practical jokes. In fact, he got his nickname from a nearly legendary prank in Ohio involving two police cars, a member of the Cincinnati City Council, a barber, seven choir members from the cast of *Cats!—The Road Show*—and a circus bear.

The chaos had been astounding but no charges were ever filed, or even considered—what laws were broken?—no one could ever work that out. A perfect crime by Bob's standards.

Cincinnati Bob bored easily.

A cigarette smoldered forgotten in a cheap metal ashtray on the desk of old Hank's shop, located in a concrete block outbuilding on his farm outside Metairie. Dan Fogelberg blared on the radio and Bob whistled along over the clacking of the printing press. Old Hank was back at work and Bob had the place to himself.

He was busy printing brochures and Grand Opening posters, phony business licenses, tax statements and everything needed to make a store seem real. Essentially a hard copy version of what Sammy was doing in cyberspace. The concept of the big store remained unchanged after a century, only the details changed. How do you make a mark see what you want him to see? By making it look like what he expects. Computers merely added a level of sophistication, the reality was in the details.

Bob was a master of the details. He knew fonts and styles and the Advertising Marketplace Standards books by heart. He could re-create an authentic poster from memory, knew what colors went with what decade, product and region.

Bob could have been a rich advertising executive in some company if he didn't have the bent toward larceny.

And, of course, the penchant for practical jokes.

He smiled to himself as the machines whirred and clattered, wondering how Sammy was doing at this moment. Did he enjoy the balloons? Bob didn't like Sammy Hensel, not that that made him the obvious target. Bob would have tried this on anyone, but Sammy being an overdressed stuck up jerk made it sweeter.

It hadn't been easy setting up. He had to find out where Sammy was, decide on the appropriate prank and get the details right, all while working on the project. Fortunately, the job pressures weren't great; just a few easy things for Patty like the magazine and credentials, and the business checks for Ray. Kid stuff.

He couldn't ask Dani, of course. He'd never worked with her before, but from what he knew she wouldn't take this well. She struck Bob as a little up-tight, not the easy-going girl he recalled after working with her father. Pops Logan, now there was a character!

Bob let himself drift in a fog of pleasant memories as the posters printed.

## PATTY

Patty Krill simply could not get Hailey Briscoe into her pants. Or even close to them.

They were now at Clark Brothers Steak House, a five-star restaurant on Palmetto Street, and Patty was beginning to think she'd only gotten him here because of the food. They'd parted at lunch, she with a gentle kneading of his bicep, he with the excuse that he had the Lord's work to do, and a promise to do dinner sometime. Sometime, due to Patty's insistent phone calls and messages, happened on Thursday at eight-ish when he came to her table and apologized for being late.

He looked over the choices. "My," he said, peering at her through the dim light over the book-like menu. "A little pricey, isn't it?"

And this, she thought, from a scamming millionaire. She thought about his house, the Cadillac, the lifestyle he lived and her brow furrowed. He's bitching about fifty bucks for a steak? But she said, "Don't worry about it, Hailey; I'm on an expense account."

In fact, the magazine story was the only thing that got him to come. He'd hemmed and hawed but gave in to the lure of vanity; his name in a national, if small circulation, magazine.

"Tell me more about yourself." Patty wore an appropriate evening dress that fit her character; dark blue, cut only so far in front, back and length. Her shoes weren't flat but close enough, her jewelry subdued.

"Well, the church is really taking off," Hailey said. "I simply can't believe the response. The Lord has truly blessed us."

"Us?" She asked. Did he have a partner?

"My congregation," he said. "The charity work we do. Did you know that nearly a million dollars went out to needy organizations just last month?

"A million! I had no idea."

He nodded his satisfaction. "Yes, almost a million. And we'll do better next month. The faith in the Lord is truly an amazing thing."

"Well, surely a lot of the credit has to go to you?" She touched his hand, but he surprised her by pulling away. He declined the offer of a drink, instead asking for a, "Co'Cola, no ice, thank you."

Patty had a daiquiri.

"No," said Hailey. "None of the credit goes to me. I'm a servant of the Lord. Didn't he say that no man gets into Heaven by good deeds? Only by believing in his name shall a man pass through the Pearly Gates."

A comforting idea thought Patty, if it works. Be nice to have her sins not counted. Maybe she should ask him. But for now, this was the single worst seduction she'd ever had. She'd done vanity, touching, flirting, eye contact...Hailey seemed immune. Patty was baffled. *All* these techniques should have worked. She considered that he was gay. Maybe the trophy wife was a cover-up. But no, she saw the way he ogled the hostess.

Sure, a look wasn't proof of infidelity, but a third-floor tryst at night certainly was. The Ace said he saw them and that meant Hailey liked women and why the hell didn't he make a move on her?

It was enough to make her doubt herself, if only for a short time. Meanwhile she listened and smiled and batted her eyes and got nowhere.

After he left—"sorry," he said, checking his gleaming silver watch, "But I get up early,"—she dialed Dani from her cell phone to report her failure.

"I don't get it, Dix; he should have tumbled by now."

"You can't win them all"

"I damn well have before."

"You gave it your best, Patty. Come on in."

"I'm not finished with him," Patty snapped. She waved to the waiter, pointed at her glass and he went off to get her a refill.

"What are you going to do?"

The waiter returned with her drink and she swallowed it whole. "I have no earthly idea."

## Sammy

Sammy Hensel sat at the second chair to the left in the conference room. The table, stretching to infinity, surrounded by six-hundred dollar chairs, was dark mahogany that gleamed with polish. The lights were muted, the atmosphere solemn, the inquisitor—Landry Calhoun, VP of Management and Personnel Placement—insistent on an explanation.

Did Sammy have one that covered all this? He did not. He poured water from a carafe into a cut crystal glass, watched it sparkle like jewels under the halogen overhead lighting.

"Well?" said Landry. His arms crossed his chest and Sammy almost laughed out loud at this posture of authority. "I'm waiting."

"I have to say," said Sammy, waiting for inspiration, "That I'm impressed with you."

"What?"

"That you found me out." Was this something? Why, yes; it was. "So quickly." He sat up to better appear in command. "My name is Ed Quisman. I'm with internal security." He took out his wallet and showed a driver's license showing his picture and Ed Quisman's name over the official stamp of the state of Delaware. It was one of a dozen he owned, available for just these moments.

"Security?" Landry said, confused.

"You betcha," said Sammy warming to the task. He admitted to himself that he lived for these close calls. They made him feel superior. For a moment he was young again, a slender black boy growing up in Philly with no prospects, no money and not much of an education. At times like these that kid raised a small fist and pumped it in victory.

"I've been assigned by headquarters to investigate internal security at our satellite offices." Amazing how this stuff just poured out, like water, which he sipped. "They're concerned with identity theft and corporate spying."

"But why wasn't I informed?" asked Landry. "I mean, shouldn't I have been informed?"

"No, sir. I'm sorry, but your department has leaks. We're covering all the bases here and I know you'll appreciate that we can't let the word get out. It would compromise the entire mission." Compromise, he thought; what a terrific word.

"Well, of course," Landry fumbled. He'd come in expecting to nab a crook. Now, faced with a company watchdog he was feeling startled and off balance. "I wouldn't want to compromise anything..."

"And you certainly can't tell anyone else about this. There are spies everywhere. Can I get your cooperation on this? Landry?" Sammy held out a hand full of lying sincerity which Landry took.

"Yes, yes. I'd be happy to help all I can."

"How about I brief you on..." Sammy considered. Today was Friday. If he worked through the weekend he could be finished before Monday. But Cary was having the retirement party for Phil on Monday and he didn't want to miss that. "Wednesday? Would that be acceptable?"

He stood up, concluding the interview and Landry hastily got to his feet.

They walked to the door, opened it and Sammy gestured, you first. Landry walked past him and suddenly stopped.

"But," he asked. "What was that all about? The strippers? The balloons?"

"Um," said Sammy.

# Dani

Ray Sanchez sat at the table eating an omelet I had cooked. He had a list. "I'll need a crew for remodeling the store. Painters, drywall, cleaning. I'll need laborers to set up the books and the shelves."

"Where'd you get the stock?"

"An auction house in Vegas. Bookstore there went under and the Feds sold off the inventory for a tax lien. More than we need but I got a good price on it."

Thank God for that, I thought. "What else?"

"Posters, paper..."

"Bob's on it."

Ray shrugged, forked some eggs, sipped his coffee, a thick dark brew spreading a comfortable odor that reminded him, he said of cinnamon and alfalfa. It tasted like crap but the smell was wonderful. "That's it for me. When do we hit the mark?"

"When will you be ready?"

"Thursday next week. Friday at the latest."

"Monday," I decided. "The twelfth."

"You sure the guy's going to go for the store?"

I thought about Patty and her failure to lure in Hailey Briscoe. What was *wrong* with the guy? Sex should have worked. They should have had an insight by now into the way his mind worked, his needs and wants. But, woulda/shoulda; what are you going to do? I covered my deep anxiety with a gulp of the heavenly coffee. I adored the taste, though the smell could gag a wharf rat. It was one of those things I grew up with, an imported blend Pops got somewhere.

"I'm sure," I said. I had to be sure. The essence of leadership was confidence. That's why we're called confidence men, right? Pops was the definition of self-assurance. He could convince you things were peachy while the ship was sinking and the water was at your lower lip.

Again, I wished he was here. And I was relieved that he wasn't. I buttered toast and considered Ray who was slouched back in his chair reading Christopher Moore's *Bloodsucking Fiends – A Love Story*. He licked his finger and turned another page.

# PATTY

Patty, more grimly determined to seduce a man than she'd even been in her whole life, marched up the three stairs to the school building, clacked her heels down the long echoey halls to the office. She pushed open the door, adjusted her expression to one of a timid woman wondering exactly what she was doing and said, "Hello?"

The office was empty and she came further in. A rustling from the other room and Hailey Briscoe himself entered with an enquiring look on his wide face. "May I help you?"

He didn't recognize her. Patty was certain he wouldn't. She was dressed in housewife frump, an older shapeless dress, tennis shoes and just slightly disheveled hair, blond again since it was her own. She wore tinted contacts and had done things with makeup that made her appear as if she wasn't wearing any.

"I found a wallet," she said.

"Yes?" Hailey asked, looking interested.

"Uh, it says it belongs to..." she held it out, folded open. "Somebody named Hailey, uh..."

"Briscoe! That's me!" He beamed at her and held out his hand. "Where did you find it?"

"On the street about a block from here. See, I go to the Piggly-Wiggly and I decided to walk since I didn't need much and near the corner over on Fourth Street? Where it crosses Delany? I saw this in the weeds and I picked it up and it had this address and..." She trailed off and shrugged.

"I can't believe it! I never thought I'd see this again. Can I give you a reward? Some small token...?"

"Oh, no; I couldn't, Mr. Briscoe."

"Please. The church is not without its resources." He beckoned. "Come into my office."

Said the fly to the spider. Patty couldn't keep the predatory smile off her face as she walked past him into his private room. It was what she expected; square, dark and manly with a big desk in front of a shaded window, book cases, framed testimonials and degrees on the vanity wall.

He urged her to sit, went to his own chair, sighed as he settled in. "Can I give you a check? We don't keep much cash here, I'm afraid. Say a hundred dollars?"

She widened her eyes as if this was an enormous sum and tried not to appear too eager. She had only the basic outlines on how to go from here to seduction but he'd turned down an obvious invitation from the reporter, an even more obvious one from the hooker. Maybe he just liked the common folk.

Half an hour later Hailey Briscoe escorted her out the door, one hand on her back and not even feeling her bra strap, gently nudging her out. He was still happy about his wallet but hadn't responded to anything else.

Walking to her car in a daze Patty wondered, what the hell? No man—or boy—since Mickey Sullimark back in seventh grade had ever—ever!—turned her down. And Mickey had been so into action figures that he probably never even knew she existed. But this guy hadn't tumbled to anything.

Patty got in the car and turned the key. Dani was *not* going to be pleased.

# CHAPTER 19

## HERE COME THOSE TEARS AGAIN

Leroy Logan, Pops to his friends, who were legion despite a half century of long cons, showed up at the same time that Patty arrived to tell me her latest failure. Ray Sanchez had moved to the sofa and was engrossed in his book. He looked up at Leroy, his eyes grew wide but he said nothing.

Patty studied him as well. She'd never met my father but quickly realized who he was. To say Pops was a legend in the con man circles was like saying, "I saw Sir Paul McCartney today at the market. He was buying Corn Flakes." She let him go by while miming at me. "Oh, my God! Is that him? Is that really Him?"

I gave her an "oh; grow up," eye-roll and said sweetly, "Pops? What brings you here?"

I was wondering how he found me, but knowing his experience and resources I didn't ask. Leroy came and left by some obscure rules of his own.

"Dani." He greeted as I came into his arms for a bony hug. It always felt odd to embrace him, both because he'd been gone so often and because I was now taller and basically engulfed him.

He adjusted his fedora, eyed Patty approvingly which went far to raise her self-esteem and cocked an eye at Ray. "Esteban," he said.

"Leroy," said Ray. He went back to his book.

"You got any food in this place?" Leroy asked.

"Some. What do you want?"

He settled for the same breakfast we'd recently finished and I headed to the kitchen area to crack more eggs. Patty followed and, to my annoyance, so did Pops.

"Is there any coffee?" He lit a cigarette from his ancient diamond studded Zippo and began telling Patty stories, some of them true.

I cooked, served and stewed. What awful timing. Just before my first solo long con, when I wasn't even certain of turning the mark, Leroy turns up like a bad penny. Surely, I thought with paranoia, it couldn't be an accident; he knew something. He was here to check up on me. He was...what *was* he doing here?

I made more toast and hoped that Patty had good news.

She didn't. I sat down and nibbled the edge of a slice of browned bread as Patty explained how she could not get through to Hailey Briscoe.

"Maybe he's a fag," said Leroy.

"He's not," insisted Patty.

"You didn't play him right," Pops said this like the pro he was, as if it was obvious.

"Pops!" I yelled.

"I did, too!"

Pops sipped his coffee, indifferent to the outburst and Patty turned to me for support.

"I did play him right. I did. All three times. Nobody's ever run the raggle like I did and the man didn't go for it."

"I know, hon. You did your best."

"I feel so used," she said sadly. "Like nobody wants to screw me."

"I'll do it," said Ray from the couch.

"You don't count, Ray. You'd screw a parking meter if it didn't cost a quarter."

Ray considered this, shrugged and went back to his book.

"What's next?" asked Pops. "Anything in it for me?"

"No," I told him. "Nothing. Drink more coffee." I poured it for him, setting the pot down a little too hard.

"You sure you're doing this right, girl? I know I've been against this whole self-finance idea from the first. Is it possible you can't make the play?"

I was about to absolutely explode. Veins bulged, eyes widened and as hot a reply as has been served was just about to erupt when the sound of arguing came from the stairs. What now?

"I know it was you, Bob. You and your stupid jokes."

"I didn't mean anything by it."

They entered the room together like schoolboys who've been fighting and are each eager to reach the teacher first to rat out the other.

"He almost got me caught," demanded Sammy.

"It was just a little prank." Since they both were talking at once it was hard to make out what was going on. "No big deal," finished Bob.

Sammy waved a slender fist in Bob's general direction.

"You ever do anything like that again, you bastard, and I'll do better than kill you. I swear it, I will bury you. I will wreck your credit rating, file so many computer warrants on you that the police will fight over who gets to lock you up longest. I will create a computer hole so deep you'll never see the light of day."

Everybody stopped to listen to this tirade, impressed at its scope. Wrecking a credit rating didn't affect them much, theirs being mostly a cash society, but the warrant thing sounded pretty dire. Even Ray over on the couch set his book down to listen.

"Strippers," complained Sammy, in my general direction. "He sent strippers to my office. I could have been made."

"And balloons," added Bob helpfully. Despite the argument, he couldn't help laughing.

"Wipe that goddam smile off your face," Sammy bellowed. "Before I wipe it off."

"Boys!" I yelled. "Boys!"

Order was restored with the threat of a frying pan. I roughly shoved Sammy and Bob apart, picked up the pan and swung it experimentally. Even the non-combatants got the idea. Setting it back down I asked serenely, "Sammy, what's this about you getting fired?"

"Um," said Sammy.

"And you." I turned to Bob. "What are you trying to do? Screw the deal?"

"It was just a joke."

"A joke. Remember what happened in Philadelphia when you played that little prank?"

Bob grinned back at me. "Five squad cars," he said. "*Five!*

"How'd that turn out for you, Bob?"

"Um," said Bob.

"Hard-Pan Harry went to jail, didn't he? And the scam didn't go down? And you didn't work for, what was it? Three years? I heard you took a straight job as a printer to get by."

Bob ducked his head and studied the tablecloth. Sammy brightened. "A straight job?"

"Shut up, Sam, you're no damn better." I felt bitter and put upon. I trusted these guys and they acted like children. It was bad enough that the plan wasn't going right; *that* I could sort out. But to have this dirty laundry aired in front of Pops was awful. I saw that Leroy was watching with interest.

"Don't think I don't know about you. I paid for a computer system and you don't get one. So you pocket that amount. I'm okay with that, we all do a little scamming. But what are you doing in somebody else's office?"

"I like the perks," said Sam. "It's more fun to have people around, you know, not cooped up in my apartment."

"You could get busted."

"That just adds to the spice."

"And if my long con goes south, what then?"

"I don't know."

Suddenly I was too angry to continue. "Get out, both of you. The con goes down in a week. You've already been paid and I expect you to act like professionals until we're done." I waited and nobody moved. "I said get out!"

With a shuffling of chairs and no-one looking at anyone else, Cincinnati Bob and Sammy Hensel left the kitchen. Their footsteps clunked off down the stairs and soon faded out.

The silence continued until Patty said, "I think I'd better be going, too. I'm sorry, Dani. I really am."

I squeezed her hand. "It's not your fault, Patty. Sometimes the mark doesn't tumble."

"Sure." She gathered up her purse and turned away. "Well," she said. "Bye."

I went to the living room and stood over Ray. "What about you?"

"What did I do?"

"Nothing. But that doesn't mean I want you around for what's coming. Get what you need and get it done. I'll take it from here."

Ray dog-eared his page, closed the book and stood up. "Leroy," he said and Pops said, "Estaban." Ray picked up his overnight bag, shoved the book in and left.

I turned to Pops. "So," I said.

"Things don't seem to be going too well."

"I'll handle it. I don't want you interfering."

"Who's interfering? I just stopped by, had some coffee...this is good coffee, by the way." He held up his cup. "Can I have some more?"

"Sure." I poured the last of the pot and decided not to make any more since he wouldn't be here long enough to drink it. A heavy weight settled over me and I felt old and tired and wondered if, at any time in his long career, he had ever felt this way. Had he fought off the feeling that everything was wrong and there was no way out? Did he have anyone to turn to when the weight became too heavy to carry?

I studied him. An old man sitting in a normal kitchen, drinking coffee and smoking cigarettes and I marveled; he could be anyone. A straight man, retired after fifty years at a factory or an office, a wage earner and husband who worked all his life, with everyday concerns, a normal past.

But he wasn't. He was Leroy Amadeus "Pops" Logan, the most notorious con man still living. He was or had been wanted by every law enforcement agency in the country. He'd sired a half-dozen children and stolen millions of dollars from selfish and greedy men. And I was his daughter.

For a moment, I considered asking his advice. Surely, he had some; he had opinions on everything. He knew every con game ever played because he *invented* many of them. He'd know how to handle this mess. I felt things slipping out of control and reacted typically, by getting angry. This was my time. The long cons idea belonged to me and I had to make it work on my own.

"Pops," I said softly, intending to get his advice *and* be independent. But Pops spoke first.

"That's the problem when you pay your own way up front, you don't take the con seriously." He pointed the stubby remains of his cigarette at me like an accusing finger. "You didn't have to scam the startup money so you haven't put in the time to size up the mark. If you want my opinion..."

"I don't." I said in a sudden fury.

"What?"

"I don't want your opinion. You've been against this from the beginning. You don't think I can handle it. Well, you're wrong, I'm doing just fine. Next week we'll turn the mark with a big store and you'll see."

"But I just think—" Pops said.

"I know what you think and I don't want to hear it." I was angry and frustrated and it all came out in a wave of fury against my father. I said a lot of things I knew, as I was saying them, that I'd regret later, and I did regret them later, after he'd given me a hangdog look and stood up, and shuffled out of the kitchen, a bent old man who looked, for the first time in my entire life, his real age.

After the door closed with a slight click that sounded like a gunshot, I sat at the table looking at nothing, feeling nothing. I turned the radio on and heard Billie Holiday singing *God Bless the Child.* That's the thing with New Orleans; there's always sad music playing.

I smelled the damp earthy smell of his coffee, the acrid aroma of his unfiltered cigarettes and the sweet undercurrent of his after shave and realized he was gone.

"Pops, God damn it." Why couldn't I tell him I needed him?

# CHAPTER 20

## THE FAT MAN COMETH

From tears to a jazz club on Bourbon Street, a dark hive filled with sweaty drinkers only half listening to the pulsing beat, took only a few minutes, a major mood swing and an angry determination not to be depressed.

A psychiatrist would probably say I was sublimating my emotions, but then a psychiatrist would also say my choice of careers was a manifestation of father/daughter struggle. I had the uncomfortable feeling that a shrink would have a field day with me *and* my father.

But at the moment I didn't care. The band Jazz double-four time was Jimmy's All-Stars, a foursome of old black men in the requisite fedoras, with cigarettes held between thick lips, smoke curling to the ceiling and blocking their features. Li'l Jimmy The piano player did most of the singing in a guttural voice filled with whiskey, women and regret and I settled in a chair in the back to let it seep through me.

His name was James Monroe Washington but everyone called him Li'l Jimmy, because of he weighed in at over three-hundred and forty on a Five-eight frame. He was nearly blind from some cataract illness and spent his non-playing hours in one hospital or another recovering from a life making love to booze, smokes and the blues.

I'd known him since I was sixteen. Jimmy had once ejected Jiggs from his club for bringing in another woman when he was dating me and I'd used him a dozen times on the small scams I'd run locally.

He caught my eye during a downbeat number about cheatin' wimmen and smiled his wide grin while never missing the feeling in the song. All blues bands play the same music, only some are better at it than others. It all depended on the feel and Jimmy had made a life out of wringing every drop of woe from the twelve-bar blues.

After the set he waddled over ,brushing his girth between the tightly packed tables, keeping up a running apology. "Sorry, Ma'am," he'd say or, "Excuse me, suh," in his raspy tobacco voice and folks would ease out of the way with a smile or wave and an easy, "no problem, man."

Clarissa the waitress, who I also knew by sight, gave me a chin bob in greeting and set a bourbon and beer in front of Jimmy.

"Dani," he greeted with that voice and I felt at home for the first time in months. "Where you been hidin' daughter?"

I smiled. Jimmy had adopted me when I was a skinny white kid hanging out where I had no reason to be and it was through his efforts that New Orleans was my real home and Jimmy my adopted father.

"Hey, Jimmy. I've been in New York."

"The Big Apple," he said, impressed. Like every local player, Jimmy thought of New York as the Mecca of music. He sang, "If I can make it there I'll make it...anywhere," and I joined in, off key but enthusiastic, "It's up to you, New York, New York."

He giggled and downed his shot like a walrus slurping a harp seal, drank the entire beer in one swallow and pounded the table. "Whee-oo," he said. "That is good."

"How you been, Jimmy?"

"I been good, girl, I been good." He told me about his three operations and how Katrina had destroyed his house, his son's house and most of the Ninth Ward. "It didn't get the club much, though," which I knew heartened him. The club was his real life.

At a sudden idea I said, "Have you heard anything about a local preacher? Runs a TV studio down in the ward?"

"Hailey Briscoe? That who you mean?"

"The one," I answered, feeling a bit of small world.

Interest took away some of the pain and the alcohol was easing the rest. Jimmy rubbed the stubble on his wide cheeks and blew out smoke. "He's been the talk lately," he said. "Has a lot of people out in the streets pushing people to donate to his ministry. Started out with the whole "God wants you to' speech but lately it's been different."

"Different?" I asked. "How so?"

"Well, like now they're talking money. How you can give up your house, still collect the insurance, and do good for the community by helping God." He laughed. "Seems to me like God needs all the help he can get around here, just the like rest of us."

"So he's a crook?" I knew it. I tried to let the feeling of salvation wash over me but something still nagged at me.

"Oh, sure," said Jimmy. "A course he is. Why else would he be in the religious racket?" Jimmy had a strong belief in the power of bourbon and blues. "All a man needs," he said, "to get hisself into Heaven."

We talked for a few more minutes before he shoved himself from the chair with great effort. "Gotta go, daughter. My set's overdue. Talk to you after the show."

I sat there for the rest of the morning while he played his heart out for a scattering of tourist catching the early show. Jimmy felt that drinking should begin right after breakfast and scheduled his performances accordingly. The steady attendance went far to confirm his theory.

Jimmy's thoughts about Hailey Briscoe helped immensely to ease my doubts. He knew everyone in the Ninth Ward and heard every rumor, every piece of gossip. If it was spoken it went into Li'l Jimmy's ear.

We talked about other things between his sets, but I was already feeling better. The warm community, the friendly acceptance and even the booze gave me a sense that I could handle this.

I was on the right track, I told myself, and with that thought front and center in my mind I left the club and walked steadily into disaster.

"Ali?"

"Yes?"

"It's Dani."

The bellow of Texas style welcome went a long way toward restoring my self-confidence. Alison Pinckney and I had done a long con back in New York a while back and he evidently had good memories of working with me.

He was a medium-sized man in an oversized Texas ten-gallon hat, who lived in Houston and ran a most peculiar business. Alison Pinckney was a cross between a Roper—a man who brought in the mark after the contact—and an Inside Man—the grifter who sold the mark on the scam.

His specialty was being a fat businessman. He had at least a half dozen fake businesses pre-built, with fictitious histories, phony identities and easily checkable existences. If you needed someone to make a business seem real, you couldn't do better than Alison.

The fat man part came from his habit of wearing fat suits when dealing with the marks. "It's better," he said. "When the scam goes down and the mark's looking for somebody to blame, they're not going to come after a skinny car dealer in Houston are they? I just take off the fat suit and nobody can ever find me."

I got to the point. "I need a roper."

"What's the job?" Ali said which impressed me. Everybody else asked about the fee.

I explained about Hailey Briscoe and the Church of Divine Faith and the big store being set up in Santa Vicente. "Ray Sanchez is running it."

"He's good," said Ali, though his tone suggested unpleasant memories. I decided not to ask. "When do you need me?"

"Friday."

"That's damn short notice, Dani. What if I'm busy?"

"Are you?"

"No."

I laughed. "I know I should have let you know earlier." I decided to explain. "I was using Patty Kreel to set up a raggle on him and she struck out."

"Patty failed a raggle?" He said, incredulous. "I've never heard of a mark turning down Patty. Hell, I even...I...uh—"

"Right. I got it. But that's why we're behind the gun. We've got to move on him and I don't know how else to bait the hook."

"Read me the story."

"There are these Bible stores popping up all over the place. We set up a first class show in California, Sammy did the background..."

"Sammy Hensel?"

"You know him?"

"Miserable little overdressed son of a bitch."

"You know him."

"He's good though," admitted Ali. "You went first string. Who else is in?"

"Cincinnati Bob Wilkerson."

"Don't know him."

"The Ace."

"Oh God!" Sounds of real revulsion came over the line. I wasn't surprised; everyone thought that way about the Ace.

"He brings down the average, doesn't he?"

"Right down to the ground."

"Well, be careful with him. The Ace, Jeez."

After more shop talk and complaining about the schedule, Alison agreed to come out on Thursday. "Set me up for a Friday meet with the chump," he said. "I'll run him out to California on a corporate jet. Do the whole 'Champaign lifestyles and caviar dreams' number on him. He'll bite."

"It's good to hear you say that."

"You having doubts?"

"With Leroy out, Ali, it's my first."

"Bring him in, then." Alison Pinckney, like most of the con artists, thought the world of my father. Most of the police respected him as well, despite decades of trying to catch him.

"Can't do that, Ali."

"Pride, Dani? Is that something you can afford?"

I thought about my decreasing bank balance and what a disaster this would be if I failed. But I couldn't fail, this *had* to work.

"I can afford it, Ali. Trust me, I can afford it."

But I said a brief prayer to St Disthmus, the patron saint of thieves, to please watch over me.


I made the calls to Hailey Briscoe on Wednesday—could he meet with Arthur Pettiger regarding the *Golden Rule Bookstore* chain?

"What's this about?" asked Hailey. The remembered arrogance jumped down the line and I smiled, thinking how much fun this would be, bringing him down. He sounded like a well-fed lion with his loud booming voice.

"A preliminary meeting to determine your interest in representing the chain in the Southern markets." I said my name was Karen Peck and caller ID would show me calling long distance from the company headquarters in San Clemente, California. Bless Sam, I thought, a true computer genius.

"Preliminary..." Hailey Briscoe seemed to have trouble getting around that word.

"We'd like to gauge your interest in being our spokesperson, sir. Our Mr. Pettiger can explain the details when you meet. Would eleven o'clock work for you?"

"I don't know," Hailey hedged. "Who are you people again?"

"*The Golden Rule Bookstores.* "'Christian Books for Christian Lives,'" I said, reading the slogan Sammy had made up. "We're second to the Mardell chain and moving up quickly. We're expanding into regional markets and hope you might be interested in a ground floor opportunity." The words, 'ground floor opportunity' were pure gold for getting a mark's attention. Surprisingly, the response wasn't the eager interest I expected. What was with this guy? First sex, now money. What did it take to reach him?

I said, eager to close. "Friday? Say, about eleven?"

"Sure. I guess I can be there for that."

"Wonderful. In the meantime, might I suggest you visit our website to familiarize yourself of our company and its history?"

"You mean on the computer?"

I knew he had one because I'd seen it when Marcy and I first visited, but maybe the guy couldn't use it. Wouldn't that just figure? "Yes, sir. Just look up *Golden Rule Bookstore*.com or Google us. I guarantee you'll be impressed."

I'd seen it myself. Sammy had created a web of lies and misdirection that would earn him an award if such things existed. The Connies? Maybe I'd use that sometime.

"On-line, hmmm. Well, maybe I could get one of the girls to find it. I'm a very busy man, you understand."

"Of course, you are, sir." You, pompous jerk, I thought, but said, "We'll see you Friday." I hung up and blew air through my lips. "Hey, Ali!" I said. "We're on."

I drove him, in fat suit number four, in a rented Chrysler 300. The Mustang and Marcy still hadn't shown up and the little sports car would have been out of character anyway.

He played with the radio buttons. "This is a very nice automobile," he said. "And American made, too. I am truly impressed."

"Uh-huh," I said, as indifferent to new cars as I was to sports. What's the big deal? You turn them on and drive. Except my Mustang, of course. "Keep on target, willya?"

"Is this wise, you coming along? Hasn't he seen you?"

"Not like this," I said. I touched my carroty-red wig, catching my reflection in the mirror. Green contacts made a lot of difference. No, he wouldn't know me.

"You ready?"

Alison looked as annoyed as a fat man could. "Of course, I'm ready! I've been ready since you were just a child. I've been..."

"Got it. You're ready. I hope so, because here we are."

We parked and entered the little school. Alison muttered softly, "This is it? I expected better."

"They cleared three point six last year and projections say double that in another two."

Now he was impressed. His bushy fake eyebrows rose. "Really? Here? I have got to get a new career."

We entered the office, got escorted into Hailey Briscoe's personal space, took seats across from his desk and made introductions. "I'm Karen Beck? We spoke on the phone. This is..."

"Arthur Pettiger," said Alison, rising to shake hands. "Pleased to meet you."

"The same," said Hailey, not sounding it. "I read your web site. It's very impressive." He gestured to the computer and I got an even stronger impression that he couldn't operate it.

Alison said, "This little station has been a rocket, Hailey, and it has the proper demographic as well. We are deeply interested in you."

"Thank you, sir, thank you."

"Shall we get down to business?"

Alison expertly sold the story. *Golden Rule Bookstores* was looking for a regional spokesman and when the market down South was mentioned, everybody said Hailey Briscoe was the rising star. *Golden Rule* was expanding, he said and handed over a thick presentation folio with color brochures of stores in twenty-five cities and nine more under construction. As Hailey studied the eye candy, he extolled the limitless potential of doing the Lord's work alongside a partner who understood and could capitalize the venture.

Hailey grasped the idea quickly and asked surprisingly astute questions. Alison in turn changed his patter from speaking down to a back-county cracker to an educated equal. He was so good at selling

I was barely aware he was doing it. Hell, I'd buy in myself even knowing was a scam.

An hour later Hailey said, "Dinner?" and Alison agreed and the two men shook hands and we parted company.

Dinner at Antoine's led to drinks which led to an invitation to see Hailey's broadcast as guests. We were in.

I said, "I think we've got him."

"Shhhh." He touched a finger to his lips. "Never say that! Not until we reel him in. You'll jinx us."

"You believe in Jinx's?"

"And voodoo and rabbit's feet and lucky charms and anything else that'll help take money from people."

"Sorry." I didn't like to admit it but maybe I believed in superstition too. Otherwise why was I wearing my lucky bra?

I asked, "Do you need help with that?" Early Sunday morning and Alison was struggling into his fat suit, a rubber and plastic monstrosity that enveloped him like a big pink pig.

"No, I've got it. Number four's always a bitch. Better get ready yourself. This is the important part."

We watched Hailey's revival from the control booth and were impressed by his energy. Live and prowling the stage Hailey was a southern dynamo. He pointed to the audience, demanded reaction, praised the Lord and worked himself and his audience into a frenzy. Compared to the technical calm in the booth his show was stirring and memorable and I gave him grudging respect, seeing why people sent him their money. The man was hypnotic.

Well, there wasn't that great a difference between an evangelical preacher and a con man. We both sold a bill of goods that bought long on faith and sold short on truth.

Hailey, in an exhausted glow, met us after the show. He was proud of his performance and I saw him as he saw himself; a born huckster, spreading the world for God. I wondered, not for the first time, if he could possibly believe in what he was saying.

Over drinks back stage Alison made the pitch.

"I think you're a natural, sir."

"Why, thank you."

"No, thank *you*." Fat Alison sipped his iced tea, seemingly lost in thought. "You know," he said, as if it was a new idea. "I think you should visit one of the stores. See what you'd be representing."

Hailey looked interested.

"How would you like to join me in my private jet? Take a trip out to California and see what *Golden Rule* has to offer a man like you."

Hailey swelled like a self-important balloon. "Mr. Pettiger, I would like that."

"Please," said Alison with a very real smile. "Call me Arthur."

The jet left Louis Armstrong International Airport with Alison, Hailey Briscoe and me, seated in rich red leather seats.

"I have never had such a ride," Hailey confided, sounding for a moment like the back woods boy he'd once been.

"Well, strap in, old son," said Alison. "And you will."

Cruise time to Southern California was four hours and we were all happy and well lubricated when we arrived. We escorted Hailey to a suite in the Sheraton Hotel and left until morning when we took him for a ride in a new model Chevy Suburban with signs of being well used.

"It's my own car," said Alison. "Please excuse the junk.

The junk turned out to be boxes filled with Bibles and religious knick-knacks. Sales brochures and company paperwork fell out of thick folders and Hailey couldn't help but read some of them as he sat in the rear seat admiring the beauty of San Vicente. Palm trees floated overhead and traffic flowed like water in a constant stream. We passed mansions with red tile roofs, white stuccoed buildings gleaming behind high security walls and turquoise swimming pools sparkling in the summer heat.

Alison pointed out sights—"Regis Philbin lives there!"—and Hailey enjoyed the fantasy of power displayed like jewels on a beautiful woman. The Pacific Ocean rose and fell like a living thing, a constant reminder of how far we'd come from Louisiana. Nowhere was there any sign of storm damage or of reality itself. It was as artificial as a tinsel Christmas tree.

We entered a small upscale mall with stores like Saks Fifth Avenue and Harold's of Rodeo Drive and I smiled, pleased at Ray

Sanchez' handiwork. Hell, I believed in the store even while knowing it was all a false front.

We parked and walked across the lot to a brightly lit building with posters of current popular Christian titles. The shelves were stocked with books and current magazines, helpful young smiling clerks assisted the many customers and a middle-aged woman welcomed us.

"May I help you?"

Alison waved her away with a smile. "No thank you. We're just looking." She returned to her register.

Ali said, "A blind man walks into a store, picks up his seeing eye dog by the tail and starts twirling him over his head. A clerk comes over and says, "May I help you?" and the blind guy says, "No. We're just looking around.""

It got the needed laugh and I saw Hailey appraising the place.

"Pretty nice, huh?" Alison nudged him in the ribs. "We've got thirty-seven of these in California and Washington and Utah. The growth is phenomenal. Our profit share..." They wandered off, talking.

I had to hand it to Ray Sanchez. He might be a major pain in the ass but he'd created a first- class store. Everything about it, from the bright customer friendly lighting to the expensive looking display shelves to the staff itself attracted the right kind of attention. Too bad it would be gone soon.

I felt a queasy sense of anticipation, a thrill of electricity shivering down my arms. Hailey was hooked. By this time tomorrow he'd be landed, filleted and fried.

# CHAPTER 21

# THE PLAN FAILS

We placed a well-fed, deeply impressed Hailey Briscoe on the jet, strapped him in and watched each other over his supine body. Draped in the seat like a beached Polyester whale, Hailey began to snore gently.

Alison gave me a thumbs-up, loosened the neck of his suit to allow fake fat to droop over the collar and fell back in his own seat as the jet taxied into the air, heading home.

I watched the sky darken into night and studied the tiny lights below. What kind of lives did they lead down there? Were they happy? Did they ever look up and wonder what I was doing up so high?

We drove the still sleeping Hailey to his door and shoveled him into the startled arms of his pretty young wife. He woke up long enough to say a blurry, "Thank you very much," like Elvis entering the building, and I told him we'd be by tomorrow. I had no idea if he heard us.

When I called Hailey at ten the next morning he laughed and said he was eager to get it done. Good, I thought, because so am I. I decided to close the deal on home ground and suggested he come to the Longoria to meet us. I gave directions and nodded to Alison.

"He's on his way."

"Time to get fat."

Hailey arrived at 11:30 and we all went to a Johnny's Po-Boys for late breakfast. He talked non-stop about how being associated with the store would help him. "My ministry will thrive," he said. "People will flock in. Money will flock in." He looked earnestly at me with eyes that beheld Heaven. "Can you imagine the good works we'll be able to do?"

"Good works," I agreed. You, hypocritical bastard. The only "good work" you have in mind is lining your own pocket.

Hailey said, "My charities, of course. All money from donations goes directly to them. I don't even take a salary."

"What about your house?" I asked. Now that we were this close to being partners in crime I couldn't help but needle him.

"What about it?" He asked, looking honestly confused. I was amazed at his guile.

"We saw it when we dropped you off," I said. "It's a beautiful place."

"Isn't it? Thirteen rooms with a boat dock right off the back door. I could fish from the dining room if my wife would let me."

"Your wife is beautiful, too." I smiled to take the edge off the implication but Hailey wouldn't have noticed anyway. He was struck by his own fortune, wallowing in the blessings from God like the runt pig sucking front tit.

"I know! Can you believe that someone like her would marry someone like me? I mean," he made a sweeping gesture at his suit, his body...himself. "Look at this. Truly, I am a truly blessed man. And I owe it all to the Lord."

"Yes, you do, Hailey. I hope we can all be as blessed."

We walked back to the Longoria with Hailey's cup still running over. Inside, at the kitchen table, all friends here, partners even, with the paperwork being brought out of briefcases, we talked about opportunity and advancement and I said, "Art, we have to tell him,"

Alison, as Arthur Pettiger, executive Vice President of Acquisitions, made a slashing motion across his throat and shook his head but Hailey caught the movement. "What?"

"Not now, Karen," said Ali, looking both angry and guilty, as if a stack of money had fallen from his sleeve. Where did that come from?

"Hailey," I said as Karen Peck, touching him on the arm and bending slightly to get to eye level. "There's something we have..."

Alison coughed.

"...to disclose. You aren't our first choice."

Hailey, plucked suddenly from the heights, gaped at me, then at Alison who stood near the stove pretending to study at his nails. "Not your first...? I don't understand."

"Gerald McMasters," I said and looked embarrassed. Gerald was Hailey Briscoe's competition on the televised soul saving circuit, a man with major network connections, one-hundred-thirteen stations and a perfect time slot between Pat Robertson and Bass

Fishing. He had his own his own theme music and a yacht moored at the basin club in Lake Pontchartrain.

Hailey Briscoe, we knew, despised him. He opened and closed his mouth twice before managing a hoarse, "But you said...I thought...I don't understand." He turned to me for an explanation.

"Reverend McMasters was contacted a month ago about this opportunity but he's been stringing us along. Last week Corporate sent down the word to find someone else."

"Screw the greedy prick and get someone else is what they said," Alison muttered.

"In so many words." My hand was still on Hailey's beefy shoulder as he stared from one us to the other, uncomprehending.

"What they want is someone who can deliver the Christian market segment here in the South. Someone with the connections to appeal to a wide audience. Someone..."

"Like Gerald McMasters," finished Alison. He turned to Hailey. "Look, mate, I'm sorry, but this is business. I've been on the phone with corporate and they've changed their minds. They're sold on McMasters and I'll give them this, the man can deliver what we want."

"But he's not interested, is he?" I asked Ali. Hailey swiveled back to me. "We made him the stock option offer and he still isn't on board."

"Only because he wants a larger share."

"Stock offer?" asked Hailey. "What stock offer?"

I pressed his shoulder. "It's nothing, I said. "Just a participation in the profit and the risk." This was the hook. If Hailey bit we'd have him.

Hailey Briscoe, in full evangelical voice, said, "What's this about stock options?" I felt like exploding with glee. He was going for it!

"*Golden Rule* is going public," I said.

"You shouldn't be telling him that," Alison warned.

"Why not? We offered stock to McMasters. Hailey deserves the same chance to profit."

"Profit?" Hailey asked, homing in on the key word.

"Gerald McMasters wants to buy half a million in stock and option another million," I explained.

Hailey seemed to get it. "You want me to buy $500,000 worth of *Golden Rule* stock?"

"That's what we're offering, yes. Our underwriter, Morgan Stanley, set the release price at $10.00 a share and projects a first day close at $17." Words I had studied that meant nothing to me. The stock market was the biggest swindle on the planet and differed from me only in size and a severe dress code.

"But," Hailey said, "I don't have any money." Silence descended over the room.

"Your house, "I said. "Your car...?"

"They belong to my wife." I knew that, of course, but thought it to be another dodge to conceal assets. A horrible feeling of doom was growing in my chest.

Before anyone could recover, we heard steps in the hall and Marcy Garfield burst into the room singing *"the Age of Aquarius"* in an off-key alto. She took three staggering steps into the kitchen before noticing the frozen group staring at her. She stopped, teetering in place like a drunk trying to make connections and I said, "Marcy? Are you Okay?"

"Nooooooo," said Marcy. "I'm pretty sure I'm stoned though." She nodded seriously at this thought, frowned and broke into a wide grin. "Pretty sure I'm stoned though." She giggled.

I went to her, cupped a hand on her cheek and stared into dilated pupils. Marcy swayed in my grasp and made no attempt to pull away. Instead she started to hum. *"This is the dawning of..."*

"What's going on?" asked Hailey. "Is that girl on drugs?"

"Shhh," I said to both of them. The humming sounded like an electrical line. "Marcy, what happened?"

"Jiggs," she said. "Jiggs, Jiggs, Jiggs."

"Yes, Jiggs. What about him?"

"Who?"

"Jiggs."

"He gave me something." She suddenly sounded tragic. "Dani, he gave me something. I told him not to. I said I didn't want it. But he did it anyway and I got high. I got high." She staggered into my arms and we fell to the floor.

"Karen, why is she calling you Dani?" Haley asked.

"Nickname," I ad-libbed.

Hailey said, "Wait a minute." He got up and peered closely at Marcy's empty face. "I know you."

"No, you don't," I said. I made frantic eye gestures to Alison: *get him away from here.*

"Yes, I do," said Hailey. "She's the girl who came to the station a few weeks ago. With another woman, a reporter." His voice became suspicious, and he stared at me. "A blond woman." In a quick move he grabbed at my hair and pulled away the wig. Successful, and astounded, he goggled at the hair and at me, and if the scene confirmed his suspicions, it also baffled him.

Alison said, "Oh, shit."

I said, "It's not what you think, Hailey."

Marcy began to hum again from her place on the floor and my lap where we were entwined like Michelangelo's Pieta.

"It's not what I think," he repeated. "This is a fraud," he said, showing that he did know. "You people are con artists, or something." He pointed a large finger and backed away as if we were contagious.

"Marcy? Are you all right?" I tapped her cheek once, then slapped her harder. "Girl? Stay with me." Marcy began sobbing loudly, her voice becoming shrill and wailing. It sounded like a dental drill and everybody cringed except Alison Pinckney who was edging to the door.

"The jig's up," he said. "Dani, I'm gone."

I couldn't blame him. I wanted to bolt as well. Hailey stood over us all like a betrayed colossus. He said something about cops and Marcy wailed, "The Jiggs is up, the Jiggs is up."

I felt like wailing with her.

# CHAPTER 22

## ONE STEP AHEAD OF THE SHOESHINE

Hailey Briscoe, looking like a pole-axed musk ox, stood in the center of the room. "What's going on here? Who are you people? Why am I here?" He focused on Marcy, now moaning softly in my arms, and became frantic. "What's *wrong* with her?"

"I don't know," I said. "I think she's having a drug overdose."

Footsteps on the stairs.

"There's cops everywhere!" A fat and flushed Alison Pinckney burst back into the room and rushed to the balcony. Hailey Briscoe followed.

Alison watched from the edge of the glass door and ran a commentary. "There's three cop cars pulled up at the curb. Six, seven cops gathered around a fire hydrant. Water's gushing and there's a red car that hit it. Dani, is your car a convertible?"

"A Mustang." I groaned. Marcy gasped once and went limp, unconscious. Her breathing was shallow and her heart rattled in her chest like a snare drum.

"They're after us. Looks like your little darlin' crashed comin' over here and brought the cops with her."

"The police?" said Hailey. "Call them in. I demand they hear your story."

"What a good idea!" Alison turned on him. "Listen you. How's it going to look if they find you here? Television preacher caught in drug raid? Film at eleven. How's that sound?"

Hailey sagged against the wall, deflating like a balloon losing air. "Oh my Lord," he whispered. "They'll find me here." He clutched Alison by the sleeve. "They can't find me here!"

"A moment ago you wanted them." To me he said, "They're fanning out and we're stuck in here. What are we going to do? Dani?"

I wasn't listening. My attention was on the motionless girl. Her face was hot and flushed. Her right fist kept clenching and going slack. She needed help.

"Dani!"

I looked up, startled. Alison and Hailey were staring at me, waiting. "What?"

"They're outside. Cops. A whole lot of them." He looked panicky at the idea. "We've got to do something."

I took another moment to touch Mary's forehead, felt a fever, though she shivered in my arms. I slipped out from under her, gently laying her head on the wood floor. I stood up.

"What's happening now?"

"They've got the street blocked off. Evidently the young lady was being chased before she ran over the hydrant."

"What else?"

"They're fanning out...oh, shit! They're starting a door to door. Dani! They're just down the block. They'll be here in five minutes."

"Are they watching the doors?"

"Yes."

"Shit." I considered our position. Trapped in a second-floor room with no back door, a preacher who couldn't be found here, an unconscious girl being sought by the police and two con artists who didn't want any official attention.

That was the problem. Now, what was the solution? I breathed in to calm myself. Looked around the room. Cops outside. Drug fugitive in here. No way out. I walked to the kitchen counter with all eyes on me, picked up a bottle of Southern Comfort in one hand and twisted the cap off. I poured a generous splash into a glass and drank it in one quick gulp. Argh. It burned and my eyes teared up.

"Ali?"

"Yo." He glanced my way from the window. "You have an idea?"

"No."

"Well, you better get one soon. They're just three doors down now."

"Okay, lemme think. We can't be in here with her." I gestured at Marcy on the floor. "Or with him. Marcy can't move so let's start with Preacher Dan here. Hailey."

He turned with a jerky motion as if parts had been replaced, not all of them correctly.

"You need to go," I told him.

Hailey looked horrified. "I can't leave!"

"You can't stay," I said reasonably. "Do you want to be here when they come in?"

"Sweet Savior Jesus, no!"

"Leave. Go. Walk out the door as if you're interested in what's going on. Ask questions."

"Questions?" The idea made him gasp. "What kind of questions?"

"'What's going on, officers?' 'Who are you after, officers?'" I mimicked. "Hailey, you're an upright citizen. Act like one. You're not afraid of the law so just walk right out and get away."

"I can do that?"

"Sure, why not? Go."

He left. We heard the front door and Alison asked, "What if he rats us out?"

I shrugged. "It only speeds things up a little. But I don't think he wants to be involved."

"So, what's next? What are we gonna do?"

"I don't know. I can get us out of here—"

"You *can?*"

"Sure. But Marcy needs help. We've got to get her to a hospital."

"Let the cops take her."

"I can't. I have to get her out of here."

Alison stared at her. "Do you hear yourself? Why do you have to do anything for her? She brought the cops, she screwed the deal. She's the one made the difference between a lot of money and a lot of trouble. Dani, you've got to let her go."

"I can't *do* that!"

"Why the hell not?"

"I don't know." We glared at each other and I said again with less intensity, "I don't know. It's like I'm a big sister or something. I've got to look out for her." I cocked my head as if to say, "There."

"This isn't abandoning her, Dani. This is about saving her. And saving our own asses at the same time. Let her go."

"But..."

"Let her go." He took my arm and pulled. I resisted for a moment but gave in and took the lead.

"Upstairs, quick." I stopped to grab my purse and ran into the bedroom, came out with a small case. "Let's go."

We ran up the stairs and I stopped at a door at the top of the landing. I took out a key and opened the door. We went in to a furnished apartment, similar to the one downstairs but different enough to cause a sense of disorientation. For one thing, the bathroom was on the right, the bedroom on the left. For another, there was no unconscious woman having a drug overdose on the kitchen floor. We heard the sounds of heavy boots from downstairs.

"Hurry," I said. "Strip." I was tearing off my clothes as I talked and Alison began peeling off the fat suit as he followed me to the bedroom. He was down to his shorts with his arms full of clothing.

"Shove them under the bed!" I reached back to unsnap my bra and tossed it on the floor. I dove into the king-sized bed, threw the covers around until it looked like a hurricane had hit them, patted the space next to me and said, "Ditch the shorts."

I squirmed around and pulled off my own panties as Alison, red-faced, tugged down his boxers. He got into bed next to me and I snuggled against his shoulder. "We're lovers," I instructed. "We've just finished a quickie. We don't have any idea what's going on." I dropped my head onto his chest.

"How can this possibly work?" He asked. "They'll know we don't live here."

"We do live here. Leroy always taught me to have a bolt hole so I rented this place when I took the one downstairs. If nothing goes wrong I've paid double. It's cheap insurance in case something does happen."

For the first time this morning Alison smiled. He also reached down and copped a feel before the cops began battering at the door.

The police were embarrassed   Alison, in a red terrycloth robe the hotel provided was polite but oblivious. No, he hadn't heard anything. No, he didn't know who lived downstairs. A drug raid? My god, what was happening in the world?

He made it a point of leaving the bedroom door open which was ungallant but effective. The cops could see me in the huge bed, white sheets clutched to my chest. They were thorough but brief.

"Identification? Certainly officers." Alison ducked into the bedroom, found his wallet and showed them a Texas driver's license that said Herbert Boosler from Lubbock.

"Why are you here, sir?" They asked and Alison, on home ground with lying, invented several on the spot, including, "She's not my wife, okay? We met at an office party last week." He made knowing eye contact and the cop, an older man with a five o'clock shadow at eleven in the morning nodded like a man of the world. Could he, Mr. Boosler, get the lady's ID?

"Of course. Honey?" said Alison, not wanting to call me by a name until he knew what it was. "These officers need to see some identification." He shut the door to give me some privacy. I came out a moment later, barefoot and disheveled, in a matching robe. I got my purse and rummaged around, handed over an open checkbook/wallet with a current New Orleans license showing this as my address. The cops studied it and left.

"Good planning," said Alison.

"Cincinnati Bob does good paper," I agreed. "Shall we get out of here?"

"We shall," said Alison.

I flinched at the remains of my poor Mustang being tugged up on the bed of a wrecker. The front end was smashed, its little pony emblem crumpled like someone had squeezed it in a fist. I ground my teeth as we walked slowly down the block, away from the activity. At least the registration wasn't in my name so they couldn't trace the car to me.

An ambulance pulled up to the curb with sirens and lights flashing, white clothed men dashed around, dragged out a stretcher and raced into the Longoria. Alison tugged my arm.

"It'll be fine," he said. "They'll fix it up."

"Where are they taking her?"

He read the ambulance. "St. Joseph's Hospital." I stopped to watch. "C'mon," he said. "We've gotta be gone."

We walked slowly to the corner—innocent bystanders never move quickly—and left the scene. We hailed a cab and took it to the airport, consoled each other in a British pub styled bar near terminal B and waited for our planes. Alison managed an early jet to Houston leaving in an hour. My only flight to Kansas City didn't leave until nine that evening.

"I've got to go." He studied my face. "You'll be okay?"

"I'll be fine. Go catch your flight."

Alison Pinckney gave me a last hug and vanished into the crowd, a slender man with no baggage.

I nursed my drink. I called Sally and Ray, Bob and Patty, gave them the bad news, then wandered the bustling concourse. I looked at books and souvenirs, bought a new *People* magazine with a celebrity suicide on the cover which perked me up some, and a local paper. I did the crossword puzzle at the food court while eating Chinese food out of a plastic box and tried not to think about the size of this disaster.

But I couldn't let it go. Like having a broken tooth, it nagged at me and I kept poking at it even though it hurt. How could things have gone so badly? Hailey Briscoe had been about to take the bait. I could have taken him for enough to cover my expenses—there was a sore spot—and make a modest profit. Maybe even leave the crooked preacher with enough skin to allow us to come back and fleece him again some time.

The self-financed long con, I thought bitterly. What a joke.

Mentally I totaled the amounts I'd spent and was appalled. I was out of pocket for the wages to the crew, the expenses, the big store—almost forty-thousand all by itself—my poor little Mustang...two-hundred and seventeen thousand dollars. More than a third of my remaining capitol. How on earth was I supposed to justify that to myself and not feel like a complete failure?

I settled on the uncomfortable gate seats and realized I still had four hours until my flight even boarded. Airports had to be the loneliest places on the planet. Cold, sterile, empty; exactly the way I was feeling.

Marcy. There was another hole to probe and I picked at it with a sense of self-punishment. Should I have paid more attention to her? Monitored her or kept her in or... whatever you were supposed to do to keep a person from messing themselves up?

This was Jiggs doing, I decided angrily. I knew I shouldn't have trusted him. He'd been a bad seed twenty years ago and he was a bad seed now. I felt a stab of regret at having let Marcy meet him, like I was the one responsible for her being in the hospital. I realized that I'd been hasty in taking the rat at face value. Jiggs hadn't been interested in settling a score with a crooked preacher, he'd been looking out for number one. He only wanted his Moms' house back.

I'd broken a main rule of the con; never be in a hurry. I'd allowed my pride to drive me into making the mistake of speed. I felt I had something to prove to Pops and so I'd taken the first thing that came along.

It was no different than when I'd taken up with Jiggs in the first place. I'd done it to piss off my father. In a case of teenage rebellion, I had deliberately chosen the absolute worst person I could possibly find. A ne'er-do-well, cheap, thieving son of a...

Would Marcy be all right? I dropped Jiggs as a regret in favor of worry for Marcy, a much richer pain to wallow in. I thought about her, no doubt sedated at the hospital, waiting on whatever they and the police would do. I decided to call and find out as soon as I got home. Tomorrow, probably, since I wouldn't get back to Jamestown until very late tonight.

Eventually the clock reached eight-thirty and we began boarding. With no luggage or reason to get on early, I held back until everyone else was aboard, shuffled down the tunnel and into the jet. I settled into my seat and read until Kansas.

Just another clean getaway.

# CHAPTER 23

## HOME IS WHERE THE....AH, SCREW IT

My house on Fourth Street, when I stumbled exhausted through the front door at three-thirty-seven in the morning, was as cold and dark as my heart. I switched on the harsh overhead light in the living room and was struck at how bare and unfinished the place looked. Old wallpaper, shag carpet, scratched and worn vinyl; the house was a wreck.

What made me think I could undertake a project like this? What was *wrong* with me?

I switched off the light and walked through the dark hallway, listening to the tapping of my footsteps. I stubbed my toe near the kitchen door, bounced on one foot and went up the stairs. The moon gave a muted ghostly glow that allowed me to sense the squat shapes of the bed and the dresser.

I sat down on the bed, exhausted and head bowed, feeling like a failure at everything. The money was gone, my dreams were in shambles, the bed was lumpy. Without undressing I slipped off my socks and lay down uncovered. The night settled over me like a heavy quilt and in a few moments I was asleep.

I woke to sunshine as thick as warm honey. I kicked off the blankets and lay uncomfortably in day old clothes for several minutes before shrugging them off and taking a shower. I walked naked back into the bedroom and picked out old worn jeans and a loose fitting red tee-shirt and slipped bare feet into old leather moccasins. Comfort clothes.

I felt bruised inside, as if someone had beaten my spirit with clubs. Shrug it off, I scolded myself. Snap out of it. But what was the use? I'd botched this whole situation, messed it up beyond all belief.

In the kitchen, the refrigerator sat like a defeated warrior at the end of a great campaign, empty and useless. I nodded to it as if it was a comrade. "Me too," I said.

Of course. there was no orange juice or milk and the cabinets contained no food. I had no car since the Mustang lay crippled or dead in a junk yard in New Orleans. The thought of it made me want to cry. My pretty little car!

Pops was gone, my only real family, because I'd sent him away. Marcy was in a hospital.

Gack. I pushed open the front door and went out into sunshine so bright it hurt my eyes. "Get yourself going," I told myself and trudged the three blocks to the Quik 'n' Take. I stocked up on juice and junk food, sipping the orange drink on the long walk back home. The houses lining the street were as old as I felt, settled among thick oaks, day lilies, clover and blacktopped driveways. I looked at windows and wondered again; what do these people do? They can't all be con-men, can they? I mean, *somebody* has to deliver the milk.

I was alone. I blew out all the air in my lungs, breathed in new air and began to jog home, the white plastic bag clumping against my chest with every step. By the time I reached her porch I was gasping and set the groceries down with gratitude.

But my dark mood was, if not broken, at least diminished. I could go on.

I poked around in my purse until I found my address book, started the coffee, sat down at the living room table and dialed my youngest sister, Noreen.

"Hey, Noreen. It's Dani."

"Yeah?" No welcome in her voice. Noreen and I had never been close.

"Have you seen Pops? I need to find him."

"I'd think if any of us knew where he was, it'd be you." I recalled my sister, a thick-bodied resentful girl who'd become a thick-bodied resentful woman. She wore her hair short and kept her disapproving scowl close at hand, ready to use. I figured she was probably using it now.

"Can you let me know if you hear from him? It's..." I considered "urgent," settled for, "important."

I hung up, consulted my book and dialed the next sister, Adele, a Nun, at St. Mary Margaret's Christian Sanctuary in New Hampshire. She was a long shot for finding Pops, but I liked her and wanted to hear a warm voice.

As expected, there was no news—when is there ever, in a nunnery?—but we chatted for half an hour and I felt better for it. I went through the next five siblings in shorter order before reaching Petey, an accountant with some firm in San Francisco. I remembered him as an athletic boy, always throwing things at me, like baseballs, footballs and the occasional frog or spider. Impish and wild, Petey might have been Leroy's favorite.

"Pops? No, why? I haven't seen Leroy since July of last year. He was here for the fireworks."

"Any idea where he might be?"

"Have you tried Kate's?"

"Why?" Kate would be 'Fast Kate' Mulrooney, the once fiery redhead who was the constant companion in Leroy Logan's hectic life. In my memory, there was hardly a snapshot that didn't have Kate either in the background or directly in the picture.

"I thought she was sick or something."

"She is," said Petey. "With Alzheimer's disease. She's in a home in St. Louis someplace. I have the number if you want to try it. Pops goes there a lot. If he's anywhere it's probably around Kate."

He gave me the information and we traded pleasantries, neither of us liking nor disliking the other, not enough involved to ever make anything of our shared past. In a way it was sad, I reflected as I hung up. In a different life, I might have cared a lot.

I dialed the number on her pad and a voice said, "Leroy? Sure, honey; he's here. Say, which one are you?"

"I'm Dani Silver."

"Hey, honey, he talks about you *all* the time. I feel like I know you already. I'll tell him you're calling."

"No!" I scrambled, flushed out of the pocket. "I, uh... I'm coming down to visit. It's a surprise and I want to uh, you know...surprise him."

"Well, all right, if that's what you want." She gave me directions and hung up.

I made my last phone call.

"Enterprise Rent-a-Car? I need something sporty, for about a week."

The Autumn Manor Rest Home was as depressing as I expected. A low single story building shaped like a circle with rooms off long curving green tiled halls, it smelled of antiseptic and despair, Ivory soap, old people and death. I grimaced as I walked past nurse's stations where ancient people wasted away on benches and wheelchairs, unattended and uncared for, or about.

I carried a spray of bright flowers, purple aster, yellow mums and white daisies that stood in sharp contrast to the muted browns and tans and faded greens of the nightgowns and the walls. Everything here was waiting to die.

A nurse said, "Room one-seventeen," and pointed. I walked on and entered a small room with a single bed against a good-sized window, as if the occupant might care enough to look out at the world. A woman lay on the bed, matchstick thin with a mass of white hair flowing around her like a mane. She was asleep. 'Fast' Kate Mulrooney.

I felt my heart rise in my throat as I contemplated ending up like this. I wanted to cry. I wanted to run away and hide.

"Dani?"

I turned and there was Pops, sitting in a low wood and leather chair, his feet on a hassock, his fedora pushed forward as if to shade his eyes from seeing anymore.

"What are you doin' here?" He didn't seem angry or sad, merely curious.

"I came to find you. To apologize."

"No need."

"Is need. I'm sorry, Pops. I shouldn't have tossed you out."

He got up and put an arm around me and I sagged into him as if I was again the skinny girl who waited for him to show up, not ever knowing when, only that one day he would.

"I've been tossed out of better places than that," he said, with a smile. "A lot more often, too."

I smiled with him, feeling a sense of relief. "I'll just bet you have." I turned to the sleeping woman. "Kate? Is she going to be...?"

"No. She's going to die," Leroy said flatly, like it was a fact that he'd neither accepted or denied. It just was. He stepped away and shrugged; *out of my hands*.

I whispered. "Can she hear us?"

"Nah. She's too far gone. She stopped knowing who I was about six months ago, about the time I was supposed to be dead, in New York City. Ironic, I suppose. I came out here to talk to her, like I've been doing for a lot of years, but she was already gone. It's a terrible thing, girl, to see someone waste away like this."

"You love her."

"I loved her. For a very long time. But she's not here anymore, just the body she left behind."

"Pop." I was crying now, for the dreams everyone has and the lives they lead. For Leroy "Pops" Logan and 'Fast' Kate Mulrooney, the woman now living only in the memory of her dearest companion. "Oh, Pop."

There wasn't anything else to say and I got a chair from the hall and joined him in his vigil until the nurse stuck her head in and said, "Sorry, Leroy, it's getting on time to go."

We ate dinner at Denny's because it was open and we could smoke.

"Not many places left," said Leroy which made me shudder at the mortality of *that* statement. The image of Kate, always smiling and vibrant in my memories, laying in that bed so cold and worn...it gave me the willies.

"Tell me why you came." Leroy lit one of those smokes and the waitress delivered an ashtray without comment. Filled with light and bursting with activity, the restaurant gave me a shuddery sense of belonging, like I was again part of the living. "Last time you were just about to bust the preacher. How'd that go?"

"It didn't go. It went...Pops, I screwed the pooch." The admission came out in a rush and Leroy let go a sharp yip of surprise at the phase.

"Girl," he laughed. "I ain't heard that expression in I don't know how long. You used to say it whenever you did something wrong and your Momma was about to bust your butt. Remember?"

I did. My mother, faced with controlling six of the most hell-raising children ever produced, and without the help of the man responsible for them being that way, had taken to the hair brush and leather belt method early and often. Her children were, as a result, exceptionally well-behaved. Even the criminal ones.

"The deal went south," I said.

"Tell me."

"There's this girl—well, twenty-two isn't so much a girl—her husband was beating her and I sort of helped her out. She came with me to New Orleans and when I was busy with the scam she went out and got together with Jiggs Roche."

Leroy made a sour face as if he'd bitten aluminum foil. "I always hated that boy," he said. "Why hasn't anyone killed him yet?" Making it sound like somebody was falling down on the job.

"Me and Ali were about to take down the minister when she came in on us. Pops, she was stoned on something. Insisted it was Jiggs that turned her on sent her out to rob me. She did a whole car chase scene, wrecked my Mustang,"—there was that sour look again—"and passed out in my kitchen with the police right behind her. Right in front of the mark."

Pops sucked in smoke, held it, let it out.

I said, "He recognized her, then recognized me and we had to move fast to get out of there. Ali lost his fat suit..."

"Which one?"

"Number four."

"Oh, I *liked* that one."

"And I lost some money on the deal and I didn't know what to do so I came looking for you."

"I'm pleased you did, Dani."

"You're not gonna say 'I told you so?'"

He laughed out loud. "Of course, I am, but not right this minute. Probably need some more coffee first." But he made no move to order any and I smiled for the first time since New Orleans.

"Tell me," I said. We were driving with a river to the left and an old iron bridge in front. "What did I do wrong?"

"Is this like a confession?"

"Sure," said I. "They say it's good for the soul."

Leroy laughed. "I never did agree with that. My motto is, 'If I confess, then they'll arrest.' Didn't see a lot of sense in confiding to anyone."

"You talked to Kate."

"That was different, she was an accomplice. Anyway, it's not my place."

"Never stopped you before. Pops, I'm asking."

"Okay." He agreed instantly. "You never studied the mark."

"I know that, now."

"You didn't find his weakness. You assumed it was women and you assumed it was money. But you never knew."

I was determined not to get angry. I had asked for his advice and would accept it. But damn, this was hard to hear.

"You didn't bring in your team."

"What?" So much for listening. "Of course, I did!"

"No, you didn't. You talked to each one separate. You never did a group meet to discuss the mark. You thought being boss meant you had to think of everything yourself, which is stupid and vain."

"That's pretty harsh, Pops." Maybe this hadn't been such a good idea.

He shrugged. "You asked."

I did. "What else?" My teeth were grinding at this pretense at humility. People like me and Leroy struggled with the idea of humble.

"Hmmm...you self-financed but," he hurried on before the inevitable outburst, "I've already said that. You weren't sharp because you didn't have a personal stake. You weren't motivated."

"Well, I am now." Really, I felt motivated to throttle him by his skinny neck. That I'd asked was rapidly being forgotten.

"So go find yourself a real mark, take him down and get your money back."

"Sure," I fumed.

"Girl? Are you mad at me?"

"Yes." That came out harsher than I'd hoped.

"Well, don't be. I'm just saying the truth. Remember what they say about blaming the messenger."

I took my eyes off the road to regard my father. "Pops," I said. "They kill the messenger."

# CHAPTER 24

## BROCK BACK MOUNTAIN

I drove the rental car up the gravel driveway with the windows open and the radio blasting '*Maybelline*' loud enough to be heard in Seattle. I bellowed along at the last chorus and ambled out to the mailbox in the early evening heat feeling so much better. The sky throbbed with angry purple electricity and had a heavy storm feel to it. The pressure in the air said oh hell yes.

Out of curiosity I glanced at Marcy's driveway for a sign of Brock or his monster truck. There was no sign of either. I popped a beer and sat on the back porch waiting for weather. There was no trace of a breeze and the heat radiated off the side of the house. Nothing at all stirred.

I thought fondly of my father, a rare feeling. Usually I regarded him with impatience. Loving impatience, but still. My recent meeting had been cathartic for both of us. Time and silence had patched up our differences and by the time I dropped him back at the home I was already agreeing—in private—with his assessments.

I wondered how often he came to see Kate and how long he stayed each time. What must it be like to sit with somebody you'd loved for sixty years and watch them lose recognition of you? I took a sip. "Alzheimer's" I said, "Is a bitch."

A faint plop announced the arrival of the storm, followed by three more, then six hundred thousand. The roof runoff filled the gutters and overflowed, and I sat and rocked in the shelter of my own porch, amazed at the wonder of nature.

"What went wrong?" Pops had asked and I said didn't know, but sitting here alone I faced the facts. I'd broken most of the rules of the trade. Rule number two: never be in a hurry. I'd been so eager to prove my business idea that I'd jumped at this without ever considering the risks or rewards.

Rule number three: Always research the mark. I'd tried to, but admitted that I hadn't been thorough. There had to be something else about Hailey Briscoe to explain his reactions. Normal men just didn't behave the way he did. What had Angel Face said? "The money's behaving strangely." So was Hailey, there *had* to be a connection.

I crushed a cigarette butt and shivered slightly in the rapidly falling temperature. I rubbed cold bare arms to ease the goose bumps.

"The money's acting funny," I said. Maybe that needed some investigation. Could be that if I pushed a little farther I might find a way to recover? Maybe I should call Angel Face again.

Pops had said, "Dani, you put your faith in people you don't know well enough to put your faith in," which sounded a lot like the Ace. What if he'd been lying about Hailey having an affair? Why would he lie? Because he was the Ace. The rain tapered off and everything seemed muted and misty, unreal, as if I was in one of those spooky movies I hated where something always jumped out and you spilled your popcorn.

I lit another smoke to watch the flame and see the glow of the ember. Why would the Ace lie? Maybe he'd never followed Hailey. How could I know?

I'd told Pops about the meeting with Hailey at the Longoria and he watched me carefully, his eyes squinting as he thought. "Doesn't sound right," he said at last. "What did he mean, he didn't have any money?"

"I don't know; it's as if he's..." I hesitated before admitting it, "an honest man."

That was rule number one: you can't cheat an honest man. He doesn't take advantage of the temptations the con man placed before him. Was that possible that Hailey was honest? I groaned at the notion, hoping it wasn't true.

I decided I'd had enough thinking for one night, grabbed the cell on the way back to the porch and dialed New Orleans information for the number of Saint Joseph's Hospital. They connected me automatically and I asked for Marcy Garfield.

"One moment."

"Thank you."

"Hello?"

"Marcy?"

"Dani." She sounded better, not stoned.

"How are you, kid?" It was funny that I thought of Marcy that way. When I was her age I lived alone, paying my way with a series of small cons, psychic readings and real estate scams. Marcy though, seemed pathetically attracted to men who used her.

"Fine, I guess. I'm...sorry." Her voice sounded small and timid but I was unimpressed. I didn't believe in apologies. Better to not screw up in the first place.

But I said, "It's okay," although it most certainly wasn't. Even if Hailey turned out be other than what he seemed, Marcy had blown a month-long and very expensive long con.

"No, it's not. You don't know what happened."

"I know you came home stoned on something and collapsed in my kitchen. I know you murdered my Mustang. I know you brought most of the New Orleans police department with you, which isn't something a con woman wants to see."

"It's worse than that."

"Worse? How is that possible?"

"Jiggs gave me the drugs," she said, as if this was news to me. "He said I'd be all right but when I started to lose it he made me go back to your place." She stopped to breath and finished in a rush. "He wanted me to rob you. We ran out of money, see, and he figured you owed him..."

"I owed him? I *owed* him! How could I owe anything to Jiggs?"

"He said it was 'cause you said you'd get his Mom's house back and this would be like an advance against that."

The logic sounded insane, which was par for the course. Jiggs Roche could figure out the angles in a beach ball and everyone always owed him something. I counted to ten to calm myself. I should never have dealt with the low-life creep, never.

"Well," I said, "What's done is done. When are you getting out?"

"Tomorrow, they say. The police are releasing me on bond." She explained before being asked, "My parents wired the money. But I'll have to be back for the hearing."

"Do you need me to send anything?"

"No."

"How will you get home?"

"Uh," I said and I knew. I heard everything in that single pause. "You're not coming home."

"No. I'm going to stay here for a while. The hearing..."

"Where are you going to stay?" Please don't say it, I pleaded. Please don't do this to yourself.

She said it. "With Jiggs."

The storm ended and the night grew as black and moist and unforgiving as the heart of a banker. I hung up the phone in utter disgust.

"I wash my hands of you," I said, and made hand washing motions at the handset to illustrate. "You and your stupid wife-beating husband and your clinging to any man and your...argh!"

I picked up my trash and entered the dark house, realized I was hungry and looked at the clock on the stove. 8:30. Too early for bed, too late for dinner. I rummaged through what would be the pantry if I ever got this place finished and found slim pickings. A can of tomato soup, a package of spaghetti noodles and a box of Goldfish crackers. Oh, and some popcorn. That would be good.

Pleased, I opened the package and tossed it in the microwave, pushed three buttons and the thing began to whir. When it was done, I poured it into a large metal bowl. I dipped in for a few kernels, dropped them in my mouth, turned and shrieked. The bowl jerked up in reaction and popcorn flew everywhere, like a snow globe after vigorous shaking.

Brock Garfield blocked most of the doorway. He was wearing a black and gold University of Missouri Tigers tee shirt. His hair was wet, his eyes deep sunk and wild.

Without a second thought I reacted. I swung the metal bowl in a wide arc and slammed it into Brock's face. It made a loud bong and he went down like a fallen tree. I held the bowl with both hands, ready in case he got up to attack, but Brock only groaned, rolled slowly to his knees, then his feet. He stood swaying, rubbed his cheek with one hand and said earnestly, "Ow. Why'd you *hit* me?" His expression looked hurt.

I almost laughed. "You break into my house in the middle of the night and wonder why I hit you?"

"The door was open," said Brock, pointing back. "And it's only eight-thirty."

"Still. You hit me once and you're not getting another chance."

Brock appeared puzzled, like a bear worrying at a resistant garbage can. What was *with* this woman? "Please," he said with scorn. "That bowl isn't gonna help you if I decide to hit you again."

"You don't think? Brock, you and I tangled once. How'd that turn out for you?"

For a moment more emotions than Brock Garfield usually contained ran across his face. Anger, confusion, apprehension and annoyance. He flexed one large bicep unconsciously and shook his head. "What do you mean?"

"Think, Brock. Think what your life was like before you met me. Think of what happened after you met me."

"You mean the lottery ticket?"

"Of course, I mean the lottery ticket. Do you think Marcy could have pulled off that scam?"

"But..." He seemed at a complete loss. "Why would you do something like that?"

"Why? Brock, do you remember barging in here tearing up my house? Do you recall hitting me?"

"But I didn't *mean* to. I was drunk." As if that explained everything.

I considered that it probably did explain things in Brock's view. It had always worked before. Get drunk, hit someone, apologize later and be forgiven. Then fall asleep and do it all again, until you run into Dani Silver and her tricks.

"Brock, before you get any ideas that those impressive muscles mean anything to me, consider this. I'm a lot tougher than anything you've ever begun to imagine. If you hit me again I will do things to you so much worse than that little lottery game that you'll never recover."

"Never?"

"Never," I stressed, being completely truthful. If he hit me, the response would be nuclear without Marcy around to hold me back. I did not believe in turning the other cheek and I certainly wouldn't put up with being beaten twice by the same man.

But getting hit would hurt. I had no doubts that Brock Garfield *could* overpower me. He could undoubtedly put me in a hospital with serious injuries, could possibly even kill me. Far better that no first blow was ever struck, I thought.

"I'm not Marcy, Brock. Don't make a mistake you'll regret."

"Marcy," he said. His voice was hoarse, his face suddenly tragic. "Marcy's gone."

"Of course, she's gone. You beat her up."

Again, the confusion. Brock had hit her so often he couldn't understand this to be the reason she'd leave him. "Where is she?" he demanded, but with little force.

"She's gone, Brock. Gone for good."

"No," he said. "She can't be. I heard you talking to her."

How long had he been listening? "I don't know where she is."

"Yes, you do. You're lying to me." He moved from the doorway and began pacing the living room, his thick arms swinging in agitation. "You don't know what it's been like," he said, rounding the table. "I've been hiding out in my own house. The cops confiscated my truck and I don't have a job."

I remembered Brock's disastrous retirement from his job. I had to stifle a grin. That had been good.

"I'm almost out of money and I'm alone and everybody's laughing at me."

"Get another job," I suggested. And get a grip.

"I can't! Everybody's *laughing at me!*" He swung out—hard—and slammed his fist into the wall. I flinched and a picture fell off to crash on the floor. Brock began to sob. "I love her," he wailed. "I can't live without her."

I was appalled. "Jesus, Brock."

"I love her."

"No, you don't."

"I do!" Brock stood like a crumbling mountain in the dining room. His shoulders sagged and his eyes were damp. "I love her."

"You've got a damn funny way of showing it."

"I know. I was wrong to hit her. I know that now. I even got into one'a those anger management classes so I can learn to stop myself."

Good God, he sounded serious.

"Please tell me where she is. I want to tell her how sorry I am."

Please? From Brock? Maybe he really was trying to get better. No. A leopard doesn't change its spots.

"If I tell you and she comes back, you'll just end up beating on her again."

"Never!" And there it was, all the pain of lost love combined with the sincerity of a convert, bundled up and delivered in one agonized word.

Maybe he wouldn't. Besides, Jiggs was so much worse. If Marcy stayed with him he'd have her out on the streets earning his drug money in no time.

"Please?" He asked one more time and the fact he didn't threaten me was the clincher. Maybe he could save Marcy from Jiggs. Wouldn't that be fun?

"She's in N'awlins." I unconsciously pronounced it the way natives did.

"Huh?"

"New Orleans."

"Shit," Brock said. "How'm I supposed to get there?"

"Take my rental car," I offered. "I have the address." I dug in my purse and handed it to him along with the car keys.

"Thank you," he said—a death row inmate with a reprieve. He bolted out the door and into the night. I heard the car door, then the engine and Brock Garfield was gone.

"Sorry, Marcy," I said. "May the best man win."

I laughed, a manic cackle of pure delight and went back to make some more popcorn. If only I could solve all my problems so easily.

# CHAPTER 25

## REVELATIONS

Time to get back in the game. I started by calling Sally.

"Hey, babe," I said, reassuring her that all was jake between us.

"Oh, Dani." Her voice, a low contralto that always reminded me of caramel apples and corn silk, sounded worried. "I'm so glad you called. I heard from the grapevine what happened. I'm so sorry."

The grapevine, in this case would probably be Sammy, eager to lessen the loneliness of his solitary life with the juicy gossip that Dani Silver had fallen flat on her ass. I was astounded, as always, by how fast the news traveled.

Sally rushed in, eager to explain. "I have to tell you a few things. Remember how I had to leave early because Bryce was sick?"

"Sure. How is he?"

"Better. The doctors say he's going to be good for a while." I paused. Both of us heard in the silence that Bryce would never be good for long.

"Because I left early I didn't do a very thorough job. Since Bryce...well, I've been doing some digging from here about that church thing and I got something interesting."

"What?" Interesting?

"Uh-huh. I started looking at the money flow again. The income still looks legit. It's too high for a station the size of his, but say that's an anomaly..."

"I would, if I had any idea what that meant."

"An anomaly is an unexpected result that gets explained by co-incidence. It's *unusual* for a little church station to bring in that kind of revenue, but it does happen. An anomaly."

"Ooooooh-kay."

"But the money that's going out to charity is also too high. The percentages aren't right and there's too much going out. That's what bothered me."

"You said the money was behaving strangely."

"Right. Money in and money out both being too high is a co-incidence that just wouldn't happen. So; I looked further and do you know what I found?"

I played along, hoping this was going where I wanted. "No, Sally, what did you find?"

"The money that isn't being donated by individuals comes in from a dozen sources. I backtracked and found they're all owned by one corporation. And *that* company is owned by a group of investors called Capitol Funding."

"You're saying one company is giving most of the church's money? Why would anyone do that?"

"A lot of reasons," Sally said.

"Any of them honest?"

"None. But that's not the good part. I ran a search on the charities receiving the money and found that nineteen of them are getting almost all the money going out. There are a few who get small checks but I think that's just a front to make the books look good. And Dani?" Her voice rose and I knew she was getting to the point. "They're all owned by Capitol Funding!"

I considered. "That means they're laundering money through the church. Is it the preacher?"

"Nuh-uh. Nobody would be so stupid as to run this so close. If it was the preacher he'd set up another place to send the money and launder it there, a long way away. See what I'm saying?"

"Yeah, I got it." I sat down on the nearest chair, stunned. "Do you know their names?"

Triumphantly, Sally agreed. "I do. There are four of them. You got a pencil?"

I did and wrote as she said them. "Clive Dumont. Pamela Asbury. Tyler Cruz. Bisby Nixon."

"You got it?"

"I do." We made conversational noises and I hung up.

Capital Funding. A group of investors.

Hailey Briscoe was, after all, an honest man.

I'd gone after the wrong guy.

Whoa.

# CHAPTER 26

## ONE BIG DAMN FISH

"The Ace ain't in. Leave a message and maybe you'll get lucky."

God! I thought, even his voice mail was obnoxious. At the beep I said, "This is Dani, give me a ca..."

"Hey there, Sugar," he said, picking up. "Guess you just can't leave the Ace alone."

I took a deep breath and let it out slowly. His voice sounded like curdled milk and I wanted to scream curses at him but forced myself to remember about flies and honey.

"That's right, Ace. I've got another job for you back in New Orleans."

"What?"

"Guy named Clive Dumont. Same deal as before. Follow him and find out everything."

"Same fee?"

"Exactly the same fee, Ace."

"The Ace will be there in two days," he said. "So get yourself wet and wild."

I shuddered. "I can't wait," I said. And hung up.

"The wrong mark," I said again.

"How do you go after the wrong mark?" Sammy Hensel asked. "*You* chose the mark."

"That's right. I did. And I took the blame and paid all the bills, yours included. And now I'm going to fix the mess. I'm...where *are* you?"

"Minneapolis. I'm at the Union Plastics company using their computers." I heard the sounds in the background of a party. "It's retirement for Mona Clarkson," Sammy explained.

Off the phone he yelled, "Be there in a minute! Gotta work here. Yeah? Well, *somebody has to!*" Sounds of general hilarity and he returned.

"Sorry. Mona's in shipping. She is a hoot! Last week she bowled a 287. Dani, can you believe that?"

"Sammy? Are you insane?"

He actually considered the question; I could hear it in the pause. "I don't think so. Why? Do you think I am?"

"You're a mole in other people's lives, man. You act like they're family."

"Do you know how lonely it is being a hacker? Nobody to talk to, nobody who cares what I'm doing? This is so much better than sitting at home."

Was it? "I guess. But I need you to come back to New Orleans."

"Why? I like it here."

"Because..." I knew the reason. I didn't want to make the same mistakes. This time everyone was going to be part of the scam. No more screw-ups. "Because I need to gather the gang."

"Well," he said. "I suppose I could put in for vacation. I'm overdue."

"Sammy, you don't work there."

"Tell that to management. I'll be there Friday with whatever I find."

"Thank you."

Like running a kindergarten, I thought. Just like running a kindergarten.

Cincinnati Bob was easy. "New Orleans? I *love* New Orleans. What do you got?"

"The same thing, Bob, but different guy." Okay, that stopped him.

"Different guy? Same play? How's that possible?"

"A snafu. Got the wrong information. Trying to fix it." Getting tired of explaining. "Can you come back out? Soon?"

"Will there be paper?"

"There's always paper."

"Deal me out," said Ray Sanchez, fully in his hated Esteban mode. God, he could be annoying. I recalled that even Leroy had a hard time getting along with him.

"No can do...Ray," I said carefully. "Gotta have a fixer and there's nobody better."

"Is that flattery?"

"Sure," I said. Whatever it takes.

"Can we sleep together this time?"

Except that. "Just get your scrawny ass on a plane."

I hung up to the sound of laughter.


One more call.

"Crookshanks."

"Merle?"

"Yup." I remembered a tall, muscular, mean-looking man, with close-set eyes, bald as a pirate, arms like tree trunks and a way of speaking in single word sentences.

"I need muscle for a long con in New Orleans. They'll be some face action, too. Can you come out?"

"When?"

"Immediately. I want everybody in for the set up."

"Buckles?" Buckles was Merle's dog, a black lab with all the personality that Merle lacked.

"Sure, the more the merrier. I pictured Buckles sticking his nose in Ray's crouch and smiled. I liked Buckles.

"Money?" said Merle.

"Money's good," I said. It was catching. I shook my head to clear it. "And you'll get a chance to hit somebody."

"Yippee."

I hung up. Was that humor? From Merle? Hard to tell.


They came in from America. Patty Kreel from Maine, Sammy from Minneapolis, Cincinnati Bob from, well, Ohio. Ray Sanchez staggered in with a hangover, fresh from a bender on a Nassau cruise ship where he won three grand cheating at cards.

Patty said, "Thanks for letting me back in, after..." She shrugged her shoulders. "You know."

"You didn't do it wrong."

"He's gay! I *knew* it!"

"He's not Gay," I said. "He's in love with his wife." Also, he's the wrong guy, but let's not go there.

Patty sniffed as if such a thing was indecent, but I saw the load lift from her shoulders.

They filled my rented room like a balloon about to pop. Sammy sat on the divan, Patty and Ray shared the adjoining love seat, Cincinnati Bob leaned against a wall talking to Merle Crookshanks, whose bald head emphasized his muscles, and everyone but Buckles stayed as far from the Ace as they could get.

Buckles sat beside the Ace because he had food. Most of the others did as well, cute tiny sandwiches and cubes of cheese with toothpicks in them taken from a large appetizer tray that I bought at Piggly-Wiggly. But the Ace had greasy fried chicken and he dropped small pieces on the plush gray carpet while he ate. Dog heaven.

I surveyed the scene, noting the natural alliances. Cons were the probably the most gregarious and non-trusting people on the planet. "Okay everybody, let's get down to it. Ace? You've been shadowing Clive Dumont. What do you got?"

The Ace finished chewing and swallowed, wiped his hands on his slacks. "The guy's a skank. He's in some kind of land deal, spends a lot of time at the mayor's office and the building and zoning department." Buckles all but climbed up on him to get the crumbs. "Divides the rest between an office and—get this—his parents' house."

"He lives with his parents?"

"Nah, they're dead."

Buckles, at full extension, was now trying to lick chicken grease from the Ace's clothes.

"Uh, Merle." Ace struggled with the eager hound. "Can you call of the mutt?"

"Nope." Merle went back to his cheese.

"God damned dog. Get the fuck off!" He pushed hard. Buckles yelped and fell and Merle took three giant strides and grabbed the Ace by his throat.

"Ace? Don't touch my dog."

Buckles, catching Merle's attitude, began snarling a, "Can I have his leg?" growl.

Ace, with a too-close view of Merle's muscles and Buckles too-sharp fangs, was still an ex-cop. He didn't back down.

"Teach him some fuckin' manners," he wheezed.

Merle squeezed. "Easier to teach you."

"Oh, boys!" I yelled, thinking it important to maintain some control, but when Merle looked at me the Ace stuck a thumb in his eye.

Merle jerked his head back and Ace hit him under his chin, straightening Merle so Ace could slug him in the breadbasket. It was like hitting cast iron.

Merle squinted through narrowed eyes, grabbed Ace's arm, bent and snagged a leg. He straightened up with Ace on his back and threw him over the love seat. Patty and Ray ducked and the Ace sailed into a couple of wooden kitchen chairs which he smashed to matchsticks.

He groaned and tried to sit up but Merle planted a knee on his chest and a big hand around his neck.

"Ace, you've just been embarrassed. You want to try for injured I could maybe break something"

The Ace was many bad and vile things, but he wasn't stupid. He knew when he was outclassed. Besides, this was that damned dog's fault. A bowl of antifreeze and..."Yeow!"

The sound of the slap rang loud in the room.

Merle slapped him again, harder. "I didn't like the look on your face—like maybe you're still thinking about hurting Buckles. If anything happens to him I'll break your bones, Ace—all of them."

The Ace paled.

"We clear?"

The Ace jerked his head in a nod, once, accepting the terms and Merle let him up.

"Well, that was fun," I said sweetly. "You boys done now?" The Ace nodded again and Merle said, "Yes."

"Good, because you two are paying for those chairs." I turned back to the group and said, "Let's move along."

Sammy said, "Here's what I found so far. There's five of them, four men and one woman. They're the investors behind Hailey Briscoe. The first guy's named Clive Dumont."

We all waited for Sammy to shoot his cuffs and look important. "Clive Dumont," he said finally, "is a comer."

"Oh, I *like* comers," said Ray. For this meeting he was wearing all black, from his silk shirt and chinos to socks and shiny patent leather loafers. He'd placed his paperback book carefully on the end table after bending back a page.

I agreed. A guy who wanted to make something of himself without regard to the rules was the bread and butter of the con man. We usually had these guys hooked ten years before we ever met them.

"Near as I can tell, Clive Dumont started the whole scam. He found the rest of them, convinced them to put up the money. Before Clive they were more or less legitimate."

"What are they doing?" asked Patty. She was on the sofa close to Ray, quietly tending to her own knitting. I looked closely and decided it was either a very ugly sweater or a pretty nice bird cage cover.

I answered. "After Katrina, Clive Dumont came up with a great plan." If I sounded impressed, it was because I admired the man's spunk. "He figured that with the Ninth Ward was flooded and the houses wrecked, it was wide open for land speculating."

"What did he do?"

"He got money from the investment group and went on a buying spree."

"How'd he rope the bank for the money?" Cincinnati Bob Wilkerson sat perfectly straight on the most uncomfortable kitchen chair.

"Dunno...yet. But if the pay-off's big enough he could interest the Pope. Anyway, he borrows money to get the government to condemn the land he wants. That makes the land virtually worthless. Then, and this is the really good part, he uses Hailey Briscoe's ministry as an agent to get people to donate their property."

"How?" Patty again. She'd put down her needles and listened, wide-eyed and impressed. We all were, really, at the size of this scam. It made us look like penny-ante players. Well, maybe we'd be able to correct that.

"Fear of God?" I ventured. "Donate and go to Heaven. Plus, they offered tax breaks and people could collect insurance and later they sent out people to canvas the neighborhoods. Since they were first, with the money in hand, they got most of the available land."

"How'd they get it declared worthless?" asked Ray.

"Bribed the commissioners or the land bureau. Point is, once it was made useless, they grabbed it all at rock bottom prices."

"Why? That's what I don't get." Patty pointed with a needle. "What good was worthless flooded land?"

"Lemme," said Sammy. "I've been reading up." His approving smile lit up the otherwise dim room. We had only the gold colored swag lamp near the corner for illumination which gave the room a colorful tint, like we were in a cave, planning an invasion.

"If they could bribe the officials—and I got no doubts they did—it would only take a little more money to get them to change the zoning back. You get it?"

Ray whistled. "So, they buy low when people are reeling..."

"Uh-huh," said Sammy. "They sell high when the flood waters gone and the zoning fix is in."

Merle Crookshanks, looking like an ogre in the shadows over by the bed, said softly. "What are we talking here? In real numbers, I mean."

"A lot," Sammy mused. "Numbers I'm seeing say he's buying lots for maybe three thousand on average. Sells them when the government changes the rules again, for, I don't know, fifty thousand. Sixty? Sure, he'll have some survey costs, repairs, a lot of bribing, but basically, call it forty grand profit per lot."

Merle whistled. "How many lots we talking?"

"Hard to say. Others are jumping on the bandwagon, but he's in the driver's seat. Maybe seven or eight hundred."

Ray did the math. "Forty thousand times eight hundred? Thirty-two *million*?"

"About. And get this, except for the bribes and the money laundering? It's legal."

"No way."

"How can it be legal?"

"Because he's buying and selling. It's the American Way, my friends. The American Way."

They all sat back and absorbed this information. Every one of us was impressed.

"Okay," I said. "Now we know the how and the why. We got a pretty good idea of the size of the pie. Now let's learn about the players. Everybody pick someone and scope him out. We need to know everything about them. Everything. Find out, people, and meet back here on Monday."

New Orleans has a *lot* of very good restaurants perfect for having a meal, a little wine, maybe some desert, while discussing who was robbing who.

Sammy and Bob, equally disliking each other, joined me at Mercedes, a steak house near Lake Ponchartrain where the waiters wore white hand towels tucked over black pants and left you strictly alone. A lot of business was done over cigars and brandy at Mercedes.

I had a salad, the boys chose cattle. Sammy spoke first. "They're based out of a law firm called Furbisher, Skye and Rankin. Our guy is a senior partner named Reginald Skye. The other members, near as I can tell, are straight.

"Reggie's more or less a used car salesman, nothing at all like a lawyer. His specialty is personal injury suits, he's short and getting bald with some red hair and an aging jock mentality. He's the guy you don't bend over near in a locker room 'cause he'd sting you with a towel. Thinks everything's a joke, Reggie, unless you cross him. He's the guy who Clive first contacted."

Sammy paused to sip his wine, a pink Chablis that cost sixty-eight dollars. It would be, I knew, on his expenses. "Word is that Clive had to get a second on his house to get the scratch to pay to find a Reggie. They called it 'consulting fees.'"

Bob laughed at the simple humor. Cincinnati Bob Wilkerson, when not involved in a practical joke, still struck you as someone you'd want to have arrested, if only on general suspicion. He had that fourteen-year-old low humor kind of air about him, as if he'd just put itching powder in the Groom's underwear.

He was sipping a Coca Cola, nodding as he listened.

Sammy said, "Reggie's got all the perks. A house on the third fairway at Willow Run golf course, a trophy wife—his fifth—drives a new model Corvette every year. This year's is yellow."

I asked the question I would eventually ask them all. "Is he our guy? Do you see a handle?"

Sammy shrugged. "Not my job, boss. I'm just a simple technician. You decide who we take and who we fake."

I saw Bob repeat the phrase and knew it would be used again. I turned to him and waited while he chewed and swallowed enough beef to clog the arteries of Nebraska.

"Uh-huh," he said, holding up a finger and swallowing spastically. "Just a sec, just a sec...ah. Okay. I've been watching a guy named Bisby Nixon. He's this fat guy, got an alcoholic's complexion, pink-flushed nose and cheeks and tiny blue spider web veins. He owns the landfill that handled most of New Orleans waste and is reputed to be connected to the mob."

Bob cocked his head as if considering this. "I don't believe that part, but he's got this guy always around."

"What, like a bodyguard? A chauffer?"

Bob shook his head. "No, more like a leg-breaker. This guy— his name's Rundell Mapes—he's not from around these parts."

"What do you mean?" I asked, fascinated. Watching the reports come in was like election night, staying up to see the returns. I wished I'd done this before

"The guy's nothing but muscle and mean," said Bob. He stands about six-foot-seven, weighs I don't know, like four hundred pounds, none of it fat, and he seems to like playing with knives."

"I heard about him," agreed Sammy. "I pulled his jacket when I was in police files." I wanted to know what he'd been doing hacking the New Orleans Police Department but decided not to ask. "The guy's done time for manslaughter twice, three rape convictions, more assaults and violence that you can list."

"Why is he still out walking?" asked Bob, as anyone sane would. I pictured six-seven, four hundred and knives and shivered. He made Merle Crookshanks look small.

"Good lawyer," said Sammy. He sipped and looked smug. "That's my guy Reggie, done it all. Kept Rundell from the chair, man; I mean literally. Got him off a Federal racketeering charge and kept him free ever since."

"Nice," I said, hoping that Bisby Nixon wasn't our mark. "What else?"

"He likes books," said Bob. "Collects expensive books from a place called Faulkner's."

I considered. "Is this something?" I asked and Bob wavered a hand: could be.

I paid for dinner and we left Mercedes, a little wiser and down three hundred-fifty-seven dollars.

The Ace, already covered with crumbs and salad dressing after only ten minutes said, "My guy's a fag."

"What?" asked Patty, more refined. I felt sorry putting her together with the Ace but time was short and I needed to get this act started.

"A homo," explained the Ace, as if to a very warped pre-schooler. "A queer, a..."

"I know what gay is, you moron. But where do you get the idea?"

"Ah, they're all queer," said The Ace. Patty rolled her eyes and looked to me for support, which I couldn't give.

"All who?" I asked. "All bankers?"

"Uh-huh. And writers, you know. Bunch a damn fags."

"Listen, you stupid..." Patty was about to get seriously involved in Ace bashing, not an unwelcome thing, but the waitress was frowning. We were at a Denny's on Grande Boulevard, near the University. It had a small pond where students basked, like crocodiles, on the bank.

"Leave it, Patty," I suggested. To the Ace I said, "Tell me about your guy. Without the speculation on his sexual habits."

"His name's Tyler Cruz." His eyebrows lifted to say, 'see?' "He's a banker, can trace his roots back to King Phillip's Spain. The family says they loaned money to Phillip for the Armada. They're big on the whole 'I'm so much better than you' social crap."

The Ace ordered two dinners, ham and meat loaf, with mashed potatoes on both. "He's an aristocrat ass-hole with these large eyes, a big nose and thin lips and a grandfather who lost the family fortune during the Depression. He and his father, through a variety of scams have made a bundle on real estate."

Deeply disturbed by his eating habits, I turned to Patty. "You have the woman?"

"Her name's Pamela Asbury. Of the four, she's perhaps the single person most critical to the success of the scheme."

"Why"

"Well, she's chairperson of the Democratic Party and she's black. Her share would likely come from local union retirement funds. If there was any bribing of bureaucrats being done, our Pamela would know who to go to."

"Does she have anything we can use?" The Ace, finished talking, was wolfing down his food with the grace and manners of a starving root hog. He had a fork in each fist, alternating between plates. Ugh.

Patty pointedly looked away. "Nothing I can find. She has a Condo in St. Peters. She's got a steady boyfriend, stays over on weekends or she goes to his place. Neither has been married. She likes nice clothes, good art, but," she said quickly, seeing my interest, "Not very expensive. Sorry, Dani, I couldn't find any skeletons in her closet."

"Thanks, Patty. I know you did your best."

We left while the Ace was still porking away and, as a treat to ourselves, stuck him with the bill.

I caught up with Ray Sanchez at Mundy's Pool Hall on 47th Street. Snuggled between a porn arcade and a bail bond office, a couple of blocks from the Justice Center, Mundy's made the third world look prosperous. A couple of strung out junkies lay strewn across the sidewalk, asleep or unconscious in the late evening heat.

Ray, dressed in Puerto-Rican cool, wore oversized black shiny pants, a sleeveless Tee and high heeled boots. I hadn't seen him with bare arms in the ten years since we'd been together and noted with amusement that he had a barb wire tattoo on his right bicep.

He was smoking and, between shots, had his hands all over a pretty young Hispanic girl aged just this side of legal. She studied me under dark lashes when I came in.

"Play a round?" Ray said. "For a C-note?"

"Sure. Let me get a beer." I went to the bar and returned with a Corona Light and a wedge of lime. Ceiling fans disturbed the cigarette smoke and made little progress against the heat. Four guys slouched at a table, two guys at the bar and somebody poked a buck in the juke box. The Boss started singing about fast cars and long highways.

"Break," said Ray. Evidently he was in monosyllable mode this evening and I smiled at him, with teeth, showing my shark side.

We circled the table after his break and he told me his story as I lined up my shot. I was wearing a white tee and tight designer jeans. I noticed the guys at the bar admiring my ass.

"Clive Dumont is a real dirt-bag," said Ray.

"Is he now?" I dropped the seven in the side.

"Yes."

"Tell me." I missed and Ray began to prowl around the table.

"He's got everything tied up in this venture. Took out a loan on his house, dumped his long-time girl, spends all his time schmoozing the politicos." Ray cleared the table and collected a long, wet kiss from the girl, a hundred bucks from me.

"Another?" He asked.

"Yeah. Double or nothing." I racked and he went on.

"Clive's in way over his head. He thinks he's the mover but, you ask me, when this is played out, that guy Rundell's gonna see to Mr. Dumont."

I dropped three balls. Ray cleared the table, collected his reward. The chicita continued to watch me silently.

Ray said, "No way is Clive walking away alive."

"He's not our guy."

"No. He's not going to be in the last reel." He gestured at the table. "One more try?"

"Let's raise the ante."

Ray grinned through big white teeth. "What do you got in mind?"

I shrugged. Maybe, I decided, it was time to earn a little respect from my former boyfriend. "Tell you what," I said. "I'll play you for the girl."

That shocked him for a moment before competition and macho and all that bullshit kicked in like I knew it would.

"I didn't think you went that way, Dani," he leered.

"You'll never know, Ray."

He studied me over the green felt. He looked at the girl he obviously had plans for. "Yeah, sure," he said. "For the girl."

He broke and sank six, missing the nine.

I ran the table.

I took the girl's hand and led her, unresisting, to the door while Ray, open-mouthed, stared. He ground the blue chalk cube over the tip of his cue and was still motionless when we left the bar.

# CHAPTER 27

## I TOOK MY TROUBLES DOWN TO MADAME RUTH

I had some thinking to do and, as always when in New Orleans I went to see Madame Ruth. Ruthie was an old school grifter, a fortune teller and palm reader who ran a crystal ball shop down on Lexington under the freeway.

The sign above the red door, faded and cracked with age, still said, "Madame Ruth – the Gypsy with the Gold-capped tooth," a marketing ploy she'd thought up in the mid-fifties. Some rock group even wrote a song about her.

I opened the door, smiling as the bell tinkled. Standing in the red and gold wallpapered room certainly brought back a lot of ghosts. Ruthie taught me the trade when I was young and her tricks had seen me through some tough patches when the law or bad luck made me lay low for a while.

A bony hand pushed aside a cascade of clacking beads, followed by a hunched back old hag right out of the middle ages. She was dressed as a gypsy with a yellow shawl and thick red skirt, with bangles and bracelets all over her arms. There were silver-white cataracts in each eye. She grinned at me, showing three missing teeth.

"Ruthie!" I shouted. "You look amazing." I fell into her arms for a moment of pure bliss. It was like coming home.

She stepped back and eyed me critically. "Dani Silver, my God! How've you been girl? How long has it been?"

"Too long," I admitted. I'd been busy and had neglected her and felt sorry for it now. The skills she'd taught me, the stories she passed down from her long life, I missed those and said so. "The cataracts, are those new?"

She popped one out, a silvery contact. "Yeah, they are. Impresses the marks, you know? Kind of hard to see through, but it makes the act sing." She replaced it and again became the grandmother figure I remembered.

"You always were a showman," I admired. "Business going okay?" The room, always threadbare, felt sodden and damp, though the hurricane had been months ago. I saw signs of high water at knee level and traces of mud in the corners.

She shrugged, setting off the jewelry. "So-so. Katrina was a witch of trouble, girl. Too many people dead, too many troubles. Much bad water over the levees."

"Well, that's what happens when you're busy living." I said, and she laughed, a long loud bray that made her dentures nearly pop out. She had shared that philosophy with me a hundred times over the years.

"Dani, you rascal. You always could make a body feel good." She led me to the back and poured cups of weak green tea, babbling constantly as she puttered around. "...Cops tried to shut me down...like I didn't know the mayor hisself...after the flood I lost most of my pictures...Two-tone Smith hasn't been seen since...you heard about Eddie Sperling? Helicopters plucked him off his own roof! The bastard said I was a fake, can you imagine?...If I had a dollar for every time I been called that I'd have a million by now...I did the bone dance and read the tea leaves, they left happier than a drunk pissin' in the alley..."

"I need to talk," I told her as we sat down at the red satin covered table in the cramped room where she did her readings. The thick glass ball, like a marble from giant-land, sat serenely in its pseudo-gold base. I ran a couple of fingers over it in a welcoming caress and sat down across from her.

"You got a scam?" Ruth asked eagerly. She rubbed gnarled fingers together. "I love it when you have a scam."

"Biggest one ever, Ruthie. I need the cards on this one." The cards were her ancient Tarot deck, brought over from a village in the Carpathians if you could believe her stories, which I didn't. They were cracked and discolored with age but could have been bought at a magic shop in Trenton, New Jersey. Or Cincinnati Bob could whip up a deck in half a day and even mark them for easier readings.

"Biggest..." she whispered, impressed. She was a contemporary of Pops, and maybe more, a long time ago. I'd never asked either of them and never would but she'd been a looker back then. I'd seen pictures. "How is the old bastard?" she asked.

"Fine," I said. "Like always. He'll never change."

"Pity," she laughed.

"Kate's not so good, though." I told her about the Alzheimer's and she sat for a moment in silence, deck in hand, remembering things long before my time.

"Kate was a great lady," she said. "Too bad." A heavy sigh let the past go its own way. She dealt the first card, the reaper. "Oooh," she said. "Dani, what *are* you into?"

"That would be Rundell Mapes," I said. "He's a stone killer from what I hear. Somehow I have to separate him from the rest of the marks."

"Tell me everything."

"There's a group of five people swindling folks in the Ninth," I said. "I want to bring them down."

Ruthie looked comically surprised and dealt out the next card. The Fool, of course, a faded jester capering in the picture and I smiled. Ruth could still deal whatever she wanted. I felt like hugging her.

"You don't run scams for justice, do you?" The idea seemed to amaze her.

"No. I'm going after a score, Ruthie and I think I know who and how. It's just..."

"Yes?"

"I..." This was so hard to admit. "I met a guy and he's given me ideas."

Ruth dealt out the lovers, Adam and Eve, naked and entwined with a green serpent dangling like desire behind them. She raised her thick eyebrows in a question.

"His name's Nick Kuiper," I said. "He's a businessman from New York and he's screwed with my head, a little bit, and I want to do something more here than just take the mark for a lot of money."

The fool was dealt again. Ruth very seldom spoke in these sessions, preferring her audience to admit their own feelings. She was a lot like a psychiatrist in that way and that was why I came here. You could sort out your problems for fifty bucks.

"I am not," I insisted. "I'm going for the mark. I'm just..." I paused to put my feelings in order. Sure, I wanted the money. Of course I did. That was why I grifted. But after seeing the misery all around here you couldn't help but be moved. I wanted to give something back. And I thought I knew how.

"Let me explain," I said.

When I finished she gave me the wide grin and played her last card, the Ace of Cups. It was the card of infinite possibility and endless risk. It was the card of doubt and conviction, success or failure.

"Thanks a lot, I said. But inside I knew she'd palmed the right one.

# CHAPTER 28

# WELL, OKAY—WE CAN KILL PATTY

We met again, this time with pizza and beer. Pictures of Bisby Nixon, taken by the Ace with a telephoto lens, were blown up and hung on the wall. Here he was, meeting somebody in the Louisiana Supreme Court Building. Here he talked earnestly with an old black couple, waving at the ruins of their home. Here he was at a street corner café, here at a bookstore. Here was a picture of a topless young woman, smiling, smiling.

"Take that down," I said, grabbing it. The rest of the guys complained loudly. I held it at arm's length to study it, sniffed dismissively and said, "mine are better," which got me hoots of derision from the guys, a cheer from Patty.

Ray yelled, "I've seen 'em. She's right."

"Shut up Ray," I answered with dignity. "And they've gotten better." The mood was infectious, like frat night at con college.

"What do we have, people?"

"We have," said the Ace, "A real skank."

"Helpful, Ace, real helpful. Anything more specific?"

"I got something," said Merle.

I looked over, surprised. Merle was usually as interested in strategy as Buckles, who was presently curled up under the table. "Yeah?"

"I got his garbage." Merle held out some stained pieces of paper. "Most of it trash, but these are his credit card slips. He spends a lot of money at some book store." He pointed to the one in the picture.

This was news. "Book store? What does this mean?"

"Hey," Ace chimed in, before Merle could answer. Merle frowned, the way everyone did at the Ace. "I got that, too." He rummaged in a plastic bag that he kept instead of a briefcase. "Pictures of him at a place called...uh, Faulkner's. What kind of name is that," he asked, "for a bookstore?"

"Faulkner was a writer, you moron," said Patty, who was looking at Merle's receipts. "The numbers on these slips say he's a collector."

"More detail," I said. Around the room, heads turned, interest tweaked.

"We got something?" asked Ray. His own book this evening was, *Vanishing Act* by Thomas Perry, which lay folded on his lap.

"Maybe. What else is there? Sex?"

"Sure," said Bob, Merle and The Ace and Ray. Even Patty chimed in. "I haven't seen much of this guy but what I've seen says sex. He screws anything in a skirt."

"What about the Rundell dude?" asked Bob. "He seems to hang tight with Nixon."

"Don't worry about Rundell Mapes," I said. "I can handle him."

"Really?" said Bob, clearly impressed. I could see him weighing the idea of dealing with a monster like Rundell, the doubts crossing his face like shadows of birds in flight. But he shrugged and let it go.

I said, "How about we use the book interest to run a Treasure Hunt on him? We'll need a lot of prep, a first clas- store and a raggle."

Patty looked pleased and said, "Oh good, I get back in the game."

I said, "Um," and all eyes went to me.

"I'm doing the raggle," I said.

"What?" Glaciers have formed from warmer weather than Patty was projecting. I'd taken her and her inevitable protest over the window for privacy but I could feel the others watching.

"Dani, I do the raggle," she insisted. Her voice was a harsh whisper that I knew would carry across the room and I wanted to shush her but knew her anger was valid.

"I know, Patty. But this time..."

"*This* time! God damn it, Dani, I ran the damn raggle on Hailey Briscoe three times—three!—and he didn't fall for it. Do you know how that makes me feel?"

"I understand Patty, but I'm going to seduce Bisby." I could see tears of frustration forming in her blue eyes. Over on the couch Ray sat up, clearly interested. The others were pretending not to listen.

"Patty," I said, but her face was turned away. "Patty, listen to me."

"Why not, Dani? Is it because you don't trust me?"

"No!"

"Is it because I'm not sexy enough anymore?"

"Patty, that's not it." I could see her self-esteem had taken a beating with the Hailey Fiasco. I had to fix this quickly or risk losing her. "I don't want you to seduce the guy because I have something better for you to do."

She sniffed. "What?"

"I need you to get stabbed," I said. "And die. Maybe twice."

Across the room Ray's book fell on the floor.

# CHAPTER 29

# THE SCENE OF THE CRIME

"Busier than a one-armed paper hanger," Pops always said, but I never understood it until I tried to run a con on three sides.

He also told me, "Dani, there's more than just the Big Store con. You have a lot of options. Do something different."

Easy to say, hard to do. Bisby Nixon and Clive Dumont were the keys to getting paid and the Big Store was the way to sting them. That left Reggie Skye, Pamela Asbury and Tyler Cruz to deal with and me with absolutely no idea how.

Eventually, *reluctantly,* I chose the lottery-letter-scam. This was a favorite with police departments when they wanted to weed out the really stupid criminals. They would print up a very professional letter stating that so and so had won a big cash prize. They'd sent it to every known last address saying the guy had to show up at a certain place and time to collect his winnings.

They sat back and waited for the fish to jump into the pan.

The only problem was that, to do the con, I was going to have to come out in the open. If it worked, I could get the entire investment group off Hailey Briscoe's sacrilegious back, if it didn't...

For Pamela, I replaced the letter with an anonymous phone call.

Pamela Asbury?" I said.

"Yes?"

"I know what you've been doing with the Royal Capitol Group."

"What?"

"I'm a grifter named Jill Hastings," I said. No way was I giving my real name. "I'm doing a scam against Bisby Nixon and Clive Dumont."

"I don't know them," said Pamela. At this point a real citizen would hang up the phone or threaten to call the cops. Pamela did neither.

"Yes, you do. They're your partners in the land swindle in the Ninth Ward. The other two are Reginald Skye and Tyler Cruz."

*Now* she said, "Why are you telling me this? Who *are* you?"

"Come to 3757 Sunset Avenue tomorrow at nine A.M. You won't be sorry." I hung up, smiling. I just love the cloak-and-dagger stuff.

That morning I stood in a warm drizzle outside the ruined remains of Corretta Roche's old house. I was wearing a tan poplin raincoat, just like Boston Blackie wore, with a matching fedora pulled low across my face. Any more mysterious and I could be the moll in a detective novel.

I walked around the still sodden perimeter remembering old times. Jiggs severely testing my innocence in the back yard under the remains of that Russian olive tree by the torn up old chain link fence. Correta serving us lemonade and cookies while Jiggs hid the cigarette we'd been sharing. Sneaking out after dark to neck in her Buick. Ah, youth.

Now the house was a ruin, Coretta was dead and Jiggs was still a low-life jerk. Only now he was preying on Marcy instead of me. I felt a pang of regret at the thought of her and wondered how the whole Jiggs/Brock thing was working out. With any luck she'd see them together and compare.

A black Lincoln town car cruised the block like a hunting shark. It pulled to the curb and idled for several minutes and I watched the tinted window for any sign of intention. Pamela could do any number of things and most of them would be very bad for me. I felt naked and exposed standing here in the rain and wished that I could have stayed comfortably in the shadows.

But not this time. For this to work I had to be what I said I was—a grifter out to hustle her partners.

The car engine stopped. A door opened and Pamela Asbury got out. She was a heavy-set well-dressed black woman who could have been a real estate agent or the head of community relations if she didn't give the impression of something that bites. There was something predatory and hard inside her that made me want to back away and forget the whole scam.

She walked slowly over to me and pointedly studied the neighborhood for traps, watchers or police. Her voice, when she spoke, was a soft whisper I had to strain to hear over the buzzing insects.

"What do you want?"

"Do you recognize this house?" I asked.

She looked over my shoulder at the washed-out wreck, let her eyes come back to mine and shrugged. "No, should I?"

"It belonged to a woman named Correta LaRoche. I'm working for her son, Jiggs. A couple of months ago Correta donated this house to the Hailey Briscoe Ministry." I saw recognition in her eyes. "Right," I said. I pointed around at the crumbling neighborhood. Everywhere were downed trees, twisted metal and sagging porches on broken houses.

Hopeless people shuffled around the rubble, picking up what was left of their belongings.

"How can you do this?" I asked Pamela. I saw her attention become intense on my left cheek and I turned to face her. I wasn't sure if this was the best approach but I had to know. "How can you willingly steal from these people? How can you profit from this?"

Pamela snapped. "Don't judge me. You're just a small-time crook out to make a buck. I just do it bigger and better."

I knew I was hearing the real Pamela Asbury here, a woman who had to be better than any woman, better than any man, better than any *white* man. I heard the anger and bitterness at a life spent looking smaller than she was, slower than she could be. I saw the hunger for recognition.

"You don't think you should help them?" I pointed. "These people?"

"No, why should I?"

"Because they need your help?"

"That's what the government is for."

"I see," I said.

"I doubt it. But tell me your plan. How does it involve me?"

I said, "I'm setting up a sting against Clive and Bisby to take them for quite a bit of money and I had this idea that maybe you'd like to help."

"Indeed." Pamela was suspicious, of course, but obviously interested. I continued the tale like a fisherman playing out line.

"What would happen to your little group if there were fewer people in it?"

I heard the gasp and saw the tiny flinch as Pamela surged up to take the hook. She struggled for a few seconds with doubt but in the end her greed and desire to beat the boys made her come over.

"How?" she asked, and I told her.

We sat in the air-conditioned inside of her town car seeking privacy and shelter from the rain. She asked questions that I answered honestly, knowing she'd check it out. The address of the store, the time and place, how I intended to escape, how much money...

"What do you want from me?" she asked.

I turned my head to look outside and said to my reflection, "I want this piece of land signed over to me."

"That's all?"

"I'm taking them for more than enough. Getting this house back will square me with Jiggs." I didn't say that I'd deliver Jiggs to the cops before I gave him this house back.

Pamela said, "Yes," absently and agreed with my suggestions for transferring title. She seemed surprised at how much I knew about the operation and I realized she had no intention of behaving honestly. I made a promise to check the title policy for a "in case of my death" clause.

We finished and sat in silence for several minutes. The rain had become a downpour and the neighborhood emptied of people. We could have been on another planet for all the warmth and comfort of the world outside.

Or inside. Pamela shifted her bulk and faced me. "What about the others?" she asked.

"What about them?"

"Can you set them up for something as well?"

I smiled. "I thought you'd never ask."

# CHAPTER 30

# LET'S *DO* THIS THING!

With everyone freshly recovered from the Patty bombshell, we sat around the table and I explained.

*"We'll use a book as a flash roll and hook him at the bump."*

I flowed along St. Peter Street like a model on a New York fashion show runway, the skirt of my sunshine yellow dress waiving like a flag in time with the sway of my hips. I was wearing four inch "fuck-me" pumps and a low neckline and I knew that the eyes of most of the men were eating me alive.

Faulkner's Book store was a block ahead, third brick building, just past the liquor store where the Ace sat on a bus bench with a brown paper bag and three day's stubble on his fat jowls.

I didn't like teaming with the Ace but he was the best we had for being a stinky pathetic bum. Type-casting, you might say.

He raised the bag to his lips and let some of the liquor pour down his chest. A nice touch, I thought. Professional.

I finished my walk to the bookstore, went in and killed time waiting for Bisby Nixon. Our research told us that he spent Saturday mornings here, showing up somewhere between nine and eleven. He'd talk to the owner over cappuccinos he brought with him from Starbucks and get shown the latest merchandise.

Today he'd be getting a lot more than usual.

I browsed the shelves for nearly an hour before he showed up, fat and wheezing from the short walk from his car, nearly as disreputable as the Ace. From the shelter of the Mystery section I watched his ritual with the owner, waited impatiently through the coffee and talk and finally witnessed the purchase of a small volume of some old book.

Bisby paid, shook the owner's hand, and left. I quickly followed, pulling an identical bag from my purse as I reached the street. Bisby was nearing his car but would have to pass the Ace before he got there.

The Ace stretched and stood up. The arm holding the paper bag swung in an arc and hit Bisby in the chest. The Ace dropped his bag and a puddle of liquid seeped through onto the street. With a bellow of fury, the Ace shoved Bisby violently back against the nearest brick building.

"My bottle!" screamed the Ace. "You broke my fuckin' bottle!"

Bisby reacted as we knew he would, with violence. He hadn't built up a fortune in the trash business by being weak or refined and he shoved the Ace away like he was a stuffed toy.

"Get off of me, you stinking piece of shit!"

The Ace swayed but kept his balance and lurched forward like an out of control locomotive. He swung his arms like windmills, crude and ineffective and Bisby stepped under them, waited for an opening and hit the Ace squarely in the chest.

The Ace made a whooshing sound, doubled over and threw up on his shoes. Bisby clenched his hands together, raised them and aimed at the back of the Ace's neck but the Ace ducked away.

"My bottle," mumbled the Ace. Just as I arrived he stumbled forward and hit Bisby in the face. Bisby's bag fell to the cracked pavement and the Ace laughed at him. "See what it's like, you mother—"

Bisby kicked him. He'd been aiming at the crotch but the Ace, hardened by years on the force, knew better than to stand open-legged. Bisby's foot hit his thigh and the Ace grabbed him by the ankle. Now Bisby was hopping on one leg while the Ace spun him by the other. This human slingshot careened across the sidewalk, bounced against the building and collided with me.

Everybody fell. My package, as planned, dropped next to Bisby's and the Ace, more agile than he looked, high-tailed it out of there, leaving Bisby to stare at my carefully exposed legs.

I tucked my dress up as if embarrassed that he'd seen my panties and accepted his hand to pull me up to my feet.

"I'm so sorry," he said. His hand was on my shoulder, steadying me. "That bum..."

"I saw it," I said. "No need to explain. It wasn't your fault."

Bisby bent to pick up the packages, pausing to study mine. "You shop at Faulkner's"

"Um-hmmm. Thanks." I accepted the bag and turned to go. Never let the mark have an easy time of it. He has to come after you.

"Wait," he said and I smiled.

*"We'll sting him at the Big Store."*

Ray Sanchez sniffed as he we entered the house. It smelled of mildew, cat urine and abandonment. Perfect.

The agent, a middle-aged man named Peter Farbing, showed us around, pointing out, as if they were somehow assets, the narrow halls, the tiny kitchen, the impossibly small bedrooms.

The whole building leaned, the windows were grimy. Nothing resembling maintenance had been done in a decade. On the other had it stood high up on a rise and had been spared the water damage of the storm.

I imagined how it would look filled with junk. We could cover the windows to make it even darker and less appealing, make the hallway a claustrophobic nightmare, the living room a cave where only the demented would feel at home.

"I think I'll take it," Ray told the astonished Peter who managed to hold back, "why?"

He substituted a confused, "That's wonderful, sir," collected far too much cash against the promise not to return, handed over the keys and left, no doubt imagining drug labs or dungeons or whatever.

When he was gone we stood in the tiny living room, picturing what was ahead. "The carpet's pretty good," I said, touching a toe to the ratty brown pile.

"Yeah, and the walls can be covered with crap." Ray studied the room with an artist's eye. He would, I had confidence, transform this very ugly duckling into a totally horrible Stephen King swan.

"I know a guy can supply us with about six tons of mildewed newspapers."

"You do?"

"Yeah." He shrugged, no big deal, and I looked to see if he was kidding.

"Interesting acquaintances."

"Uh-huh."

"Can you have it ready in time?" I asked.

"Uh-huh." He held up his hands like he was a director seeking a good shot, imagining the possibilities and the amount of work needed. "But Dani?"

"Yes, Ray?"

"What did you do with the girl?"

"You'll never know, Ray."

*"I'll need provenance on a rifle, and some very old books."*

Sammy Hensel, the wizard of the internet, sat at the computer, creating a picture-perfect history of a flintlock rifle.

I wandered over, glancing at the screen over his shoulder. His bald head gleamed as if polished and he smelled of scented candles and cinnamon. His expression was intense.

"How you doing on the provenance?" I asked.

"Check this out." He handed me a document and I read the hundred-fifty-year-old language, the words in flowing script, following the frills and loops of a long dead scribe.

My eyes went wide. "This is great!"

"Yeah, but unfortunately it's for the wrong gun. This one will only fetch about $15,000.00."

"That doesn't matter." I considered. "Bob can use it as a template for whatever gun we choose."

"Sure, but it would have been nice to find the exact right one. Speaking of which, I did find the gun. It's a 1772 Pennsylvania long rifle by Jacob Dickett."

"Uh, huh." Guns weren't really my thing, but we needed this one for the con. I followed his finger where the screen showed a long rifle set against a red fabric for contrast. The piece was beautiful, all deeply worn wood the color of caramel with a black iron barrel and mechanics.

"Jacob Dickett was an important gunsmith back then," Sammy explained. "In the 1790's he made guns for the United States Government. The fact that this one dates from so much earlier and is signed..."

"It's signed? They signed rifles?" I couldn't imagine why anyone would do such a thing.

"Sure. Jacob built rifles by hand and he made sure they were beautiful as well as accurate. See the intricate relief carving on the walnut burl stock? And both the butt plate and patch box are engraved. Jacob signed the gun on the flat of the barrel and very few smiths signed their guns back then. Just look at how the lines flow." He took a deep breath and sighed.

"I didn't know you were into guns."

"I'm not. It's just...well, look at her. She's perfect."

"Sammy? Get a room." I leaned forward and pecked him on his head. "This is very good work. Now let's get the photo to Ray and I'll take the template to Bob. How you doing on the book provenances?"

"Almost done."

"Sweet."

"And Bisby's bank accounts?"

"Almost blocked."

"Sweeter."

*"We'll do the Mother of all Rags..."*

Cincinnati Bob and old Hank, in the printing shed behind old Hank's barn, seemed to be having the time of their lives, forging antique books and provenance papers that would pass anything short of chemical analysis. They were artists, at the height of their powers, responding to an almost impossible challenge. They were also children, running amok in a toy store.

Regarding the books, I had told him they needed to be finger and eyeball perfect. Bisby, I told them, was a collector and an expert. They surprised me by adding nose perfect.

Old Hank, in blue bib overalls and a paper hat, looked like the pressman in Hell, destined to run copy though all eternity. He took a deep sniff as if smelling the fragrance of a fine cognac.

"You got any willow bark?" He asked.

"All out," Bob said.

"Add it to the list."

I walked over. "What list?" I wrinkled my nose and asked, "What is that *awful* smell?"

Bob and Hank rolled their eyes with profession disdain for the amateur. There were two kinds of people in this world, the look said; printers, and everyone else.

"Hank's brewing 18<sup>th</sup> century iron-gall ink," Bob said. He handed me a piece of paper, adding. "This list."

I read, "Cider vinegar, boiled linseed oil, pine resin, animal hide glue, ammonia, willow bark, eye of newt...The Hell? Eye of newt?"

Bob, casual in tan shorts and Hawaiian aloha shirt covered with Hibiscus and McCaws wiggled his eyebrows and said, "Gotcha."

Old Hank chortled and wheezed like an obscene phone caller, pulled out a cigar and bit off the end which he spit on the floor.

I handed Bob the rifle provenance Sammy found and he whistled. "Cool. He set in on the cluttered work table and poked with his tongue for a moment at something in his teeth. "Do we have any titles picked out yet?"

"Ray and Sammy are on it."

"Anything good?"

"Ulysses," I said.

"By Homer or James Joyce?"

Through the haze of reeking cigar fumes Old Hank did that laughing thing again.

*"Yo, Crookshanks! We need to fit you with a scar."*

Merle Crookshanks sat dubiously in the chair, listening as I applied the long plastic scar to his cheek and explained. Again.

"Why?" he asked. Again.

I restrained the urge to hit him with a brick by bending to scratch Buckles behind the ears. The dog arched his neck for position and I thought, even *he* gets it.

"Your name's Oz Gorman," I said. "You stole a lot of very expensive books after Katrina. Since our guy is a book collector, we're going to sell him lot of old books."

"Who?" asked Merle.

"Bisby Nixon," I said, not for the first time.

"Oh."

"Old books," I said. "Cincinnati Bob is making a bunch of rare old books a lot more valuable by forging author's signatures and dedications on them."

"A rag," said Merle and I smiled like he'd said something clever.

"Exactly! Except instead of inserting an article in a magazine we're inserting autographs into books that are already rare." With his bald head and stocky build, Merle could have been the world's toughest bouncer or a heavyweight fighter, or the entire front four of a football team.

I found myself speaking to him like he was dense as concrete. "The mark will buy the books, we'll play out the tale, sting him and run a blow-off. You get it?"

He shook his head slowly, back and forth, like a statue come to life. A big dumb statue. I scratched too hard and Buckles growled a low throaty warning.

"Sorry," I whispered. "Merle, what's to get? The mark wants books. He gives us money for them. We take the money..."

"No," said Merle.

"No, what?" I snapped, my temper shattered. I'd heard such good things about Merle from Pops and from Patty. How could I have been saddled with this oaf?

"I meant," said Merle, "What is my motivation? See, I've been taking acting classes down at the free university. They say I have to find my emotional center."

For a long moment I stared at him. Merle looked back innocently, then slowly began to smile. A twinkle appeared in his close-set eyes.

"Uh-huh." I sighed. "You got me. But Crookshanks?"

"Yes, Dani?"

"You're a dick."

# CHAPTER 31

## BACK TO HAILEY

I was in the mood to kick over anthills and take no prisoners so I drove out to see Hailey Briscoe. He made a sound like a strangled cat when he saw me striding down the hall, pointed a finger like a wand warding away the devil and dashed to his office.

I followed casually, passed through the closed outer door and walked in on Hailey as he punched digits on a tiny cell phone.

"Nine-one-one," I told him. "I'm sure they'll want to hear the whole story."

He stopped dialing. "Who are you?"

I sat down uninvited in the former principal's office, with a flustered Hailey Briscoe staring as if unsure whether to call the police or spray me with Holy Water. I ignored his question and studied his face for a moment.

"You don't look good."

"I don't feel good," Hailey agreed.

"Somebody beat you up."

Hailey shrugged.

"Might that somebody be Rundell Mapes?"

Hailey looked away which clinched it for me. "You stupid bastard," I said. "How'd you let them get to you?" I crossed my leg and studied him. His face was raw and puffy as if he'd been slapped around. He favored his arms which suggested he'd been using them to ward off blows. The stiff way he was moving said he'd been hit quite a few times.

"You don't understand."

"Try me." He just shook his head, unable to look at me.

"I can get you your ministry back," I said and waited for the response.

"What?" he said. I waited some more. He said, "You *can't*." I continued to wait. He sat down. "How?"

"I know some things," I told him. "Like how the bankers are making you run this church to gain land for them. I know how the donations work, how they bribe the city, how they intend to make a killing later."

His eyes widened with every word I said until he resembled a balloon about to pop. "How can you possibly know this?"

"A lot of footwork, a little bit of guessing." Gone was the blustering hellfire and brimstone Southern preacher. Hailey had seen too much lately of the wages of sin.

"What I don't know is why you're going along with this." Despite my dislike for him, I was beginning to realize that Hailey wasn't the criminal I thought. So how had he gotten involved in something so far from the halls of the Lord?

He took in a deep breath. "What do you want to know?"

"Who's the girl in room three-fifteen?" I already knew the Ace had been lying about what he saw. Hailey wasn't a cheat. But whatever I expected, this wasn't it.

"Her name is Casey Moon," said Hailey. "They're keeping her a prisoner."

"Who's keeping her a prisoner?" And who the hell was this new card?

"Casey Moon," he repeated. "She's my sister. Rundell Mapes and the others, they say they'll kill her if I don't go along with them."

So I was right, Hailey Briscoe wasn't a cheating husband. They kept him in line by threatening his sister if he didn't play along

"I don't get it," I said. "Why don't you go to the cops?"

"I can't do that. They said they'd hurt her."

I felt a moment of sympathy for him and wondered what I'd do in his place. Certainly not give in. Blackmailers never stop, if you paid them they sucked on you for life. "Surely the police could get her away safely."

"You don't get it!" Hailey ran a hand through his white hair, making deep furrows in the usually perfect wave. His hand shook with tension.

"Tell me," I demanded.

"She gay, all right? My sister's a lesbian!"

I still didn't get it. "What?"

"She's a lesbian." Hailey got up and leaned his knuckles on the desk. He bellowed the word, his voice regaining its Biblical power. The word trembled in the air between us as if it had a huge meaning.

"So what?"

"I can't let anyone know," he said, turning down the volume to low loud. "It'll ruin my ministry. Everyone will point fingers and I'll be disgraced."

Okay, I admit it, I was shocked. Down here, in this Parish with his particular flock, being involved in any way with a homosexual was career suicide. But so what? To go along with Bisby and those guys meant that he had to love his sister. But to deny her for something as stupid and petty as her sexual orientation was insane.

I became angry. "Oh, you poor miserable sap," I said as Hailey sank deep into his shame. "You're betraying your beliefs, betraying your ministry, all because your sister is gay?"

"You don't understand."

"You're damn right, I don't."

"They'll take away..." He made a circle with one sagging arm, a man defeated and worn. "This is my life. I built it up from nothing. I was doing fine until they came along. They said they could make the ministry grow and I'd be able to help people. They said..."

"Yes?"

"That I'd be a star."

That was the missing piece, I realized. Hailey had fallen into one of the seven deadly sins: vanity. "You wanted to be a success."

He nodded. "Sure, the thought of doing better for people was part of it, but mainly I wanted to be number one. I wanted to be bigger than Gerald McMasters and his TV show. I wanted to..." He paused and seemed on the edge of tears. "...To have my own show right after *Bass Blasters*."

I wanted to cry myself. So much grief over such small potatoes. "You wanted to be on TV after a fishing show? People are hurting out there, Hailey, you pitiful jerk. They're seeing their lives float away and sinking into misery and you're worried that you'll lose a TV slot?"

"But my sister," he said. "She's gay."

"So what?" Honestly, I didn't understand this.

"The Lord says it's an abomination."

"The Lord says a lot of things." I was clearly close to blasphemy here and I heard Pops voice clearly. "Never mock another man's religion. If you push too far, he'll kill you."

"Hailey," I said. "Listen to me. You seem to be sincere so I'll make you an offer. I'll get rid of the investors. I'll give you back your church to run the way it should be run. It'll be smaller without all their money, but it will be real."

"And me? What do I have to do?"

"Stop lying. Be the man your parishioners expect you to be." Instead of the screwed-up mess that you are, I thought.

"But my sister...?" I could see him adjusting his thoughts and wondered if I was making a mistake. Still, the devil you knew...

"Tell or don't tell," I said. "Maybe your flock will be bigger minded than you think." I doubted it, but it was possible. "But whatever you decide to do, do it honestly, because Hailey?"

"Yes?" Already the wheels were turning as he considered his opportunities. I felt, on the whole, rather depressed at the state of Humanity.

"Whatever you decide to do had better be honest. Because I will be back. Do you understand me?"

"Yes. But what are you going to do about the investors? About Rundell Mapes?"

"Watch," I said. "And remember, what I do to him, I can also do to you."

I at least got the satisfaction of watching him go pale.

# CHAPTER 32

## GOOD LORD, THE PEN *IS* MIGHTIER

"Ray, where the hell are you?" I sat in a chaise lounge near the pool, trying to relax and not succeeding. My teal bikini was drawing admiring glances from men near and far and deservedly so. I felt better than I had in weeks and looked even better.

"I'm in Philadelphia."

"Of course you are. And why are you in Philadelphia, Ray?"

"Bauman Rare Books."

"Use longer sentences, please. Explain it to me as if I didn't know what you're talking about."

He sighed eloquently. "I am at Bauman's Rare Books here in the City of Brotherly Love to purchase a quantity of used and/or rare books to convince our mark that he has discovered a treasure."

"Ah. Sammy's list." After much study, Sammy Hensel had created what he said was the perfect antique book list. Ray had looked it over and handed it back saying, "I've never read any of them."

"You haven't read *To Kill a Mockingbird?*" Shocked, horrified tone.

"Nope."

Not *Ulysses?* "

"Nuh-uh."

"Not even...?"

"I said I hadn't, didn't I?" Ray said, pissed.

Sammy read the list himself. "Well," he said, "Neither have I."

To me Ray explained, "Bauman's is the only place I could find enough rare old books we can make rarer. And Dani, they have what we need and the books come with genuine provenances. Bob'll only have to add a few words."

"Great. How's the budget holding up?" I'd given him $37,000 to purchase our flash roll and the idea of Ray Sanchez running loose with thirty-seven grand made me shudder. Pins and needles was putting my feelings about *that* mildly.

"We're a little over."

I inhaled sharply imaging what "a little," might mean to Ray.

"Relax. I said little and I meant it. Just two grand and I made it up out of my own pocket."

Well, that was interesting. "What did you get?" My tone was that of a mother in a grocery store telling a toddler to put it back.

"A Carrie Watson," he said. "Gotta go."

I pocketed the cell phone thoughtfully. A "Carrie Watson" was con lingo for the best ever. Ray Sanchez, I thought with wonder. What *are* you up to?


"Dammit!" Cincinnati Bob threw a goose quill into a trash can already half-full of them. We were again sitting in the back of Old Hank's garage/workshop with the door open to let in the cool breezes. A dark sky writhed with swollen clouds, suggesting hard weather coming.

"Trouble with the split again?" Old Hank asked.

"Yeah, now I know why so few things were written down back then. By the time you made a quill pen you forgot what the hell you wanted to write."

"Or maybe goose feathers weren't so brittle back then?" Old Hank said, being kind.

"Nah. It's just a lost art, that's all. But I'll get it."

"It isn't a lost art. I told you, you can get them on the internet."

"A gentleman always makes his own pens," Bob said, with his nose in the air.

"Thomas Jefferson," old Hank said, "Could afford to raise his own geese just for their quills." He picked one up and studied it by holding it three inches from his glasses. "Where'd you get these, anyhow?"

"Hobby Lobby."

"Uh-huh, but you won't buy pens on the internet."

Bob, not having an answer that didn't involve admitting he was a stubborn SOB, went back to work.

"What's the problem with the pens?" I asked.

"I'm having trouble with "snapping the slit," he answered, telling me absolutely nothing.

"Tell me what that means."

He opened a folder on his laptop called "Pens" and checked off the steps he'd followed just to be sure he hadn't missed any.

"Burn fingers tempering the quills in water and hot sand – check; find the "top" of the pen so it fits comfortably in your hand – check; chain sneeze when stripping the plume back to make room for your hand – check." He gave me a solemn look and went back to the list. I refrained from laughing out loud.

"Slice finger making that first, completely unintuitive, cut *away* from the top of the pen toward the tip, less than forty-degrees angle – check; slice finger *again*, "opening" the tube with a long, shallow, curved cut along the bottom until it intersects the first cut about half way through the tube – check; fold the "horns" produced by the intersection of the two cuts together to make the slit; uncheck."

This, he explained, was where it always went wrong. He'd fold them together and press them flat and hear the faint snap – and curse when the slit wound around the shaft instead of going straight.

"See," he said. "The quillers in the 1800's used "pen" knives because...Oh, God." His shoulders slumped.

"Pen knife," he muttered, with a dark glance at his Exacto. He read on some more, leaned back in his chair, pushed his hat back on his head. He glanced sadly at the Band-Aids on his fingers.

"Hey, Hank, you got a pen knife?"

"Sure," Hank said. He rummaged around in his roll-away toolbox and came up with a leather-wrapped bundle that he handed to Bob.

Cincinnati Bob unwrapped it and saw an "Old Timer" folding knife and four obsidian-tipped tools. They didn't look like scalpels, exactly.

"What are these?"

"Paper trimmers," Hank said. "Leaves a line so fine you can't see it. Great for cut and paste work - driver's licenses and ID badges and such."

"Cool."

True to its name the pen knife gave Bob better control making cuts, and straighter, cleaner cuts made for straight slits. Soon he was happily shaping the tines and nib, success its own reward for a job that consumed both time and patience.

"Hey, Dani! Little help here." The pens were finished, the storm had decided to move on and the air was pregnant with the promise of nightfall. I wandered over from studying the books laying all around.

Bob picked up a sheet of paper with the name *Jackie* scrawled all over it. "My hand's too heavy, too masculine. I need a woman's touch."

I stopped like I'd slammed into a wall, waving one hand in front of my nose to ward off the fumes. "Wow! And I thought it was bad in here last time."

"Yeah," Bob said. "We'd vent it outside but the neighbors would probably think we were running a meth lab and call the cops."

Eyes watering so hard I blinked away tears, I said, "Well, here's the rest of the list we need." I handed it over. "How long before you're finished?"

"Three days."

"Really?" I bent to examine the papers. It seemed a long way from a finished book to me. The room was shadowy except for the bright work lamps over the cluttered work tables. It looked like a hobby shop of a mad scientist.

"Yeah, we press it, flash dry it, spray lemon juice on it and bake it under ultraviolet lights. Nothing ages paper like lemon and UV."

"I'll take your word for it. How about the others?"

"Done, except for the Kennedy." He pointed to a pile. "Ray brought 'em in last night."

My eyes roamed the titles, *Catch-22, The Old Man and the Sea, Moby Dick, The Big Sleep, Of Mice and Men*...it was even better than I'd hoped. Several covers were propped open so the freshly forged signatures and dedications would dry properly. Small changes that added great worth.

I stepped up to Harper Lee's *To Kill a Mockingbird* and read, "To Jackie, best wishes always, Harper Lee."

"Jackie Kennedy?" I asked.

Cincinnati Bob pointed proudly to *Catch-22* and said, "Got one to Bobby too. But I need your help with this one."

He handed me a typed letter from Jackie to Harper Lee, thanking the author for the book. "We thought it'd be better if the letter was handwritten, but I can't catch her hand."

I studied it, then compared a real signature with the copies. I picked up a blank sheet of practice paper the same weight as Jackie Kennedy's White House stationery. "Okay, give me the pen."

Bob handed me an original Esterbrook cartridge pen with an engraved shaft that read, "The President. The White House."

"Are you kidding me?"

"God is in the details, Dani. It's important to get it right."

Truer words and all that. I hefted the pen for balance and tried a practice run. Over my shoulder Bob said, "A little lighter. And notice how the 'k' has a faint skip to it? That's why we got this pen—it makes that skip."

"Right. Okay." I took a deep breath and wrote Jackie Kennedy's name in one fluid move. It was critical not to go slowly or be hesitant and when I was done Bob and old Hank nodded.

"Perfect," they said.

# CHAPTER 33

## THE BIG STORE

I pulled up outside the old Victorian Ray had rented and watched as Merle supervised a group of temporary laborers hauling things from a U-Haul truck to the house like a line of ants. Merle followed with an armful of civil war muskets.

I grabbed a brass parakeet cage out of the truck and came inside, stopping in the living room to stare in awe at piles of mildewed newspapers and walls that sprouted black mold like a Salvador Dali Rorschach test. At least fifty clocks hung on the wall, all with different times, their clicks and whirrs morphing into a sound like dental drills. One was a black Felix the cat with a tail swinging one way, bulging eyes swinging another and a tongue that kept sticking out.

I heard banging from the sitting room and saw Ray, in a tool belt and knee pads, on a rickety wooden step ladder trying to mount a stuffed lion's head on the wall.

He'd wrestle it in place and it would slip out of alignment as he reached for the electric drill. I watched with a trace of amusement as he repeated the process three times and was just about to lend a hand when he succeeded in getting the drill up to it without the head sliding.

"Eureka," he said and pressed the trigger on the drill.

"Dammit," he said when nothing happened. He ran his eyes along the cord to see if it was plugged in.

"Need a hand?" I asked.

Ray swiveled his head the other way and said, "Oh, hi Dani. No. I need a drill."

The lights came on, the drill drilled, startling Ray, the lion's head slipped and Ray grabbed for it and the whole shebang toppled majestically to the floor.

Thud, snap, crash and oof assaulted my ears like one single sound. The thud was the lion's head hitting the carpet. The snap was the drill bit breaking. The crash was the stepladder and the oof was Ray - who jumped up mad, kicked the lion's head and danced around the room on one foot saying "Damn" over and over again until he tripped on the drill cord and fell again.

I tried to hold it in. I really did. "Are you hurt?"

Ray rolled over and sat up and waived the drill at me like it was my fault. "Don't you dare laugh."

"I'm not," I said and slapped both hands over my mouth.

Merle poked his head into the room and said, "What was that crash?" He added, "Oh, good, the power's on." Then ducked as Ray hurled the drill at him.

Chaos, I thought between chuckles. Everything is in chaos. We're running a nice neat job on a mark so hooked he'll reel himself in and our "store" looks like someone put it together in a Mixmaster. Why *was* our store such a mess? That one I could get an answer for.

"Merle, why is our store such a mess?"

"Because Oz Gorman is a crazy packrat."

"But you're Oz Gorman."

Merle crossed his eyes and stuck out his tongue.

It almost set me off again. I closed my eyes and took a deep breath. My crew. My highly skilled, professional, well-paid crew. Cincinnati Bob's practical jokes weren't bad enough. Now he'd gone and infected Merle. I'd have to do something about that.

"It's a knock-apart, see?" Merle pulled the rifle apart and shoved it back together. "Made of balsa."

"I don't know," I said. "It looks massive. Why can't you just shoot him?"

Merle looked at me like I was crazy, which was possible, running this mob. "Well, noise for one. And at such close range the flash powder could set his shirt on fire."

That put a distinctly uncomfortable picture in my head. "Oh."

Without warning, Merle swung the rifle at me. I screamed and dodged but it hit me anyhow and I collapsed to the floor, eyes staring blankly, blood running from my mouth.

"Dani?" Merle stood there for a second, stunned, then dropped to the floor beside me. "Dani!"

Buckles ran over and started licking the blood and my face. I pushed the dog away, spit out the blood squib and said, "Yuck! Can't they make these things in peppermint?"

Merle closed his open mouth and started chuckling. "Guess I had that coming, huh?"

"You bet," I said, climbing back to my feet.

He reached out a hand and I helped him up and he said, "Dani?

"Yes, Merle?"

"You're a dick."

# CHAPTER 34

## DANI RUNS THE RAGGLE

I leaned over in a short skirt and low cut chiffon blouse on the arm of the plush chair. Bisby Nixon sat in front of the gently burning fire, sipping brandy, idly caressing my left knee. He picked up a cigar and puffed out fragrant smoke that reminded me of a chemical dump and I said, as if innocently, "Paper?"

"That'd be nice."

I leaned way over, feeling his eyes as well as his hand on my thigh and picked up that day's New Orleans Times Picayune and handed it to him. I leaned back on the chair to read over his shoulder while idly twirling strands of his long hair. This was the critical part, the bait to lure him in. Would he take it?

Bisby, looking uncomfortable in tight dress slacks after a heavy dinner, absently turned pages, stopping occasionally to scan an article. In the second section, on page three, near the bottom, an article caught his eye and I felt his shoulder stiffen.

Lost Book Recovered. The story explained how a rare autographed copy of *To Kill A Mockingbird*, believed to have been lost during Hurricane Katrina, had been discovered floating in a storm sewer catch basin. The article said the book was wrapped in a water tight zip-lock bag. "It's a mystery," said sanitary workman Joel Spellman who discovered the valuable book while cleaning the system.

Authorities speculated the possibility that the book, one of nearly a hundred missing from several locations during the hurricane, might have been stolen. "I believe this could be the work of thieves," said Officer Juan Cabrillo of Orleans Parish. "It makes no sense otherwise."

"If they were indeed stolen they would be worth in excess of five million dollars," said antiquarian book dealer John Dunning. "Possibly more."

"What is it, honey?" I asked. Bisby looked up at me, back to the paper and I could feel his interest in the story by his lack of interest in me. We'd spent the evening at a nice restaurant and, at my suggestion paused for a drink to relax before sex.

Patty, in explaining to me the fine points of the non-seduction, had said, "Men have a strong interest in sex."

Bob, listening nearby, agreed. "It's true. We do."

"However," continued Patty. "They have other interest as well. If you can balance a pair of conflicting interests correctly you won't have to take off a stitch. A flash of thigh when he's thinking about money will distract him but not make him stop what he's doing."

It was her idea that, if the article I planted in the newspaper caught his attention, the lovemaking would never happen. It was a dangerous ploy but Patty felt confident.

"This book," said Bisby pointing as I leaned in to look closer, exposing an expensive lace bra and delicate perfume. The trick was to push both greed and lust and hope that greed won.

"Huh," I said with a clear lack of interest. I squeezed his shoulder and got up and walked slowly to the bedroom, paused at the door and leaned on the frame. I frowned slightly with the tip of my tongue between my teeth, a Marilyn pose, and said, "I know a guy says he's got a lot of books like that."

"Like what?" asked Bisby, rising as he watched me undo the third button of my blouse.

"In zip-lock bags," I said. I opened my shirt, flashing him. "Are you coming to bed?" I turned and vanished into the bedroom.

As it turned out, no; he wasn't.


"This is it?" asked Bisby.

We sat in his BMW in front of the supremely ugly house on Lessepes Street, just a few blocks from the canal. The neighborhood was low income. The house looked like a punch drunk old fighter, battered and weary, ready to give up. It might have once been a Victorian painted lady, but the colors had faded and any trace of her beauty was long gone.

"Wait'll you meet the guy who lives here."

Bisby had been all over me, and not sexually. "What do you mean? What guy?" He'd been so persistent that I threw a fit, getting upset and walking out in the middle of an argument, turning off my cell phone with a brief smile as I drove home alone.

This morning he called, apologetic but just as intense. I listened, stringing him along, and made him wait until nearly five in the afternoon before relenting. I realized why Patty loved the raggle. This was a lot of fun.

Bisby, I noticed, watching him duck his head to see the house better, was really and truly hooked and I was well out of the danger of sleeping with him. From now on his attention would be focused where we wanted it.

"What about him?" asked Bisby, not taking his eyes off the house.

"He's...different."

"What's different about him? Is he like, crazy? De-formed? What?"

"No, he's just—oh, there he is."

A big bald guy ambled down the shady street. Despite his size he seemed nervous, glancing around constantly, looking into cars, into house windows, ducking under low hanging branches. He reminded me of an alley cat, wary of everything.

Bisby got out of the car, motioning me to follow. The guy reached us as I closed the door and he paused, suspicion in every muscle, eyes darting from me to Bisby. He backpedaled away from us.

"Oz," I said. "It's me."

He peered through the evening mist like a myopic ogre. A long red line of a fresh scar slashed across his right cheek. "Donna?" He almost smiled, saw Bisby and frowned again.

"Who's he?"

"He's..."

"I'm Bisby Nixon." Bisby came around the front of the Beamer, hand out, welcoming smile on his face.

Oz said to me, "What do you want?"

"I heard you had some books." I spoke softly, playing my role. I was certain we had him but marks had slipped the trap before. Bisby wisely kept his distance, which seemed to calm the big guy a little.

"Books," Oz repeated. "Books. Yeah, I got books."

Bisby breathed in sharply. "Can I see them?"

The big man studied him and said, "No." He turned and made for the door, bending at the waist to reach the low black iron gate. It creaked as rusty hinges protested, in need of maintenance, care, or a little WD-40.

Bisby made shooing motions and whispered, "Stop him! Make him talk to us. Hurry!"

"Oz," I called. "Wait a minute, honey." The hulking man stopped, shoulders hunched, but turned back. "It's all right, Oz, he's cool."

"I don't know him."

"You know me, Oz."

Reluctantly Oz nodded and gestured for us to follow. He pulled out a thick ring of over a hundred keys, flipped through them, unlocked a dead-bolt, flipped more keys, opened another dead-bolt, flipped again and unlocked the handle. He twisted the knob and went inside, not waiting to see if we followed.

Inside, the house was a junk yard, a bazaar, a flea market, a dump. It stunk of mildew and fresh urine and a scrawny cat ran from one pile of garbage to disappear behind another.

Yellowing newspapers lined the narrow hallway, pictures hung all over the upper wall, and dark antique furniture squatted wherever. A stuffed lion's head leaned precariously against a wall next to a shriveled brown philodendron. Dead leaves littered the floor nearby.

The living room was a dark cave and Oz the ogre who lived in it. He clicked on a bronze floor lamp with a Byzantine shade and a muted amber glow, like firelight, made a pool of light around them. Everything else was plunged into frightening shadow. Oz sat down in a battered red chair that huffed dust as it settled. Belatedly he offered, "Drink? Anything?"

"No, thank you," I said. "I heard you had some books, maybe for sale."

Oz looked wary and shrewd. He licked his lower lip and nodded a barely visible agreement.

"Could we see?" I spoke quietly as if to soothe a baby or calm a monster. Oz got up with a grunt, motioned to Bisby and another chair, said, "Sit," which Bisby took as a command. He settled gingerly into the embrace of a low overstuffed chair that snuggled around him like an octopus, looking dirty and claustrophobic and catching my eyes with a "What have you gotten me into," look.

Oz rummaged around in the papers on a roll-top desk and came back with a gray plastic milk crate, handed it to me and sat back down.

I looked at it, gasped, and handed it to Bisby. He plucked out a small package, turned it right side up and read aloud.

"*Of Mice and Men*," he said, reading the cover of gold leaf inset onto brown leather. "By *John Steinbeck.*" The greed and desire he fought to keep from showing rose off him like mist on a swamp and I knew he was mentally figuring how incredible this discovery was. His heart would be pounding, his hands feeling cold and tight, his throat would be dry and clogged.

The book was an autographed first edition with a dedication to Mae West –worth a small fortune. Bisby looked up and saw Oz watching him with a devil's grin.

He grinned back.

"Do you have any others?" I knew he meant to say it casually but his voice betrayed his lust.

"You'll be wanting that drink now," said Oz. He went somewhere and we heard sounds of glasses, the clink of ice, the avalanche of a lot of somethings falling followed by a muffled curse.

Bisby pointed at the book. "Do you know what this is?" He whispered. I nodded.

"Is it worth a lot?"

"A lot? This is the single most important thing I've ever touched. Donna, this is a museum piece."

I looked confused, usually an easy task. "You're gonna give it to a museum?"

"No! I'm going to keep it! I wonder if he has any more."

Oz returned with two mismatched glasses containing some brown liquid. He gave one to me and one to Bisby who sipped gingerly and smiled. He drank half the glass and asked again, "Do you have any more?"

"I might have," answered Oz. In the dim light he could have been a pirate on the Spanish Main or an Arabian trader in Damascus. The scar on his cheek rippled like a snake and I thought that all he needed was an eye patch. "Why do you want to know?"

"I'd like to buy them. I mean, if they're like this."

"You mean if they're valuable?" Oz laughed. "Oh, they are, my friend. They truly are."

"Then you *do* have more." Bisby was having trouble with his voice.

"You want to see?"

Bisby said, "Sure," like it didn't matter but I knew that inside he was a kid at Christmas, bouncing on the mattress at three A.M. waiting for Santa Claus.

Oz lumbered around the room, poking here and there in the detritus, causing tiny whirlwinds of dust. He handed Bisby a baggie without comment and went on searching.

Joseph Heller's *Catch 22,* a first edition with a dedication to Bobby Kennedy. Another baggie was dropped unceremoniously on his lap. Faulkner's *Soldier's Pay,* again a first edition in the original, unrestored dust jacket, signed with a dedication to his friend William Spratley.

Oz began to talk as he rummaged, dropping books on Bisby as he came to them. They were all classics, they were all worth a fortune. They were designed to represent, not mere treasure, but a holy grail of treasure. A prize undreamed of to book collectors.

"I like to keep things hidden, here and there," Oz said. "So, if the police get nosy—" He grinned at us on the word nosy— "They won't find anything. Who could find anything, eh?"

Bisby nodded mutely, his right hand gently on the gilded leather spine of a first edition, first printing, autographed copy of Hemingway's, *For Whom the Bell Tolls,* as Oz dropped a copy of H.G. Well's *The Invisible Man,* bound in mottled calf, on top of the others. There were now sixteen books on his lap.

"How did you come across these?"

"Come across?" Oz laughed. He reached into a pile of decaying newspapers and pulled out another book and kept on talking. "I *stole* 'em, that's how I come across 'em. You want to hear the story?"

"Uh-huh." The last book was *Ulysses* by James Joyce, an almost non-existent copy printed on handmade paper. Bisby removed it from the baggie and opened the front cover and a folded slip of paper slid out. A provenance from Sotheby's declaring the book an original first edition and one of only twelve known to exist with a misprint on the title page. He looked and there it was, "Ullyses", misspelled.

I watched him carefully, gauging the reaction. This book alone, if genuine, was worth a quarter of a million dollars.

"It was before the hurricane," said Oz. "I was working for Miller and Sons Moving Company as a laborer. Week of the storm they had us picking up stuff and moving it upstairs in these secure buildings. I guess they was afraid of the flood waters rising. They didn't have time to get it to more secure storage so we packed it all away.

"I got a hold of a lot of keys and when Katrina came I ducked over there and I picked up as much stuff as I could. I went with small things so I could carry 'em better, except for this."

He went to the cluttered fireplace mantle and took down a long rifle that gleamed in the dim light like a thing alive.

Oz handed him the gun and Bisby took it, surprised at its weight. Several small packages slipped off his lap to land on the floor.

"It's a genuine Pennsylvania Long Rifle, made in 1772 by Jacob Dickett. Only three left that were signed by Dickett himself, you know."

"Uh-huh."

"You don't know much about guns, do you?"

"Point this end at the other guy and pull the trigger."

Oz chuckled. "Hey, that's good." He took the rifle back and leaned it against the wall. "That thing damn near got me killed that night. The storm was a lot worse than anybody'd thought, myself included, and when I finally went to all the places I'd flagged it was like Hell's own kitchen out there. Cars overturnin', buildings blowin' down, trees fallin' and me out there in the thick of it.

"I was scared, I'll say." He pointed at the jagged tear on his face.' Got this that night. A body came by and I dropped some packages..."

"The ones they found," Bisby whispered.

"Yeah, that bummed me, too. Anyhow, I got home and loaded stuff out of the boat and that's when the shutter came off the window and almost took my head off." He turned and gestured at four long scratches down his neck that disappeared under his shirt. "The nails from them shutters," Oz said. He found one last book, tossed it at Clive and sat down.

*Travels Through The Two Louisianas*, signed by Perrin Du Lac himself, the first English language edition, issued in London in 1807. Bisby gulped. "So you have some idea what these are worth?"

"Some idea? A course I got some idea!" He looked to me for compassion. "Jeez, Donna, what's with this guy?"

Bisby said, "Would you be willing to accept a reasonable offer?"

"Depends on what reasonable is, don't it?"

"I'm thinking...Fifty thousand?"

Oz stared at him for a long while. The room became so quiet that we could hear the clicking of the furnace, the rasp of the big man's breath, the mice scurrying in the walls.

"Get fucked," Oz said. "And get out."

"Wait, I can go higher."

"You can screw yourself, too." Oz got up, an act like watching the Eiffel tower being built in fast-frame, just getting higher and higher until he loomed over us. He glared at me angrily. "I thought you vouched for this asshole, Donna." He shook his bald head and marched out of the room.

Bisby, looking like a man having a seizure, hissed, "What should I do?"

"Better to leave," I whispered.

"I can't leave," Bisby squeaked. He picked up *Ulysses* and shook it. "I can't leave this!"

"I'll talk to him. He'll listen to me. C'mon and let's get out of here before he gets madder."

Reluctantly, like pulling himself out of quicksand, Bisby let himself be dragged from the chair, from the room, out of the house and into the car.

He kept looking back all the way until I turned the car around the corner and out of sight. "We have to go back," he said.

"We can't."

"I can't leave those books there in that...that squalor."

"You should have bid higher."

"I know. I don't know what came over me. I should have said five hundred thousand. I can get that much. Would he take that, you think?"

My heart beat faster. "Right now," I said, "He wouldn't take five million from you. Weren't you listening? He's pulled off this incredible heist, the score of his lifetime, and you insulted him. We need to let him calm down."

"But..."

"And apologize."

"But..."

"And *then* pay him."

# CHAPTER 35

## THE ACE GETS HIS JUST DESERTS

"Why me, Dani? That's all I wanna know. Why's it always me?"

The Ace and I were in a rented Toyota Tercel parked at a meter on Renwick Parkway. The car was too small for the Ace and he crowded the center, making him uncomfortably close to me. I could smell alcohol and tobacco and something long unwashed in the air.

The windows were closed against a steadily falling drizzle and the gray skies made our vigil feel like those nights at summer camp spent hiding out from the rain under the cloak of heavy canvas tents.

I said, "You're the only one tough enough to do this, Ace."

"What about Crookshanks? He's a mean mother."

"He *is* a mean mother," I agreed. "But he's also set to run the store tonight. I can't spare him."

"Sanchez then. How about him?"

I laughed. "Can you picture Ray mixing it up with Rundell Mapes?"

"Um, I guess...no." Defeat oozed from his clammy pores, making the car even more unpleasant. If Rundell didn't make an appearance soon I was going to go into the bar alone.

"There he is," said the Ace and I looked out the fogged window to see the giant come bobbing down the street heading for the Viscount Liquor store. I looked at my watch. Right on time.

He was wearing a black pea coat and pale green pants. His hands were tucked in his pockets and his shoulders were hunched against the rain. He looked like a moving van with feet.

"Whoa, he's a big one," said the Ace.

"You're not afraid of him, are you?"

"Noooo, but..." He watched for a moment and added, "You know that song? The one about the guy?" He started to sing a few lines of *Bad Bad Leroy Brown* until I shushed him. "He's like that guy, you know? The baddest man in the whole damn town."

Clearly the Ace was having cold feet about his assignment. Since taking down Rundell was critical to me for several very good reasons, I had to get the Ace out of my car.

"You can do this, buddy," I told him. He gave me the look that deserved. "I mean, go out there and give him a hundred and ten percent." I chucked him on the arm.

"The fuck you doing?"

"Win one for the Gipper," I said.

"What?" His expression went to concerned.

"There is no 'I' in team," I said.

"You're crazy, you know that?" The Ace grabbed the door handle and squirmed out to the sidewalk, like toothpaste being squeezed from a tube. I got out and joined him, noticing he stood a little farther away from me.

"You know the plan," I said. "You've got to steal his cell phone..."

"I got it."

"And switch out his..."

"I know! Jeez, you're like my mother." That was an unpleasant image.

"And make him really, really mad," I finished. I gave him a shove and he shambled forward, a reluctant St. George out to face a particularly nasty dragon.

I watched him for a moment and hurried to catch up, with *Bad Bad Leroy Brown* playing over and over in my brain.

Viscount Liquors was more of a low rent tavern than a liquor store, with a long bar down one side, cheap vinyl booths down the other and a big glass cooler on the narrow end wall next to the door marked restrooms.

A skinny black guy with a graying mini-afro was behind the bar vacantly twisting a dirty white rag around inside a glass. He didn't look up when we came in. A juke box along the side wall was playing a loud ZZ Top song I didn't know and Rundell Mapes had his back to us as he rummaged in the cooler for a twelve pack of beer.

The Ace walked over to the next refrigerator case, opened the door and took out two bottles of wine. He held one by the neck, made a casual chop with it to test the balance, turned and smashed it over Rundell's head.

The bottle broke, Rundell sagged but didn't go down and the Ace hit him with the other bottle. Glass and wine splattered and

Rundell, driven to his knees, shook his head to clear it. The Ace waded in and started to hit him like a man punching a heavy bag. The bartender yelled, "Hey!" but stayed where he was and I watched from the door near an orange neon Budweiser sign.

The song ended and I could hear the Ace grunting as he pounded away at Rundell. His arms moved like pistons and I had a terrible image of him as a cop doing this to some poor fish caught up in a vice sweep. Laws against back room confessions were created exactly with the Ace in mind.

Rundell wasn't a small-time hood though. He was a very large, well-muscled mutated freak of nature who was showing signs of getting into the uneven fight. I sauntered over to the bartender, took a seat on a stool with my back to the bar and leaned on my elbows.

"Fifty bucks on the fat guy," I said and he shot me a wild-eyed look, shrugged and nodded. He went to the register, rang up 'no sale' and came back. He dropped a pair of twenties and a ten-spot next to me.

"I'll have a Bud," I told him and dug out some cash as he was getting it. He poured my beer and we eyed the activity like we were watching the fights on TV.

Rundell, though obviously hurting, had risen from his knees to a short of crouch and huddled in on himself to block the shots the Ace was delivering to his midsection. He straightened a little more, let a short jab slide of his right arm and swung his left like a ball player going for the stands.

His wrist caught the Ace across the chest and sent him sliding on his ass across the dirty white tile floor. Rundell paused to get his breath, the Ace rolled to his feet and charged back in. It was obvious that the Ace felt his only chance was a quick all-out blitz, which might have worked if he hadn't slipped on the wine.

With full momentum and the benefit of his considerable bulk, the Ace hurled himself at the still shaken Rundell but as he got there his left foot went out from under him and he did one of those comical ass-over-teakettle falls and landed flat on his back.

I could hear the air whoosh out and I winced. The bartender, laughing said, "that's gotta hurt," and I slid my money closer to him.

The fight was over. Rundell, though unsteady and bleeding from several cuts on his face, grabbed the Ace by the collar and hauled him up. Amazingly, Rundell managed to lift him completely off his feet and I saw the Ace look down at the floor, then back at Rundell.

He said, "Aw shit," and Rundell threw him at the juke box. When the Ace hit it a bunch of lights flickered, which I thought was kind of pretty, and it started playing *Sunday Bloody Sunday* by U2, which was both appropriate and ironic.

I let Rundell waltz around with the Ace for a while until I felt that he had time to accomplish his goals and I slid off my barstool, smiled at the bartender and walked across the room. I rummaged around in my purse.

Rundell was occupied with shaking the Ace's teeth out when I pounded on his shoulder to get his attention. He turned and I sprayed him with about six quarts of mace. He let go of the Ace but I kept spraying until he was nearly blind. Hands over his burning face he turned and fled, as overwhelmed as a bear that's knocked over a hornet's nest.

I knelt down next to the Ace who was lying in a bloody heap on the floor and tapped his cheek to get him to focus on me.

Ace? Yo, Darren!" I saw his eyes fix on my left ear, tapped again until they moved to my eyes. "Ah, "I said. "You're back with us. Wonderful."

"Dani?" he said.

"Right here, buddy." I smiled at him. "Did you get them?"

"Yah," he muttered. Honestly, he looked awful. "I switched it..."

"And the phone?"

"Busted."

"Oh, goody," I said happily. "Now Ace, let me explain something to you. Are you listening? Ace?"

"Uhhh."

"I take that as a yes. Remember how you asked, why you? Well, here's why. You told me that Hailey Briscoe was having an affair with the girl in room 315. Remember that? Darren? Your exact words were, I believe, 'sure, he's porking the broad.'"

"But I talked with Hailey and guess what? Ace? The girl in room 315 is his sister! Imagine that. And—this is bonus material here, Darren, you might want to pay close attention—she's also a lesbian. So even if Hailey was as sick a bastard as you, I doubt seriously he'd be doing her."

The Ace, dazed and bloody, was developing a growing look of apprehension.

I continued, "So, we have a case of you lying to me. The information you gave me cost a lot of money, not to mention some personal humiliation. I set you up to get punched out by Bisby Nixon and I set you up to get really punched out by Rundell, and didn't he do a great job of that?"

I was having trouble controlling a sense of jubilation. Things were going just swell. "So here's the thing, Ace. I want the money I paid you returned. And if you ever decide to fuck around with me, I'll make this evening seem like a very nice dream. You'll actually look back on this night and think, 'I wish I was there again, instead of now.'"

I stood up and looked down at him. Only his left eye seemed capable of movement and he used it to stare at me. He blinked slowly which I took as 'lesson learned.'

I went back to the smiling bartender, handed him a couple of hundreds for the juke box and walked out to the car feeling generous.

Now, if the rest of the night would go this well.

# CHAPTER 36

## HAILEY SETS THEM UP

Hailey Briscoe, when I met him in the enormous den of his McMansion, was drinking a Rum Collins, looking like a shipwreck survivor. His shirt tail was out, his jowls unshaven and the Bose stereo on the built in oak bookcase was playing some operatic dirge that made my teeth ache.

"Turn that off," I demanded and a fat lady immediately stopped caterwauling. I placed my bag on the desk and regarded the preacher. "You don't look so hot."

"I don't *feel* so...I can't do this."

"Sure you can," I said, trying for reassurance.

"I don't even know your name," he cried. "How can I trust you with this?"

"You don't need to know my name. Just keep focused on what we're doing. Do you want your sister to be safe?"

"God, yes!"

"Then we have to kill her." I glanced around. "Where's the missus?"

"She's out. I sent her to her mother's house until this is over."

"Good choice. Means we can talk freely." I picked up the phone and held it to him. "Call him."

"I don't know..."

"Cold feet, Hailey? Think it over. If you do this we have a chance to get your sister out and for you to do right. If you don't do this I guarantee I will call the cops and the media and you'll lose everything."

"You'd do that?"

"Yes, I would," I agreed happily.

He sat back in his massive chair in his fairy tale house, torn between flight and desperation. He sipped from his drink, a man as far removed from the image of a preacher as possible. Eventually, as if bowing to the will of the lord he nodded and sighed.

"Sure," he said. "Sure. I'll do it."

I glanced at my watch and calculated times. This would be close. "Call him," I said.

He pushed a button on a telephone so sophisticated that NASA probably used them to call Mars, pressed another and a dial tone whined on the speaker box. A series of beeps made the call and a voice said, "Hello?"

"Clive, this is Hailey Briscoe."

"Oh, hey." The voice sounded pleasant and normal, not that of a man responsible for blackmail and land theft. "What do you want?"

"I want out," said Hailey. He drew in a deep breath, realizing he'd just taken the leap.

"No way, man. Not gonna happen. We've been through this before, man." Man, I thought. Like dealing with an overgrown frat-boy. I thought of the information Sammy had brought us. Clive Dumont was a player, he liked nice things and nice people. Time to shake that world. I nodded Hailey to go ahead with the script.

"Not any more, Clive. I'm out. I don't care what you do with the ministry. I'm walking out and taking my sister with me."

"You can't do that Hailey. Remember Rundell is watching over her."

"I don't care anymore, Clive. I'm blowing the whistle. The cops can deal with Rundell Mapes."

The speaker said, "Hailey, Hailey, listen to me. You can't—" and I motioned Hailey to hang up. An eerie dial tone filled the room until Hailey hung up the receiver.

"Got to leave him in the dark," I said. "Makes people crazy."

"Will this work?" Hailey asked. He sank back in his chair, deflated.

I considered for a moment. "Are you going to go back to being a good guy? Use your ministry to help people?"

"Yes." I could barely hear him.

I smiled brightly. "Have a little faith. It'll be all right."

"What about you?" he asked.

"If it works out, you'll be a minister again and never see me."

"And if it doesn't."

"Then we're dead."

I left him sitting there with that to digest and drove off into the night. A few miles later at a red light at a deserted crossroad I had an amazing thought.

I was doing the Lord's work.

# CHAPTER 37

# THE AUCTION

Three days. Three agonizing days during which Bisby suffered nightmares about that old house burning down or a water pipe breaking or, God forbid, Oz selling the books to someone else.

"Calm down, Bisby."

"I've got to have them." He circled the room like a tiger in a cage, pausing to make the same point. "Those books are worth a fortune."

"Uh-huh," I said.

"You've got to get me another chance."

"I dunno, he was pretty mad."

"Well, get him un-mad."

"How?"

"I don't know, whatever."

I sighed theatrically. "Fine, I'll try. But don't get your hopes up." I went to the other room, placed a call and made sure I said Bisby's name with a short laugh. He'd be listening, I knew. He wouldn't be able to help it. I came back to find him posing self-consciously by the fireplace.

"He'll do it," I said.

"When?"

"Now."

Bisby was already getting the car keys.

Nothing had changed. The house still looked like a dump, the owner like a pirate, the interior like a land fill. Oz Gorman greeted me at the door and stepped aside, pointedly ignoring Bisby's attempt at warmth.

We returned to the dingy living room. The plastic shades were rolled down in case a stray beam of light tried to get inside. The smell of coffee almost overcame the smell of mildew but Oz didn't offer any. He sat in his chair and waited with a mulish expression on his face.

"First off," said Bisby, "Let me apologize for my offer the other day. It was unfortunate."

"It was insulting," said Oz.

"Insulting," agreed Bisby. "But now I have an offer I think you'll like."

"I doubt it."

"I'm prepared to offer," he paused and I knew he was debating whether to make the low offer and get a bargain or go immediately to the high end. If he botched this he'd never get another chance. I saw the wheels turning until he came to a decision.

"Five," he said. "Hundred," he said. "Thousand."

Oz sat up a bit straighter in the horrible ratty chair. "Yeah?"

"Cash," Bisby finished.

"I think," Oz said, letting the silence fill the horrible room until I felt I couldn't stand it. I was thinking that Merle was overplaying the hand when I saw that Bisby was poised on the edge of his seat, ready to explode. "I think, eight."

"What? Eight? Eight what? Eight hundred thousand? Are you out of your mind?" Bisby looked at me. "He's out of his fucking mind."

"Hey," barked Oz. "I don't have to listen to you. And I don't have to sell to you."

Bisby looked stricken, knowing he'd gone too far. Furiously he waved his hands, trying to placate. "No, don't get mad. I was surprised that's all. I can...I can do it. I'll raise the money."

Oz settled back, considering. "Cash."

"Yeah, sure." Bisby looked feverish.

"When?"

"Um...uh, well...Thursday?" Today was Monday. We didn't want to give him time and I was pleased when Merle answered.

"Today. Tonight. At Nine O'clock."

"I can't!"

"Then no deal. I got other people you know." A lie, but Bisby wasn't in a place to question it.

"Tonight," he said, as if to himself. "Sure. Tonight. I can do it."

"Then we have a deal," said Oz.

I couldn't tell, as we walked through the afternoon rain, whether Bisby was relieved or depressed.

"I gotta to drop you off."

"Why?"

"Why?" He yelled. "To get the money! God, don't you ever pay attention?" Anger and frustration, like crows on a clothesline, seemed to be his constant companions. His emotions were probably scraped raw and I imagined he felt broken inside, like a sock full of glass shards. This was a huge risk for Bisby, far from the quiet deals he made with his investor friends.

It was a very long way from the boardroom to a suitcase full of cash. "Never mind." He jerked the car to the curb and shoved me. "Get out now."

"What?" I protested, for real. "Bisby, what the *Hell?*"

"Out," he said. "Out. Get OUT!"

I pulled the handle, cursed at him and stood on the street as the Beamer sped away. I watched it disappear, a silver missile heading for imminent destruction at my hands.

I picked up my cell, pushed the button and said, "Sammy? He's heading for the bank. Are you ready?"

"Sure. I put a Federal Income Tax hold on his account. There will be no money available for the guy."

"For how long?" I asked, though we'd covered this already. Nerves, I supposed, making me restate the obvious.

"A couple of hours," Sammy said. "At least until close of business, but no longer."

I told him I appreciated his genius and meant it. It couldn't be easy to forge a federal bank code and convince another computer you were the IRS. I shuddered to imagine the complexities. Give me a simple scam any day.

I flagged a cab with a loud whistle and went home to wait for Bisby's call.

It came at six-fifty-seven, interrupting me while I flossed my teeth after a very nice dinner of Chicken and mashed potatoes courtesy of Swanson. Good dental hygiene is important and I almost didn't answer the phone, but Bisby had stewed enough. I probably didn't need to make him more agitated.

He picked me up, a man consumed with greed and sweaty desperation and I got in the seat without commenting on the suitcase in the back seat. He shifted the fast car through the gears and spoke to the windshield, not looking at me.

"You would not believe what happened," he said through gritted teeth.

"Hey, I had a bad day too," I said. After you threw me out, in the rain, you know? I had to call a cab and it took them an hour...a whole damn hour standing under an awning waiting..."

"Shut up! He glared in my direction. "Jesus! My bank account was seized."

"Seized?"

"By the Feds. The damned IRS locked up my accounts. I don't know why, probably 'cause of some deals I'm doing. But they have no right."

We didn't have any actual information but we all agreed, a guy like Bisby Nixon would have no trouble believing the IRS would stake out his accounts.

I touched his knee and he almost flinched from the nervous energy. "Poor baby! What did you do?"

"I went to my business," he said. I figured he'd be so tanked up he'd want to talk and I was right, he wasn't able to shut up. "I've got this side business...me and a few others...we're investing in land...I took some money from the account."

"You stole from your partners? Won't they be upset?"

"They would," he admitted. His smile was demented, teeth and gums in a pasty face. Bisby was a man very much consuming himself. "If they find out. But it's my guy who does the books and he won't tell them. By the time there's an audit I'll have sold the books, made a profit and no one's the wiser.

His accountant was a creepy little guy named Gum Pepys, a Ukranian in his middle-forties who lived in a dreary apartment by the airport. We would have chosen him for the scam but frankly, he weirded us all out.

Bisby jerked to a shaky stop in front of the house, got out and pulled the suitcase, hugging it to his chest. We took a few steps in the dark in the shadows of the thick trees and I said, "I'm scared. What if this doesn't work?"

"It'll work," said Bisby.

"How do you know?"

"Because I've got this." He slid a small black pistol from his left side pocket, showing me the edge and dropping it back. He looked satisfied at having shown me.

Finally, I thought, seeing the gun. Showtime.

# CHAPTER 38

## THE TRADE

With eight hundred thousand in a silver case Bisby felt free to enter the house without knocking. He walked down the narrow hallway and into the living room just as a long-barreled rifle turned to point directly at him and fired.

Flame belched from its muzzle and a cloud of cordite rose above the gun and Bisby dropped to the musky carpet expecting to die. When nothing happened, he looked up to see Oz Gorman, the giant madman, stomping out a smoldering spark.

Oz studied him on the carpet as I helped him get unsteadily to his feet, making sure I pocketed the pistol as I did. "It wasn't loaded."

"How the hell was I to know that?"

"Thought you was burglars or something." Oz Gorman stood in the dark room wearing tan pants and an incongruous grey tee shirt with the yellow Batman logo emblazoned on his chest. He looked like a scarred, bald, eight-year-old on growth hormones.

"Is that it?" He asked eagerly, pointing to the case.

Sullenly Bisby held it out, stiff armed with fury and embarrassment. Oz set in down on a pile of papers that immediately slid to the floor in a minor avalanche, clicked the latches and stared. "Oh, my," he said. "Oh, my my my."

Stacks of green currency banded with red paper, they filled the case completely. I wondered where Bisby had gone to find that much cash.

"Count it?" He said sullenly.

"You bet!" Oz was all smiles now. He leaned the enormous rifle against the mantle next to the mounted lion's head that growled up from the floor. Oz picked up stacks, thumbed them and set them back again, as happy as a kid with a new bike.

He did this with each packet. When he was finished, he replaced all of them in the case, closed it and clicked the latches. "Fine."

"The books," said Bisby.

"In here." Oz led him away and, after a moment I followed them into a tiny cluttered room where a cardboard beer box sat on top of an oak dresser. "These are them."

Bisby studied them. The room was stifling and the smell of cat urine was even greater in this room. He touched the plastic bag containing the misspelled *Ullyses*, reeling from the odor.

Satisfied, he picked up the box and we returned to the living room. "All right," he said. He picked up the milk crate of books and turned toward the door.

It burst open and a cop in uniform stood there, his arms outstretched in the classic shooters stance. In his hands was a very big black gun.

# CHAPTER 39

## A WHOLE LOT OF SHOOTING GOING ON

Bisby dropped the case and muttered, "Shit." Oz stood frozen near the mantelpiece. I spoke soothingly to the cop.

"It's all right, officer. There's nothing happening here."

"What's he got there? Put up your hands." Waving the gun around, it was clear the cop was terrified. He made waving motions and pointed the thing in everyone's general area. "Get over there. Hands where I can see 'em!"

Bisby and I turned to the wall and the cop went with us, forgetting Oz, the giant luring in the shadows, for exactly one second too long. Oz, breathing in and out like a bellows, sounded like a boiler about to explode. With the cop's attention distracted, he picked up the huge rifle by the barrel and swung it in a wide arc.

I screamed.

The cop, too late, fired his weapon. The explosion boomed and through the smoke we saw the rifle crash down, chopping through the cops raised arms to smash to bits on his skull. He went down like a pole-axed cow. Blood spurted on the wall and dribbled from his mouth. A pool began seeping from under his head.

"Oh, Lord," I said. I put a hand to my mouth. "I'm going to be sick." Without another word, I ran from the room and made retching noises.

I heard voices yelling. "You killed him!" Bisby.

"I had to!" Oz Gorman.

"He was a cop!" Bisby again.

Silence and "Hey, what are you doing? You can't...wait a minute. Put that down."

Another gunshot rang out and I raced back into the room to see Oz Gorman, our own Merle Crookshanks, standing against the wall with his hands to his chest. Blood was running from under that ridiculous Batman logo and his expression was one of total surprise, as if he couldn't understand what had just happened.

"What did you just do?" I squeaked from the doorway.

Merle slowly settled down the wall, like an inflatable doll losing air. He ended up in a heap on the crappy brown carpet. I felt real tears forming in my eyes and blinked to be able to see.

"Donna?" Bisby appeared to be in shock. "We gotta get out of here." He shoved his pistol back in his pocket and grabbed the milk crate. "Get the case," he demanded.

"What?"

"The case! Grab the god-damned case! We've got to go."

"Why are we taking the case?" I asked. I kept staring at Merle's body, unable to move. Bisby tugged at my arm.

"Somebody has to have heard the shots. The cops'll be here any second. We've got to get away."

"But why are we taking the money?" I asked.

"He doesn't have a use for it," Bisby laughed with an edge of hysteria. "No sense leaving it behind. He turned and ran for the door and I grabbed the case and lugged it after him.

# CHAPTER 40

## CASEY MOON

Bisby Nixon drove through the rain swollen streets like the devil was chasing us, oblivious to the danger he posed to himself or others. At a light on Garmaine Boulevard he rested his head on the steering wheel and sobbed in great gasps of relief and terror.

His cell phone rang and I gasped silently as yet another tumbler clicked in my plan. It rang again as Bisby tapped his head against the wheel, uncaring. And again.

"Um, I said. "You want to get that."

He didn't answer me, or the damn phone.

"Might be important," I said. Bisby just kept tapping his head. The phone rang once more and went silent as I closed my eyes and said a prayer to St. Disthmus to please...please! Call back.

The rain tapped against the roof rather soothingly if you weren't in the middle of a scam or contemplating how you recently killed someone. With those in mind it was annoying. I clicked the fan on high to clear the fogged windows and Bisby's cell rang again. Relief!

"Answer your damn phone," I growled, feeling real anger. Shape up, man, I thought.

Bisby shook himself, pulled out one of those really tiny phones and poked a button. Immediately I heard a whiny little voice making insistent sounds that slowly got Bisby's attention.

"What?" He said. He listened. "No way. He didn't say that. How could he be doing this?" I heard in his voice what he was thinking: why now? Why to me?

"No, Clive. I don't know where he is. Why didn't you call him? Maybe he turned it off!" Bisby was shouting with frustration now and I sympathized, a little, with the creep. His whole world was about to fall down on him if I had my way.

I said softly, "We could just go there." A subliminal trick Madame Ruth used in her act.

Bisby said to the phone, "I'll go over there. Yeah, right now. I said so, damn it!" He shut down the phone, picked third gear by mistake and the car eased forward instead of flashing away in a spray of gravel. I tried not to laugh.

We pulled up in front of a porn store called "*XXX Books*" which was direct, I supposed, if not entirely creative, and Bisby dashed out of the car. He ran to a door next to the whitewashed windows, (*Naked Girls! Magazines! Sex Toys!*) crashed through it and vanished.

I was working on the idea that things would happen so fast to Bisby that he'd never realize I was with him. Otherwise I was going to have to talk fast to avoid being thrown out again and missing the last act.

He came back a moment later with Rundell Mapes, the bruised giant. Quickly, before they could make any comment, I ducked into the cramped back seat with the money case, hiding in the shadows to be forgotten.

Bisby got in and Rundell shoved himself with some difficulty into the passenger side. He came close to filling the entire space and with his knees against his chest, his breath laboring like a broken pump, he cursed the night and the car and even the *Live Nude Girls*.

Ten very cramped minutes later we pulled up in front of the Hotel Mirabel where Casey Moon spent her time in room 315. A tan Chrysler idled at the curb and, when we pulled up, disgorged a very agitated Clive Dumont. Bisby and Rundell clambered out and I followed at a discrete distance, a fly on the wall.

Clive began yelling before they got there, making a small scene on the mostly deserted street. A uniformed doorman frowned at them and picked up a phone which I thought wasn't all that good a sign, and began to push buttons.

Clive, oblivious, was shouting. "He's going to take her! He'll call the cops."

Rundell said, "They aren't taking anybody." He shoved past the doorman and we all ran after him into the hotel.

Up three flights of stairs, left turn down a narrow hall with wine colored carpet and dark brown wood trim to a door marked 315. Rundell didn't knock. He pulled back a size fourteen boot and kicked. The door splintered, crashed open and we all raced in.

A young woman in blue jeans and white peasant shirt jumped up from the couch like a startled fawn and gaped at the intrusion. Casey

Moon. I saw the resemblance in the thick blond hair, the wide eyes, now staring in amazement.

"Oh my God," she managed before bolting to the slim chance of escape through a side door. Rundell, fast for someone so huge, grabbed her shoulder and threw her to the floor where she rolled and got up again in one gymnastic movement. She obviously knew what Rundell was here for as she began throwing plates and chairs, anything she could lay hands on.

Rundell walked through the storm and Casey retreated to a small kitchenette where she picked up a huge butcher knife. She held it in both hands like a weapon and a shield, crouching low with her back to the stove.

Rundell Mapes laughed, twisted an arm behind and pulled out a six-inch handle. He pressed a button and a long wicked looking blade sprung out. Casey Moon's eyes got even bigger, like a deer caught in the headlights of her approaching doom. As Rundell took a step closer Casey let go of the knife, grabbed a pot of coffee and smashed it over his head.

The she grabbed the knife again, leaped forward and slashed at the big man's throat. It looked like it would work. Rundell, gasping in pain at the second assault on his eyes, barely evaded the thrust. His own knife rocketed forward and plunged into Casey Moon's stomach.

Everybody froze. Casey Moon, the hilt between her fingers as red blood poured from the new hole in her belly, staggered forward, past a stunned Rundell Mapes, to the living area. She stumbled over a coffee table and fell to her knees.

She turned to look at us, making contact with her killers for a final moment, then sagged to the floor with a fluttery sigh.

Casey Moon was dead.

# CHAPTER 41

## THINGS GET WORSE

There's nothing like cops to clear a room. We all stared in silence at the bloody corpse on the floor, Rundell shaking his head in denial at Bisby who was covering his mouth against throwing up. Nobody noticed me at all.

"Bisby," said Rundell. "I didn't mean to kill her."

Just then, two uniformed cops arrived with drawn guns. One was a thin man with unruly brown hair sprouting from beneath his cap. The other was a medium built black man who gave the impression he was poorly dressed. The room lights glinted off his perfectly bald head.

This time they were real cops.

Both had the blue uniforms with wide black belts jangling with all their cop stuff. The wild haired cop stepped forward, grabbed Clive Dumont roughly by the sharp lapels of his serge suit and shoved him face first against the wall. The black cop pushed Bisby next to him. Nobody noticed me along the other wall and I waited, trying to resemble flowered wallpaper.

The black cop said, "You got 'em?" and the wild haired cop said, "uh-huh," and the bald cop holstered his gun and pulled a pair of shiny handcuffs from his utility belt.

He walked with authority to where Rundell was waiting over the motionless body of Casey Moon.

The cop said, "Hands behind your back. You know the drill." He came closer as Rundell obeyed, clicked open one cuff and Rundell clubbed him across the chest.

The cop fell like a broken doll, the cuffs skittering across the polished wood floor to hit the body of Casey Moon. The other cop turned and raised his gun but Rundell was moving now.

He barreled past the startled cop like a self-contained stampede and sped through the still open door. The cop managed a shot that splintered the wood just over his head. Then he was gone.

Clive Dumont and Bisby Nixon reacted when they heard the shot. Each spun from the wall, dropping their raised hands, and made a desperate run for freedom. The bald cop, possibly angered by being blind-sided, tripped Bisby who sprawled face down on the polished floor and skidded in a circle. The cop rose to his knees and grabbed the handcuffs, snapping them on Bisby's wrists. A track of Casey Moon's blood smeared from the cuff to Bisby's coat as he lay there in ruins.

The other cop didn't treat Clive Dumont any better. He jerked Clive's coat down, pinning his arms to his sides. He glanced around at his partner, saw a slight nod of encouragement and drove a meaty fist into Clive's belly. Clive gasped, bent over and threw up on his shoes.

With both suspects in cuffs the wild haired cop led them away out the door and the bald cop turned to study me where I was plastered against the wall.

"Dani Silver," he said.

"Rory Munson," I answered and smiled.

It's very important, if you're a grifter, to know about the police. There are cops so strict they'd bust a jaywalker, cops so fair they act as judge and jury. There are cops who give an honest crook an even break and some—like the Ace back when he was on the force—who will beat a man in a small back room. There are cops who will take every advantage...

Rory Munson and his longtime partner Carl Finch were bent cops. They'd been on the force for thirty years and crooked for all of them. They shook down merchants, curried political favors, let bad crooks pay them off and put innocent people in jail. I had hated them since they busted me for running a crystal ball scam with Madame Ruth and they took our fix money and busted us anyway.

Pops had taught me about them, all the cons knew them and avoided them like the contagious vermin they were. But, beggars can't be choosers and when I needed the worst of the worst, these are what I got.

Rory said, "Heard from your father lately? I'd sure like to see *him* again."

"You wish," I said. Back in the seventies Rory Munson almost got Leroy on a blue law beef for co-habiting with Fast Kate. They were dragged from a hotel and arrested, charged with violating the sexual decency laws under a statute written in 1864. Leroy beat the rap of course, but Kate had spent a particularly unpleasant night in Women's Prison.

"You did good, Rory," I said, through gritted teeth. "You good on our deal?"

"I arrest them and keep the money they bribe me with to let 'em go. Sure, I got it. We still talking a half-million, Dani?"

"Uh-uh." I shook my head and Rory, the predatory bastard, got a very angry look on his face.

"What the hell you doing here, Silver? Our deal..."

"Shut up, Munson. Our deal was you get what they have to bribe you with. And that, since we bargained him up, is not a half-million, but eight-hundred thousand."

"Eight," he said weakly.

"Hundred," I replied. "Thousand. But only if they walk free." I had to let Bisby and Clive get away or they'd rat out Hailey and ruin the ministry deal. But there were other ways...

Rory Munson was all smiles, as unpleasant to consider as a snake with a wounded rat. "How do I get it?"

"Ask them. They've got the money—in cash—nearby. How you get it from them is up to you."

"Oh, I'll get it," he said and I had no doubt about it. Clive and Bisby were in for a very bad evening before they gave up the suitcase. The best part would be that Clive, having nothing to bargain with, would have to be grateful to Bisby, even as he found out about Bisby's theft. That turn felt good to me, almost like justice.

Rory, smiling like a well-fed vulture, strutted out of the room and, hopefully, out of my life and I turned back to the room. Casey Moon still lay where she'd fallen in her own gore and I hurried over to her, feeling suddenly guilty.

"Get up, get up get up," I said quickly. I dropped to my knees and apologized. "Sorry for leaving you like this so long. Are you okay?"

"I'm fine." Casey Moon sat up, looked at the fake blood all over her peasant blouse and said, "Yuck. Dammit Dani, do you know how hard it is to lay there in this fake blood without moving? I thought you were never going to get them out of here."

She rolled over, rose to her knees, up to her feet, a kind of creepy reenactment of the resurrection. "I know, Patty. But you did that so well. Thought you were dead myself and I planned all this."

"And you planned great, Dani! That was more fun than any raggle I've ever run. I don't know how to thank you." She gave me a hug that smeared the fake blood of the cackle-bladder all over my shirt. "Oh, my God! I'm sorry. Here, get that off and I'll run it under cold water."

"Later Patty. I think it's a better idea to get the hell out of here."

"Why?" she asked, confused. Her mind was still focused on the blood stain. "You bought off the cops, didn't you?"

"I did, but with those two vipers there's no telling how long they'll stay bought. But that's not the problem." I hurried her to the door and took a last fond look around. My first major con scene. I was so proud.

Going down the back stairs Patty asked, "Why are we in a hurry?'

"Well, you know, the reason the cops are letting them go?"

"Bisby and Clive? Because you bribed them."

"Uh, no, not exactly. I set up a deal where Bisby is going to bribe them. With the money he brought for the book buy."

"Oh Dani," she said. "I get it. We're going to lose the payoff when Bisby gives it to the cops."

"Nope," I said. We reached the main floor and ducked out the back way. Patty had her rented Nissan parked at the curb and we got in and drove away.

"I switched the cases as soon as we entered the store," I said. "I have the eight-hundred large that Bisby brought in."

"Then...?" I let it hang for a moment, a major discovery just waiting to burst into view. Patty turned my way, her mouth opened as she got it.

"Bisby is bribing the cops with counterfeit money!"

"Yes," I said.

"Dani, you swindled the cops."

"Yes," I said.

"But won't they go after Bisby and Clive?"

"Certainly," I said. But those guys will be long gone. And with cops like Munson and Finch after them they will never ever be heard from again."

Patty glowed with delight. "Dani, you are amazing!"

"Yes," I said.

# CHAPTER 42

## THE WINDUP...AND THE BITCH

I thought of loose ends that need clearing up as we motored slowly through the Louisiana darkness. I didn't know how long it would take Bisby Nixon to crack or if Munson and Finch would tie me into their troubles this quickly, but I was not about to take any chances.

I was worried about Merle Crookshanks, since the last time I'd seen him he was holding on to a bullet wound to the chest. Sure, I'd swapped the guns and set up Ray Sanchez as the phony cop, but Merle looked so real crumpled on the floor that I felt a stab of anxiety whenever I thought of him.

Patty drove us to the house of the madman Oz Gorman, a fellow about to disappear forever. As we drove I told her about the events we weren't going to stay around to see.

"Bisby's convinced that he's got a fortune in rare books," I said. "He'll get out of town so fast he'll leave his shadow behind. Clive Dumont..." I wondered.

Patty said, "He doesn't have a lot of money does he?" I shook my head, considering the angles.

"No, and I can't predict what he'll do. He doesn't have a hold on Hailey Briscoe anymore and he thinks he saw Casey Moon murdered. He won't realize the money is fake until the cops bust him and by then they'll be so pissed they won't believe anything he says."

"So what do you think he'll do?"

"I dunno. Run away early? I can see him doing that. But staying around? He was born and raised here so maybe he'll stay. Doesn't matter to us either way."

Patty said, "That Rundell Mapes creature..."

"I know," I said. "Isn't he a piece of work?" The melody for *Bad Bad Leroy Brown* ran through my brain like a bad tape and I cursed the Ace for putting it there.

"He thinks there's a murder rap waiting for him. He's already gone."

"I think so," I agreed. *Baddest man in the whole damn...* Argh. "Maybe something will catch up to him, somewhere, someday. But it won't be me. I've had more than enough of Rundell Mapes.

As we neared the old house Patty slowed to a crawl. "What about Pamela Asbury? What do you think she's going to do?"

"Pamela?" I said. "Oh, I have something special planned for her.

We ran into the house with worry for Merle scrambling our imaginations. The door was open and I flew inside with my stomach twisting. The room was as dark as I'd left it, lit by that damn dim bulb

Ray in his cop outfit was already gone but as I reached the living room my worst fears were realized. Merle Crookshanks lay on the floor where he'd fallen, bloody and dead.

"Oh, shit." The bright yellow Batman logo, worn to attract Bisby's bullet, was torn and a gaping red wound lay beneath it. The blood had long since dried and as I dropped to my knees I began to cry.

What had happened? The gun should have had blanks in it. I changed it myself. Merle was supposed to trigger a flash-bang mounted under the logo which would rip the shirt and look like an impact. He should have triggered the cackle-bladder to spew blood and fallen.

What had gone wrong?

I reached out a tentative hand to touch his shoulder, feeling sick inside. Oh Merle, I thought dismally. My first caper and you go and die on me. You bastard...you utter bastard.

Just as my hand reached him his own hand reached up to grab it. In every ghost story Pops ever read me when I was a young impressionable girl, they used the expression, "her heart stopped."

My heart stopped. I screamed and fell back on my butt, scrambling backwards like the devil himself was after me.

Instead of the devil, Merle Crookshanks, bald and grinning, sat up with his back to the wall. His face, macabre with the fake scars in the eerie lighting, looked like a jack-o-lantern on the world's worst Halloween. He began laughing so hard that tears poured down his cheeks.

"What?" I said through a suddenly dry mouth. "What the *hell*..."

Singing from the kitchen drew my shocked attention. A flickering light floated down the hall as I made out the words. *"For she's a jolly good fellow...for she's a jolly good fellow."*

Ray Sanchez entered the room carrying a flat cake. On the cake was a single candle. Behind him came Sammy Hensel, Cincinnati Bob Wilkerson and old Hank. They were all smiling and singing off-key.

I gaped at them, then at Merle who was leaning on one elbow on the floor. "You set me up," I said.

"Yuh-huh," he agreed.

"You guys were watching at the window," I said.

"Yeah."

"And you got into position to scare me half to death."

"You bet."

"Merle?" I said.

"Yes, Dani?"

"You're a dick."


We sat on the filthy floor amid the decaying newspapers, the hundred ticking clocks and the reeking cat urine and I asked the question I should have asked a lot earlier.

"Ray? Where'd you get cat urine?"

"It's eucalyptus scent," he answered seriously. I found a lab over in Chattanooga makes it."

"Why?" asked Patty. "Would anybody want this smell?"

"That I don't know."

I had to say it. Despite my deepest misgivings I had to say it. "Ray, you are one hell of a fixer."

Everybody cheered in agreement and Ray leaned in close. Softly, his voice a near whisper, he said, "What did you do with the girl?"

I laughed. "Not telling."

"Dani...c'mon."

"All right. If you must know."

"I must, I must." I laughed at the line from *Blazing Saddles*.

"I let her go. Took her to a bus stop and gave her twenty bucks for a ride home." I looked into his eyes and shrugged. "I let her go."

He studied my face for a moment and sighed. "Figured. But," and now his face lit up. "That's not what's going to happen in my dreams."

The party broke up early since cake—devil's food, appropriate choice—and cat piss don't go well together. Merle carried the duplicate case to Patty's Nissan and I told them I'd wire their shares to whatever accounts they wanted. There was no issue of trust. A grifter's word was his bond; they all knew they'd be paid.

Patty drove me to my motel and I hugged her tightly.

"You did good, girl," she said from a firm embrace. "I'm proud of you."

For the second time in one night I felt tears in my eyes.

I felt them again twenty minutes after she'd gone as I lugged the case to the trunk of my rented car. Four-hundred thousand dollars, a huge score. Even with bonus payments to everyone I'd still make up my losses and have a profit. Add the Ace's money and I was well ahead.

Add the hundred-thousand I got from Pamela Asbury...

Pamela. I pulled into a Texaco truck stop on a deserted stretch of road where the white lights made a bright puddle of safety in a dark world. I slid the rented car into a space near the restrooms and went to the pay phone bolted to the white ceramic brick wall.

The money Bisby had stolen was not his own. That had always been part of the plan, although no one but me knew it. It was critical that Bisby be denied the use of his own fortune just long enough to make him go to the one source of cash available in a hurry.

The Investment Group's money. The start-up capital came from Pamela Asbury who in turn embezzled it from the retirement fund of the local Teamsters. Pamela was a high-ranking officer and had access to their money. It must have been an easy decision to take it. Retirement funds are invested for long term growth and an audit might not discover anything for years.

Easily long enough for Pamela to pay it back when the flood waters finally receded and the politicians did the work they were paid for. When the Ninth Ward was declared safe to build Pamela would make millions.

With the investment group broken and the male members fleeing like the cockroaches they were, Pamela was now in sole command of an illegal fortune.

Or maybe not...I had scammed Bisby and Clive for money. I'd driven away the brute Rundell Mapes to keep Hailey and his sister safe. I had allowed myself to be used by Pamela to disgrace and frame Tyler Cruz and Reggie Skye. None of them would pose a threat to the new ministry or talk about their connection to the church.

No one but Pamela Asbury stood to collect from the events I'd set in motion. Unfortunately—for Pamela—I had planned to betray her from the start.

I dropped a couple of quarters in the slot and dialed a memorized number.

"Teamsters Local Fifty-Three," said a woman with a deep Southern drawl.

"Yes," I said. "I'd like to report a theft of the retirement fund."

Pamela Asbury wouldn't last a week.

I left Louisiana in no hurry but with no interest in staying either. The grifter's guidebook, if there was such a thing, mandated a hasty retreat from the wrath of the mark. In this case, I had no fear. My marks would be too busy to come looking for me.

With a light heart and a trunk load of cash I turned the car onto the open road, heading for home.

# CHAPTER 43

## ONE LAST LITTLE THING

"Gee it's good to be back home again," I sang, with perfect pitch and style that would make Madonna blanch with envy. I'm not as a rule a big John Denver fan but he sure pegged it on that one. I sang the last line again as I pulled into the driveway of my very own place. Perfect timing.

Everything was coming up aces, and not just the ones I usually palmed. Hailey was again an honest phony minister, Bisby and Clive were having unique and wonderful relations with the New Orleans Police Department and I was up a couple of hundred grand.

A couple of hundred grand! It made my heard skip just thinking about it. Queen's *Bohemian Rhapsody* came on and I sang lustily in the privacy of the car, breathing like a balloon about to burst.

I was just at the high part, you know; the one where everybody thinks they can hit it but they can't and it always sounds like cats sucking helium as their tails are stepped on.

A hard rapping on the window just as I reached for the note made me shriek and lurch back in the seat, totally freaked out. Wide-eyed I followed some knuckles up an arm wrapped in red flannel to the straps of a faded denim coverall to a face peering down through my window with as worried an expression as I have ever seen.

He rapped again and said something I couldn't hear. I held up a finger—not that one—to suggest he wait, turned off the radio and hand-cranked down the window.

"What?" I said, not pleasantly.

"You ok?"

"I saw you pull in," he said. "Been wanting to talk to you. I thought you were having a stroke or something."

"Or something," I agreed, though I hadn't until he showed up. "The hell do you want?"

"I'm Garland," he said, holding out a well-creased hand. "Plumtree."

His handshake was as firm and full of promise as any Pops had ever given and, I decided, as honest. He pumped it four times and let go. "I'm the general contractor around here," he said.

He pointed toward the road and I looked. A red pickup sat at the curb covered with built on metal cabinets and ladders and handles of tools sticking out. It looked like a tomato designed by a government committee. A magnetic sign on the side said, *'Plumtree and Sons— General Contractors'* in black block letters. Under that it added, *'You'll be plum happy when you hire Plumtree!'*

Good God. I turned back to him to reject whatever approach he was about to offer but somehow, he managed to lightly touch my elbow and turn me to the house. His spiel, no doubt a practiced part of his bag of tools, swept over me like one of my own and I smiled with sudden amusement.

"This here house," said Garland, in a voice of the working man, "Is a beauty. One of the last of a dying breed, Mrs…?" He paused and I waited until he realized I wasn't offering a name.

"Mrs..?" He said slowly, as if to a sheep.

"Yes?" I asked, wide-eyed with innocent confusion.

He said again, "Mrs.…?" stretching out the syllables and I watched him, leaning in with bright curiosity, shaking my pretty little head as if I just…didn't… get it.

"Mrs.…," he said, stood up stiffly and frowned. "Oh, fer…what's your *name?*"

"Mona," I said, like I was just now catching on. "Mona Pasternelli from Queens, New York."

"Finally," he muttered, and resumed his pitch.

Which was, I discovered eventually, after he talked me into my own house and led me around each and every room, that the house needed work. A lot of work.

"See that?" He said, many times. He pointed to drywall needing patching, wallpaper hiding all manner of crawling things, bathroom fixtures that sure; weren't leaking *now*, but what about in the future? "Do you really want to take that chance, Mona?"

"This kitchen," he explained with grave solemnity, "will require a complete redo. Those cabinets. The countertops." He guided me to the living room.

Which, "Needs more light," He explained. "We could jut out that wall there, put in a bay window, extend the outside porch, make it a wraparound…"

"I don't," I said, "Need any of these things."

"Sure, sure," agreed Garland. "But this wall here…"

"Mr. Plumtree," I said.

"That's a bearing wall." He had his orange measuring stick out and was unfolding like a magic box. He held it against a wall, took out a fat red pencil and scrawled something in a tiny pocket notepad.

"Mr. Plumtree," I said. My amusement at this odd person was beginning to fade. I was tired from the long drive wanted a good dinner, with wine and a fattening desert that I wasn't likely to get here in Jamestown. It was already past six and Kansas City, where all those things could be found, was an hour or more away.

"Garland!" I out two fingers in my mouth and gave a sharp whistle. He jerked and dropped his orange stick. "You need to go."

"I'm just finishing my measurements," he said.

"Fine. Go. Send me an estimate." I wasn't going to hire him but didn't want to make a scene.

"I'll just write it up in my truck."

"Do it later," I said, leading him in the direction of the front door, which he explained needed to be replaced.

"Get you one of those new ones with the built-in screens."

"Just send the estimate."

"You want me to drop it off in the morning? It's not a bother."

It was to me. I intended to sleep until noon.

"Why didn't you E-mail it?" I asked.

"Wassat?"

"The internet."

"Wassat?"

"A computer?" I suggested.

"Oh, *that*." I'd never heard such disdain before. "I don't do them things. What I do is fix up old beauties like this one. See; if you just think about how easy…"

## THE END

Hi all, I hope you enjoyed this first book in the Grifter's Daughter Series. The sequel, GHOST COACH is coming soon. Check out the first chapters below.

I'd be grateful for any comments and reviews you can post on Amazon. The reviews help me get promotion which helps a lot in the sales of the books.

There's a couple chapters from MISSING AMANDA, the great Lou Fleener Private Eye Novel.

There's also a glimpse at another new book, this one written by my longtime friend and co-writer Raymond Dean White. It's called Tap Doubt.

By the way, feel free to check out Ray's work. If you're a fan of apocalyptic books – and who isn't? – his 'The Dying Time' and sequels are amazing fun books to read.

You can find him at

http://www.RaymondDeanWhite.com

And me, of course, at:

http://www.DuaneLindsay.com

A Comic Thriller — Dani Silver - # 2

# GHOST
# COACH

DUANE LINDSAY

## CHAPTER ONE
## DANI MAKES A DEAL

The problem with a small town is that the same guy who tried to pick you up last Friday night at the Hoot 'n' Holler will likely be the guy trying to sell you that new yellow Prius at the October Toyotathon.

"Mona!" He greeted me, that being the name I gave him— and everyone else—here in the tiny hamlet of Jamestown, Missouri. I couldn't tell if the enthusiasm was for Mona the potential date or Mona the potential commission. Either way his smile lit up the night like a bug-zapper when he saw me next to the car. "Looking to buy some new wheels?"

I was, since my last car, a perfectly restored '64 ½ Mustang convertible, had been towed to a wrecking yard in New Orleans, victim to too much trust on my part and too little sense on Marcy's. Drugs and alcohol contributed; hers—I don't do drugs. My little car was DOA.

Hence the evening visit to Burt's Auto World on the corner of Packer Blvd and County Road 119. I was bored and felt the need to do something impulsive. And I needed a car.

Matt Langly, car salesman and bar troller, rolled his eyes at the Prius and tried to steer me to an enormous SUV, maroon colored, with all the charm of a box of weeds. I herded him back to the Prius.

"What's your best price?" I asked.

Matt cocked his head like a sparrow or a slave auctioneer sizing me up for market. "Well, this is your lucky day, Mona." He touched my elbow to lead me closer to the office, a tactic used by sales people and con artist alike. Also by preachers and politicians. If there's a difference, I've never been able to tell.

Matt said, "Little Lady, I'm sure we can come to a price you're gonna love. If you'll just step into my office?" Said the spider to the fly.

I was also sure we'd come to a price I loved because I was a con artist, trained by the best in the business—my father, Leroy

Logan. Eating people like Matt Langly had been Pops' and my full time meals for a long, long time. As we entered his office, a cubicle only slightly larger than my proposed Toyota, Matt was already rubbing his hands with anticipation.

I could see him totaling numbers, already convinced he had the sale and a sizable markup as well. I was, after all, 'the little lady.' Fresh meat to a hungry shark.

I sat, he leaned on the counter to better look superior, offer pad held ready in expectation. "So," he said, pencil poised, "what kind of payments do you have in mind?"

"None."

"What?"

"Cash." This was first misstep in a complicated dance but Matt recovered nicely, painting the smile back almost before I saw it slip.

"But," he said patiently, "it's a forty thousand dollar car."

"No it isn't," I said. "MSRP is forty-three-five. Your advertised price is Thirty-seven-nine. You'll let it go, for cash, at twenty-eight even." I smiled my best Sunday-go-to meeting-smile, the one that left them breathless with desire.

Matt's smile faltered but he recovered smoothly enough. "That's below our cost." He chuckled, always amused at the ways of women. "I can offer you an interest rate of only one point nine percent. Or a discount of…" he paused, looked reverential and breathed out in wonder, "six thousand dollars." The amazed expression was almost sincere.

I said, "If I bought this car, Matt, how much would you get as a commission?"

Frowning, he said, "I don't understand."

"You commission, Matt; how much." I knew how much. I'd been at the Hoot 'n Holler specifically looking for him. Matt Langly had been fishing that night but so had I. As he sized me up as a potential meal, I had appraised him in turn. A greedy man, I determined, with an appetite that was never satisfied. When I had turned down his sexual advances he had easily drifted away, certain that he'd find another.

It was that hunger for more that I was playing here. I had learned, in my lifelong experiences as a con artist, that people who crave more than they deserve or need are the easiest marks. Matt, I saw, from the slight sheen of perspiration on his upper lip, sensed profit.

Like bait to a shark I thought. Like a mirror to Narcissus.

I said, "Let's go back and look at the car, shall we?" and he followed like a hound on a scent. Inside the Toyota, the black bucket seat snuggling around me and that new car smell overpowering even the scent of money, I took and envelope from my purse and began counting out one hundred dollar bills on the console. I noted that there were two cup holders, which pleased me. I liked my coffee when I drive.

Matt said weakly, "What are you doing," but stared as I got to fifteen bills and stopped. "The car," he said, swallowing, "costs…"

I counted out another five bills and put my wallet away. Matt stared at the money, sighed, and came to a decision. He scooped up the bills as smoothly as any dealer in Vegas clearing the table.

He said, "Shall we get to the paperwork?"

That, I thought, as I drove away in my new Prius, as yellow as the sun on a new morning, was fun.


Fun is another thing that doesn't last a long time in a small town. At least if you're a big city girl like me, raised in the bustling center of new Orleans. I missed the crowds, I wanted the opportunities afforded by a lot of people all bent on getting something for nothing. I wanted some excitement.

Dammit; I wanted Nick.

I drove, far too fast, down a country lane just like the other four country lanes that led out of Jamestown, north to Bodkin's Corner, south to Harper, west to Plymouth and east into the blinding sun. Nick Kuiper, multi-millionaire businessman, philanthropist and general all around swell guy and I had been lovers, not so long ago in New York City. I met him when this rich family had tried to swindle his company and I helped him swindle it back.

We celebrated by him proposing marriage, offering me luxury, love, security and peace, but not freedom. Marrying Nick, it was implied, meant giving up my larcenous streak.

It meant giving up my freedom. My answer, I am ashamed to say, was to steal the $600,000 dollars we had scammed from the bad guys, along with an additional 600 grand Nick had put up as a convincer. Driving along these arrow straight gently rolling roads in middle America I felt a small sense of guilt over that.

But I had, in my way, made it up to him by proposing a game. I would hide from him and Nick could find me. If he did, I'd be his, a prize in a game of hide and seek. If I kept the game going long enough to work through my issues of freedom/matrimony, a struggle faced by more women than anyone realizes, I would, I hoped, get to the point of wanting to be with him.

So I moved here to Jamestown, Missouri, bought a house under an assumed name, hid my tracks with amazing ingenuity and waited for Nick to make an appearance. I had been waiting now for three months and was getting bored and a little angry.

I mean, the man was a *millionaire*; how hard could it be to track a single woman in a red Mustang and two fat suitcases full of cash? Sure, I'd avoided the usual mistakes; no credit cards to leave a trail, no airplanes to record my real name. I had avoided speeding and stayed out of trouble, except for a little scam down in Louisiana.

Or that lottery scam with my ex-neighbor and lost friend Marcy. I thought of her, a mousy young woman I'd taken under my wing after her brute of a husband beat her up. I'd stung Brock, the husband, pretty hard, making him believe he'd won the state lottery. The following train wreck, when he quit his job, left his wife and insulted everyone on national television had been his own doing.

But Marcy couldn't handle independence and gotten involved with a creep nearly as bad as Brock, a no-account jackass named Jiggs Roche. The last time I'd seen Marcy she was trying to decide which of these idiots she was going to throw her life away with.

Not that I'm bitter, mind you, but did she have to take my car with her? To say nothing of nearly getting me arrested and blowing the long con I'd been setting up for weeks?

"Not hardly," I said aloud. My voice sounded small in the cool breeze pouring in over the windshield. I began to wonder, for the first time, just how hard Nick was trying. Did he even think about me anymore or had he written off my theft as a lesson in life and moved on?

I had an overwhelming urge to find out. I turned around at an historical marker inexplicably placed in the middle of nowhere. I saw that it had something to do with a wagon train that had stopped here in 1873 but I drove on without reading further. Who cared, I wondered? I mean, who *cared*?

So I drove, still too fast for someone trying to keep a low profile, back to the large old country house I'd been living in instead of the ecologically friendly McMansion Nick owned on Long Island. As expected, Garland Plumtree, my lazy contractor, was parked in the driveway, casually assembling tools to begin his arduous workday. It was, after all, ten-thirty.

"Hey, Ms. Pasternelli," he called out with the cheerful good will of a man who knows he's got you by the balls, metaphorically speaking. "Beautiful morning, isn't it?" He raised a well-tanned arm toward the heavens as if it was his own personal accomplishment.

"What's left of it, "I answered, a bit more short tempered than I'd intended. His large face, mostly jowls and sagging skin, settled into a kicked puppy wounded expression, one that I knew he used to good effect in getting out of the many promises he made all over town. "Sure, Mr. Johnson; Friday at eight's fine. I'll be there tomorrow, Mrs. Smith; first thing in the morning. The project will only take a couple of weeks, Ms. Pasternelli; I'll have her buttoned up in jig time."

But first thing in the morning to a contractor meant anything between ten and two, the couple of weeks was now at two months and counting and I still had no idea what 'jig time' meant.

Nothing quick, certainly. In the meantime my kitchen was mostly in the backyard, my living room was uninhabitable and only by threatening violence had I managed to keep the upstairs bathroom undamaged. Garland Plumtree, as a general contractor, shared that view of his fellow tradesmen that a house should be completely taken apart before any repairs could possibly begin.

And though he hadn't achieved his preferred goal, I had twice had to stop him from taking down a ceiling or removing all the electrical wiring. He walked over, admiring the new car by nodding with thumbs hooked into his measuring tape suspenders. On a man as taken to flab as Garland, these were not a sensible fashion.

"New car?" He asked as I got out.

"Finished with my house?" I said, by way of not answering. He laughed, as if this was a joke, which I suppose, to him, it was. I'd never had any idea how he made a living, never completing a project, and I had a suspicion that Garland Plumtree was as much a con artist in his way as I was, in mine.

"That's a good one, Ms. Pasternelli," he said companionably and I fled to the ruins of my house, utterly defeated. I went upstairs to the only working room in the house and threw my keys on the bed. The door was open and I saw that Maximillian had once again managed to get in.

Maximillian was a huge black tomcat who had wandered into my house a month ago and declared it his own. I'd been his servant ever since and he came and went as he pleased, as free a spirit as any ghost. I catered to his every whim and spoiled him and would feel awful on that inevitable day he decided not to return.

He rolled over on his back on my bedspread, stretched mightily and agreed that I could rub his belly. He asked if I'd brought him anything and shrugged when I said no. Maximillian and I had an arrangement—he could do whatever he wanted and I'd allow it.

"No, he's not done," I explained to the cat as I wandered around the room, straightening things that didn't need straightening, putting away my shoes, slipping into moccasins and jeans. I made sure the shades were drawn as I'd twice been surprised by faces in the window; men on ladders hardly working hard.

The idea of calling Nick both excited and unnerved me and I was unused to the sensation of dread. Normally I'm as shy as Maximillian there, lying on someone else's bed with the calm assurance that it's really his. Stealing Nick's money had been an impulse that came straight from my true nature. I'm a gypsy, trained to commit felonies, minimizing damage by doing only what I thought was right. Nick didn't need the money, I'd return it if and when he caught up with me and we'd both have fun in the meantime.

Except...he didn't seem to be enjoying it as much as he should. What fun is a game of hide and seek when hider isn't being sought? As I paced I began to get angry, my usual response to ambiguity and by the time I picked up the phone I was in a state of smoldering fury. All it would take is a small breeze to fan it into flame.

That breeze was supplied by an annoying secretary who, upon my request to speak to, "Nick Kuiper, please," informed me that he wasn't taking any calls, "at this time."

"He'll take this one, sweetie," I said. "Tell him Dani's calling."

"Who?" She asked.

"Dani," I said. "Silver. Trust me; he'll want this call." But would he? I wondered. Had he written me off as just another bad investment? Would he still be interested? A rare sense of doubt hit me and I felt like hanging up but I'd come this far.

Not that my resolve mattered. In an annoying New York voice that grated like a nail on a chalkboard, little miss efficiency announced, "Mr. Kuiper gave instructions not to be bothered." Her tone strongly implied, "especially by you."

I was about to make one *honey* of a response when the phone went dead in my hand. I pressed redial and heard no answering tone. The damn thing was off.

"What the *Hell*?" I said, startling Maximillian into giving me a vocal complaint.

I glared at the phone and apologized to the cat and went looking for someone to throw it at. I found the target in the smiling face of Garland himself, casually walking alongside the house winding a cable around his arm into a compact coil. He wore the bemused look of a man who's done a good job but stopped when I held the phone in front of his face and shook it.

"Oh," he said. "You were making a call?"

"I was," I said, with what passed for dignity. I fought off a desire to strangle the man with my own phone cord. "Why are you tearing out my phone line?"

"I needed to move it," he explained, pointing back toward the garage, "over there."

"And you didn't think maybe I'd need the phone?"

He didn't appear to have considered that. "I thought," he said, "that you had one of those cordless phones."

"I do," I said, showing it to him. But even a cordless phone needs a phone line."

"It does?" He pushed his ball cap back and scratched a nearly bald head, puzzled. "Then why do they call them wireless?"

"Because they're…" I stopped and gaped at his innocent face, completely unable to continue. I wanted a beer at that moment, or a cigarette, which I hadn't in over two decades. I wanted to scream at him to get finished and get out. I wanted to…

What? What did I want? Certainly not what I had, which was a ruined house in a tiny town and a love affair with a man who didn't seem to care that I was gone. The game, which I'd thought would be so exciting, felt like ashes in my mouth and I turned about face, marched to my new car and drove off without another word. Behind me, a shocked and wounded Garland Plumtree held out my telephone line like an offering to an angry God. As I roared out of the driveway in a very satisfying spray of gravel I heard him say, "You want me to put it back?"

# MISSING AMANDA

## WE HAVE YOUR DAUGHTER

### DUANE LINDSAY

A LOU FLEENER DETECTIVE THRILLER

# MISSING AMANDA - PREVIEW

## 1 - August 19, 1958 – Chicago

"Gotta go, gotta go, gotta go…"

Paul E. Smalls, in a two-room flat near Bryn Mawr, frantically stuffed clothes into a battered leather grip. His tan cotton pants were dirty, the white wife-beater tee stained and his brown shoes were scuffed. Everything else went into the case or onto the floor.

He paused at a picture of his sister, tossed it in the bag, scanned the room and decided enough was enough. He threw on a shirt, tails out and unbuttoned, and slapped a fedora over his thinning hair, closed the bag and ran for the door.

The mob, he thought as he dashed down the stairs two at a time. Jesus Christ, being chased by the damn mob. A choked sound came from his throat as he careened from the wall, off balance, and legged it down the last flight at the back of the building. He looked both ways and dashed for the black Ford Fairlane convertible across the alley.

He almost made it. The case was in the back seat, his keys in his hand and his mind already on the road when something heavy hit him between the shoulder blades. He went down like a wet sack of cement, his back screaming in agony.

Feet came into view, black tie-ons, argyle socks, brown cuffs above them. Paul E. cringed and tried to scuttle backwards, crablike but hands lifted him, not gently, to his feet.

Paul E. felt the harsh acid of rising bile. So close, so goddam close. If only he'd rabbited sooner.

The guy shook him, making Paul E's head roll around. From nearly closed lids Paul E. saw the goons' hard expression and knew there'd be no mercy here, no sympathy. The ox was low grade muscle, paid to beat people and bring them to his masters.

The mob. Fear like he'd never known went through his gut. The ox worked for Cermak. Guzman Cermak – *Cermak the Surgeon*. Stories of Sadism and torture attributed to the crime boss were legendary and if even half were true, Paul E. was in for a world of hurt.

Cermak. They say he carried a scalpel in his lapel pocket...

The ox shook him again and Paul E. pretended to be out, thinking of what he could do. He could scream but who'd listen? He could fight but why bother? It would be like hitting the brick wall behind him.

But...Ox didn't have a gun, or didn't have it out, which was the same thing, In Paul E.s world, if you don't pull a gun you didn't intend to use one. So that was one good thing. And here was another: the guy was alone.

Probably didn't expect trouble from a private dick with a camera. Good. There might be a chance after all. He willed himself to stop shaking.

He groaned again, theatrically, making it sound worse than it felt. His right shoulder where the ox had hit him was numb and useless, maybe broken, but his left felt okay If he did this right he might live to see Wisconsin.

He waved a hand feebly – no acting there – as if to ward off the goon.

He heard a laugh like the braying of a not particularly bright mule, but the vicelike grip on his arm lessoned. Paul E. slumped against the Fairlane, across the open window and slid down as if falling inside. His left hand scrabbled for the gun...

Ox said, "Hey! Get up," like a junk yard dog who could talk. He grabbed Paul E. by the shirt and yanked, expecting dead weight. The unbuttoned shirt ripped off. Paul E. came up fast and the goon overcompensated. Paul E. swatted at the horn in the center of the steering wheel and the Ford made a loud blatting noise, further startling the goon. Paul E. spun around with a silver .22 and pointed it straight into the guy's startled face.

The ox stepped back suddenly, like he'd been stung by a bee, the alley exploded with sound and a bullet shattered the Ford's side mirror. There *was* another one.

Paul E. reacted with the Army training from the war not that many years ago. He pulled the trigger twice and the little .22 cracked in the alley. The ox went down bellowing in pain and Paul E. swiveled left and dropped to his knees, feeling a bullet flash over his head even as he heard the blast.

Five more time he fired his pistol, emptying it. A shadow teetered over a garbage can and fell into a shallow puddle of muck. Just like at the target range Paul E. thought, blessing his foresight in keeping up with his training. What would a private dick be without it?

Dead, that's what, and not pleasantly. He tossed the now empty gun into the back with the valise, opened the door and cursed. He couldn't just leave the dead guys, not with his apartment just across the alley and himself about to vanish. The cops would put that together like lightning and the search would be on.

No, gotta do something else. With his left arm useless the chore would be difficult but not impossible he pushed and pulled and dragged the nearest thug to the car, thanking Ford for the size of the trunk. He fit neatly, just above the spare.

Paul E. went to the other guy – ox – and was surprised to see him still breathing. Well, not for long. Paul E. went back to the trunk, took the gun off the body, a nice silver plated .38, went back and shot ox twice in the chest. The gun jumped in his hand and Paul E. flinched at the sound.

Farther away, ox took a bit more effort to drag to the car but soon he was slouched in the back seat like he was sleeping off a drunk. Paul E. pulled the ragtop into place, lugged it down with some difficulty, rolled up the window and got in. he drove carefully down the alley, made a left on 54th and hightailed it to the safety of Baraboo.

Hey Rube, he thought. I'm coming.


"It's open."

Lou Fleener was admiring the White Sox coverage in the Tribune when a shadow darkened the frosted glass of his office window. The Sox were in second place, the Cubs in third. Louis Aparicio was hotter than the August weather. Was there a God? Could it happen?

" Lou called to the shave-and-a-haircut rapping at the door. He set down the paper and watched with interest as a big guy in a new Poplin suit pushed the door and shoved it closed with his hip. He shuffled across the dusty green and white checkered linoleum and sat in the guest chair. If an elephant wore summer weight cotton, it would look like this guy. The chair creaked.

"You Fleener?"

"What it says on the door." *'Lou Fleener – Private Eye –'* backwards in gold letters, painted on by a cousin of Monk's.

"Smart guy," said the suit.

"Lou shrugged modestly. "It's true." He put his feet on the scuffed wooden desk and leaned back. "What can I do for you?

"Word on the street is you're good."

"Word's right."

The guy cocked a jaw and bit his lip. His hair was cut short like a Marine, flat on top and razored on the sides. He didn't look like a customer, but what does a customer look like? There had been so few lately that Lou lacked perspective.

The suit fidgeted, took a pack of Lucky's from an inside pocket and lit one from a gold Zippo. Lou pulled an ashtray from the drawer and slid it across the desk, a thick chunky glass souvenir from the Palmer Hotel. The bottom said 'A handy place to stay,' in red ink under a pair of black dice. Classy.

Lou studied the visitor for a moment as the smoke filled the small room. Nice suit, good cut, one of those new polyester fabrics, it covered the muscles as if tailored and concealed the gun under the left armpit. The guy was a blond with the features of a body builder gone soft.

"Hey," he said. "I know you!"

"No, you don't."

"Yeah. Yeah I do." Lou snapped his fingers. "Wait a minute, it'll come to me."

"It doesn't matter who I am. I've been sent –"

"Got it! You're Milt Stiltmeyer." Lou slapped the desk in delight. "I'm right, right? Milt the Stilt?" Lou sounded like a fan at Comisky meeting Minnie Minoso. In a moment he'd be asking for an autograph.

The guy made hands down motions, like quieting down a rowdy dog. "It don't matter who I am," he said. "I'm here to bring you to –"

But Lou wasn't balked. "I know I'm right. Millie the Killer they call you. 'Cause you killed that guy, what was his name? Stubbs, right, while you were wearing a dress.

Milt looked pained.

"Sure," Lou said, "I know all about you."

Now Milt looked concerned. "How?"

"I read about you. In the Trib. I got a scrapbook,"

"The hell you mean, a scrapbook? You got a scrapbook of thugs?"

"Sure." Lou didn't mention that it was Monk's idea and that he'd been against it.

Monk said, "If you're going to do this – be a private eye –the least you can do is be prepared. You've got to study, know your enemies."

Monk talked like that, like he graduated from Loyola or someplace. "It could save your life." Then he'd gone off to his used book store down on Clark street and came back with this huge pile of old musty newspapers and made Lou go through them every Thursday night. The company had been good, the beers cold and Lou had gotten into it, learning the names, nicknames and habits of the current Chicago mob scene.

And now, here was one of them - in person! Lou could hardly contain his glee.

"Bummer of a name, man," he told Milt with real sympathy, meaning it. "Other guys have cool names like Sammy 'the icepick' or Bugsy Siegel or 'Scarface' Al. But you got saddled with 'Millie.'" Lou shook his head at the unfairness of the world. "Coffee?"

"The name's not important" Milt said through clenched teeth, like he'd been explaining this most of his life, which he probably had. "I'm here to take you to see –"

"Duke Braddock," Lou finished for him. "You're muscle for Duke Braddock."

Milt looked uncomfortable with that, pursing his lips around the cigarette and puffing like a '53 Buick Roadmaster. He started through the growing haze until Lou thought he'd maybe quietly choked to death. But, "Okay," he said. "I work for Duke Braddock. You heard of him?"

"Course," said Lou. He sat up straight and his office chair creaked. "Who hasn't?"

Even without Monk's research Lou would have heard about Braddock. Bookie, prostitutes, marijuana, some said Coke and the big H – heroin. If it was illegal or killed you it was probably connected to Braddock.

"The mob guy," he said simply.

"The *businessman*," corrected Milt.

"The businessman then," Lou agreed, smiling. No way, he decided, was he going to take this case. Duke Braddock was a major player. People who slept with Duke Braddock tended to wake up dead.

Lou wasn't afraid – hadn't been for years, since those long months slogging through the Pacific theater – but still. "What's a guy like Duke want with –"

"A two-bit gumshoe?" Milt grinned like he'd been waiting for the line.

"A private investigator," Lou said with Dignity. His practice was small – just him – and the office wasn't in the best part of town, and the El did rattle the windows twice an hour, but it was approved by the State of Illinois. Said so right on the license.

The mentioned El chose that moment to rumble by the window, shaking the glass and making conversation impossible. The tracks were second story, just like the office. It kept the rent reasonable and there weren't that many paying customers anyway.

Mocking, the guy kept talking. Lou could see his lips move. Ha-ha, cute joke. Lou upgraded his opinion of the guy from hired muscle to idiot. No way would he take this case, whatever it was.

When the train noise had faded to a muted rumbling he said, "Whadaya want?"

"The boss wants to see you?

Lou had maybe seven minutes before the next train so he rushed it. "No,"

"You haven't heard what he wants."

"Don't need to. If Braddock's involved, it's dirty."

Milt actually looked offended. A cheap thug in a turtleneck – in this August heat; how was that possible? – offended for a boss who killed people. Honor among thieves, Lou supposed.

Milt stared around the office; a short trip it was true – you could just about touch both walls if you stretched. "A punk like you," he said. "Turning down Duke Braddock?"

"Amazing, isn't it?"

Milt shook his head like he was clearing gnats. "A small time, no account piece of crap like you?"

Go figure," agreed Lou. He was actually enjoying this. Few enough people came here, an actual gangland celebrity was a treat. Since opening the office two years back Lou hadn't met anyone more dangerous than the bartender at Billie Goat's, steamed about the bar bill.

Milt stood up, stretched, his fingers brushing the ceiling. "You gotta come with me."

Standing he was bigger than he looked sitting, filling out the suit like a stuffed sausage. Worse, he balanced lightly on his feet and turned sideways like a fighter. A pro for sure.

Lou's smile became a grin. This was getting better and better.

"Get up." Milt motioned with the front fingers of his left hand. His right hand was resting on the edge of the desk.

Lou stood. He exhaled through his lips, blowing out all the air, sagging as if resigned and Milt relaxed, seeing the expected obedience.

Lou said, "Sorry," picked up the ashtray and slammed it down on Milt's fingers. Cigarette butts flew across the room in a spray of spark and ash.

The glass broke, Milt howled and automatically stuck his injured paw toward his mouth, Lou grabbed the wrist and pushed along with it, the motion making Milt bend back to avoid slapping himself in the face.

Once Milt was off balance Lou shoved him – hard – in the middle of that broad chest and kept pushing. Milt fell back, hit the door head first and the frosted glass shattered, the lettering gone with the wind. Monk was not going to be pleased, Lou thought, especially since his cousin hadn't been paid yet.

Milt hung there, half supported by the remains of the door, then shrugged himself up and out. He brushed glass from his coat and glared.

"Tough guy," he said.

"Yeah," Lou agreed, He took a gun from the desk drawer and pointed it.

"Okay," Milt said. "Okay, you're a tough guy. Maybe that's why the boss wants to see you."

He stretched his shoulders around in a small circle and twisted his neck. Muscles bulged and bones cracked loudly. The heat came in through the open window and shimmered between them. The air hung heavy and expectant as if waiting.

"I'll send Braddock a bill for the door," Lou said finally.

Milt laughed, a short bark. "You do that." He pulled open the door and walked out, heavy shoes crunching on glass shards. He turned back, framed in the space where the window used to be.

"I'll be back, tough guy. Depend on it. I'll be back."

"Great meeting you," Lou said. Come back any time."

Duke Braddock, he thought. Hot damn.


Later, Mickey said, "Duke Braddock?"

Mickey Jablonski was a stoolie, a paid informer who'd sell his dog to a butcher for pork chops. He was short and skinny and walked with a limp from a meeting with a very dissatisfied customer. The guy had actually tried to chew through Mickey's leg. Took three of Chicago's finest to pull him off and cuff him. Of course, the cops hadn't been in all that much of a hurry – nobody cared much for Mickey.

"Braddock," agreed Lou. They were eating a late lunch at a corner booth at the Billy Goat Tavern at lower Michigan by the river. The Billy Goat's was a newspaperman's hangout and a bunch or reporters from the Trib were making noise at the bar. The place was old time, with dark wood crown moldings somewhere up there in the haze. If it weren't for political connections, the place would have been closed down years before it ever opened.

Mickey scratched a kitchen match on the scarred table and fired up a cigar, Acrid blue smoke surrounded him and he looked like an acned Satan until he coughed and ruined the image.

"Still getting those expensive imported cigars?" Lou laughed.

"Screw you, Fleener. These cost two bits for ten."

"Two bits. Big spender."

But Mickey seemed more interested in another subject. "Braddock, man. I don't know. He's about as big as this town gets anymore."

"I know. He's very hot stuff." Lou read the papers: Duke Braddock arrested for drugs, for prosties, for arson, assault. Probably murder and bad breath. But he'd walked away on every count every time, the result of great attorneys or big money. Or both.

"He lives in Evanston?" Lou asked. Where the old money hangs out?"

Mickey laughed. "Sure. He's gone uptown for sure."

Lou thought about old money and new money. He didn't have either but he picked up the tab for the beers with the last two singles in his wallet, still wondering what Duke Braddock could want with him.

# TAP DOUBT

Raymond Dean White and Duane Lindsay

## 1 - The Threat

### 13 Years Ago
### Moscow Institute of Chemical Studies

*Maria Elena Zelanskaya swallowed bile as she stood before the five men seated in the cramped laboratory. Her heart raced like a thoroughbred in the homestretch as she watched them eyeing her, each a picture of boredom, interest, patience or doubt. That they were all large men and she barely reached 5' 2 made her hands shake. That they were powerful members of the committee and soldiers had her near tears of self-doubt and worry.*

*They could make her career if they liked her presentation.*
*They could break her if they didn't.*

*"Gentlemen," she said, almost stumbling on the word. Nothing about these five conveyed gentleness or warmth or any kind of human feeling. They were killers, all of them, trained in the fields of Afghanistan, veterans of campaigns too horrible for a chemistry student like her to comprehend. They were timber wolves roaming the frozen steppes and she was a lone hare trapped between them, offering them a tempting meal.*

*Maria Elena couldn't feel more naked and exposed if she was one of the cheap slut dancing girls on display at the Western-style strip clubs that now flourished in Moscow—the result of the East/West clash insuring the worst of both cultures.*

*She breathed deeply to calm herself and said, "There is a man in America named Nicholas Kuiper who owns a company called* EnviroTech. *This company is designed for one purpose: to clean up the most heavily polluted chemical waste sites in their country."*

*Several of them stirred at this idea, shaking their heads or rubbing thick calloused hands through full beards in amazement at the concept. Mother Russia was still hiding its own poisonous wastes, burying them like they did at Chernobyl, covering up like a cat in a sand box.*

She rushed on. "This company has forty-three highly contaminated sites under contract with the American government in a project they call the Superfund." She stumbled a bit on the uniquely western word, having no equivalent in Russian. "They devise methods for how to turn their dangerous waste into safe, pure water."

"So?" Ivan Petrovsky, a hard fat man in a gray coat and beaver hat, made his displeasure known—his body language clearly stating his desire to be somewhere else. "What does this misguided foolishness have to do with us?"

"Let me explain. No, let me show you." Maria stepped behind a laboratory table and pointed at a large glass bowl filled with a yellow/green liquid. "This compound is the exact equivalent, in chemical composition, to a small lake in Pennsylvania, that EnviroTech is charged with cleaning up."

Two men sat straighter in the student chairs, making them creak a sound like someone dying, far away, in anguish. Maria Elena rushed on, trying to shake the image from her brain. If they decided she was wasting their time, she might be the next poor soul to make that sound.

She picked up a beaker filled with a sickly rust-colored liquid, the shade of a long abandoned Zil. "And this is a formula I tailored to blend specifically with the chemicals in that lake."

She paused. There was so much at stake. Her status as a student was in jeopardy due to the latest round of purges and decreasing funding of the university. She had to make them see.

A voice spoke up and she saw Alexander Krakov, a red-bearded bear of a man sitting at ease in the too-small chair, his expression guarded. "How do you know the American chemistry?"

"I...um...I asked for it. The Americans...I asked..."

"You asked for it? What are you saying? Who did you ask?" Expressions turned hard against her and Maria Elena felt like crying in fear and frustration.

"I sent a letter to a friend in America." An exchange student named Ron Driekman she had met last summer when he was a tourist. A science student, his major was particle physics, they shared a love for the classroom and had written several times to each other, long letters from worlds so far apart.

"My friend asked the American government about the chemical composition and they gave it to him..."

Loud grumbling and sounds of disbelief flowed toward her. "They gave it to him? What nonsense is this?" Oleg Mechel, a skeletal old man with a reputation that made the others fade into insignificance—some say that he once worked directly for Stalin himself when he was young and hungry—snorted. The idea that someone could ask a government for anything and the government would simply hand over the information was so foreign to Russian experience that it sounded like a fairy tale. His derision made her hear that death-shriek again.

But Alexander waved a paw of a hand, quieting them before they got too far out of control. "I want to hear this."

Maria Elena, grateful for his interest, played the rest of her presentation directly to Alexander, ignoring the crude remarks and guttural barking of the others. Animals, she thought. But such dangerous animals. They reminded her of the massive sea lions in the frozen north.

She said, "Perhaps you should put on the masks in front of you." Each man had a brightly colored plastic respirator. Gold, purple, red and blue, with green filters on the side, she had gotten them from her professor before staging this meeting.

Holding the beaker clumsily in one hand she picked up a small cage with the other. In it several white mice raced back and forth, whiskers twitching, noses testing the air, sensing danger. She held the cage over the bowl for a full minute before setting it back on the table.

"You see? The chemicals, which the Americans think are so deadly, are only a problem if they make direct contact with the skin. They cannot harm you through the air. However..."

Gesturing like a Gypsy magician she held up the beaker for display. She could see their attention focus as she tipped the rusty brown liquid, letting it pour slowly into the bowl. The colors merged, swirled together in unholy patterns that reminded her of the cancerous cells she'd been forced to study in biology. Sick cells all of them, twisted and foul.

She set down the empty beaker and grasped a long-handled spatula, using it to stir the mixture. With one hand she held a respirator to her own face. She picked up the cage and again held it above the bowl.

This time the result amazed them. The mice began to thrash around in a frenzy, clawing at the cage in a desperate attempt to escape. They slowed, twitched and their bodies curled as the poison they were breathing overwhelmed their lungs. In seconds all of them were dead. Ventilation fans kicked in and removed the remaining gas.

She had the men's attention now. All of them sat upright, wide-eyed and incredulous.

"A chemical weapon?" asked Oleg, her harshest critic. "You have made a chemical weapon?"

"I have done much more than that," said Maria Elena, her voice firm now that they'd seen her proof, her eyes glowing with triumph. "I have created forty-three chemical weapons."

"Explain, please." This from an intent Alexander Krakov.

"Instead of this small bowl full," she gestured, "each EnviroTech site contains millions of gallons of waste.

"Imagine," she told the group of feral men facing her, "What would happen if we captured those pumps that are cleaning these places and pumped in our own chemicals to convert each site into a small factory of death?"

An uproar. Four voices each trying to out-bellow the others. A cacophony of discord and dissent struggling for dominance, all directed at the idea that Maria Elena had proposed.

"Madness!" cried one. "How could it work?" demanded another. "Foolishness," and "Insane," and "The Americans would never allow us near these places. How would we deliver the poisons? It isn't possible."

Finally, the verdict. "Belongs in an asylum," said Oleg, followed by angry glares as four men gathered themselves and clumped from the room

Maria Elena felt her shaky scholarship crumble and die, just like the dead lumps of mice lying in the cage. Her eyes stung with tears of failure but when she wiped them away she was surprised to see one man remaining.

Alexander Krakov sat watching her. On his face was an expression Maria Elena could only describe as wonder.

# Chapter 2
## Let the Battle Begin

The punch flew straight and true into the jaw of Richard Blackwell and sent him flying. He landed on his immaculately tuxedoed backside, slid across the sidewalk and bumped off over the curb to lie limp and motionless in the gutter.

A world-class blow, it started from somewhere way back there, a windmill sweep of the entire body, as classic and elegant as any comic book art, with legs akimbo and grace completely absent. It was Captain America draped in the flag smashing Hitler on the jaw.

The punch was the small fist of every fourth-grader on every playground whose lunch money has been taken once too often by the sixth-grade bully. That it was thrown by a middle-aged out of shape chemist at a forty-five-year-old tycoon did nothing to lessen its importance or its poetry. It was a longing for justice and a scream of rebellion, summed up in one great surge of muscle and bone.

And in the end, it was as futile a gesture as it was fleeting and beautiful; a rose spreading its scent on the boot that crushed it, a butterfly wanting to matter.

Nick Kuiper overbalanced by his own momentum grabbed a wall for support, astounded at what he'd done.

A voice behind him said, "Put 'em up," and he turned to see James Blackwell, seventy-four and silver haired, standing before him in an old-style pugilist pose, left fist in front and guarding, right hand a trip hammer waiting to strike.

"Jeez," Nick said, "I don't want to fight you."

"You should have thought about that before you decked my son."

They stood on an empty street outside of the conference hall where the Blackwells had just stolen his company. The time was nearly midnight and a light drizzle gave the scene a Hollywood feel of deep shadows and smeared red and green lights reflecting off the wet pavement.

James Blackwell, in a black tuxedo, looked dignified and important. Only the cauliflower ear and battered nose suggested he was anything but a businessman.

"You're too old," Nick said, and a fist he never even saw coming smashed into his nose, breaking it.

"You don't," punch, "know much," punch, "about boxing," James said, landing a right cross that spun Nick into the ground. "I was Golden Gloves champion two years running, you know. Won forty-four of forty-six bouts."

Nick shook his head and climbed to his feet. His ears were ringing. He swung a wild one that James blocked and counter-punched with a jab that rocked him back on his heels.

"You swing like that, you never hit anything," James said, as Nick found his feet again.

"Short quick jabs are the key." He demonstrated by pounding blows into Nick's arms and body. "Don't watch my hands," punch, "or my eyes," punch, "watch my shoulders. The shoulders never lie."

Nick followed his advice and managed to block a punch and land a feeble blow of his own.

"That's better," James said with a smile as he bored in.

Nick was on the ground again and didn't know how he'd gotten there. He felt the scratch of damp concrete and a piece of candy wrapper stuck to his cheek. Stubbornly, he climbed back to his feet. His legs were rubbery but they still held him up.

James moved around him, jabbing at will. "Look boy, I know you're pissed off at losing your company." He landed a left hook that dropped Nick in his tracks. "But it's not our fault; you're the one who made charitable donations instead of buying back EnviroTech stock."

Getting up was harder now. Nick used both hands to push against his knee so he could stand, raised his head and his fists and said, "What you do is still wrong."

James danced in and delivered two quick body shots. Nick's legs buckled and he landed on his butt.

"I won't debate morals with you, but what we do is legal. I see to that."

Nick pulled himself up, somehow, and said, "Law's wrong." He spit blood. "And screw you." He took another feeble swing and James hit him in his mouth, loosening a tooth.

Things got a bit vague after that. He took a fist in his mid-section that knocked his breath out and sent him to his knees. He saw

James back off and wait for him to recover and was surprised at the old man's sense of fair play.

"You should stay down, boy," James said. "You keep getting up, I might hurt you."

That made no sense at all to Nick, who hurt absolutely everywhere already. He climbed grimly to his feet and James batted his arms aside and pushed Nick so hard he fell, landing in a puddle with a great splash.

"Dammit! Stay down."

Nick rolled over and used a parking meter to pull himself up. He staggered away from it and put up his fists. One of his eyes wouldn't open all the way and the other was a bit blurry.

"Jesus," James said. "You have guts, boy. No brains at all, but yards of guts."

Nick saw Richard struggling to his feet, but it didn't compute.

"I'm going to put you down now," James said with a touch of regret. "It's for your own good."

Nick felt the punch slam into his chin and then he was flat on his back looking up at a too-bright streetlight, blinking rain out of his eyes. His clothes were soaked and his mind clouded. But he knew he'd been knocked down so he had to get up. "Get knocked down six times, get up seven." Words from his father; words to live by.

He heard footsteps approaching as he rolled onto his side and saw Richard's shoe coming straight at his head. Richard got in three more vicious kicks before his father pulled him off.

The war had begun.

Manufactured by Amazon.ca
Bolton, ON

17946746R00148